DOOMSDAY'S CHILD

PETE ALDIN

To my boys.

You, more than anyone, have taught me
what it is to be a man.

Monday's child is fair of face,
Tuesday's child is full of grace,
Wednesday's child is full of woe,
Thursday's child has far to go,
Friday's child is loving and giving,
Saturday's child works hard for a living,
But the child who is born to survive Doomsday
Is blessed and cursed in every way.

- Children's Rhyme circa 66 PC (Post-Collapse)

I

Harrietville

.

1

Hunger made a man do dangerous things.

Elliot should have faded back into the hills behind the Lotus Petal Day Spa. He should have retreated into the bush. Instead, he hugged the shadows, camouflaging himself amongst trees he'd once only known from the Discovery Channel, wattles and stringy barks. Selecting a spot across the wire fence from the health retreat's herb patch, he took a knee on dry grass, pressed his shoulder against a eucalypt, and he watched, and he waited. Nothing moved in the gardens this side of the two-story homestead or along the driveway, nothing but a single crow hopping along the roof. But there *was* noise. On the far side of the house: male voices, coarse and careless. The noise meant no deaders. He hoped.

A gunshot. He pressed tighter against the trunk, folded in on himself, glad he'd left his pack behind another eucalypt up-slope. His rebellious stomach gurgled—lucky no one was close enough to hear it. An̄ gunshot. Some laughter, whooping. One man ʼted another on his accuracy. Someone ʼuse. Not the kind of men who'd likely ᵊrb gardens. He hoped.

the hill where he'd left the pack, he'd had ꓒ view of the health retreat: ten acres of walks, spas, gardens, a free-range chicken pen, a horse paddock and the long driveway out to whatever local highway that was. The two horses were dead, and that meant a full belly if he could get to them. Yesterday's birds—tiny striped things like quail—had barely affected the chasm of his hunger.

Amongst the herbs, bees nuzzled stamens. The crow cawed and hopped from sight. Metal clanged—pots or a barbeque cover. Glass broke. Someone cussed out someone else in earnest. More laughter. Deaders or not, the racket was careless, even this far from an urban centre. A motorbike started up, and a second, proving the recklessness. One appeared from behind the house, puttering up the driveway in first gear. He might just get that meal yet. Another bike followed. More engines started up, car doors slamming like rifle fire. Four more bikes appeared, riding in tandem. All six were low riders, the men on them clad in leather or denim cut-off vests and without helmets. Three cars followed. A van without windows in the cargo space—a matt black slab of steel and rubber. A gas-guzzler V8—red with flame decals. A mud-spattered white pickup with an enclosed tray on the back housing the tools—what Aussies called a *ute*. He shifted sideways to watch the convoy regroup at the highway and accelerate from view.

Elliot decided to wait ten minutes despite his stomach nudging him with a jab of hunger. He told it to man up and wait its turn. A half hour earlier, four gunshots had drawn him across the hill, the noise promising him—well, he wasn't sure what. Human activity might mean food, was all he could think. An there *was* meat in there—whoever those assholes were, they hadn't taken the horses.

Maybe one of the gardens grew vegetables too. He knew that his basic training made sense, that living off the land you should only eat things that run and swim and fly. More simply put: *if it moves, eat it*—which was pretty much the undead's philosophy too. Meat meant calories.

But Holy Mother, if he didn't crave a salad. A potato. A carrot. Vitamins. Fibre.

Man cannot live on meat alone. Not for long anyway. It was a recipe for colon cancer. Be just his luck to survive history's most devastating pandemic, overcome hordes of undead to escape Hobart and then die of the big C or scurvy or some shit like that.

He sat back, straightened his legs in front of him, the coolness of the earth pressing through his trousers. Around him hung the mossy scent of the lantana; the orange-flowering bushes flourished despite suffocating heat and lack of recent rain. From a small hollow to his left there grew a dark-leafed shrub taller than him and thick with berry clusters. The lantana was no doubt introduced—it grew back home—but the glossy black berries may have been native for all he knew. The tiny fruits were shaped like butts, complete with ass-crack. Were they edible? Aborigines had lived here for thousands of years before the Brits came, so there had to be food around. He could be five feet away from a feast in this wilderness and never know it.

He sighed, plucked at grass as rough as straw, crushed it. He'd left it too late to find info on what locals called bush tucker. The visit to Tasmania had been unscheduled—and he'd been here mere hours when shit began hitting fans. In the eight weeks since, he'd learned so little about the big island. Why hadn't he visited a library in Hobart and researched? Used an internet kiosk while there was power? Grabbed seeds from a gardening supplier?

Yeah, well, maybe I was a little distracted getting out of Dodge before a hundred thousand deaders chowed down on my ass.

Beyond the fence, nothing had moved for five minutes, nothing but circling birds and bushes responding to breeze. The crow had not reappeared, though he'd heard it call again. The sun brushed the tops of a band of cloud to the west, setting off a riot of color. It was beautiful—and its low angle meant dark was coming. Another night in the open made his stomach clench with a different concern.

Food, water, *shelter*: it was all on the other side of that fence.

He forced weary legs to climb the hill. He grabbed his pack. He checked the property one more time from high ground, saw nothing of concern and made his way downhill. The pack stayed by the fence when he climbed over. He skirted the main house, came around the building and into the open space of a pool and dining courtyard.

He froze, gorge rising.

Most of the black flies swarming the three bodies clustered on the man and the dog. Man and beast had been shot in the back and their heads hacked off, providing a smorgasbord of choice for insects. Two crows stood on either side of the woman, pecking at her eyes. One raised its head, wary. Elliot stooped, pulled up a pebble from a garden bed and tossed it. The birds lifted, cawing their objection as they headed for the roof.

Elliot ventured closer. The woman had suffered more: the blood around her thighs, her hiked up dress, the stab wound to the abdomen, the bruising on her throat. Defensive wounds—cuts and nicks—striped one hand and forearm around a banged up pandora bracelet she wore.

"Give 'em hell, babe," he managed to say and—though he'd seen a shitload of death in his time, in diverse shapes and sizes and permutations—he had to turn away.

The yard was a bloody mess. Luggage sliced up, personal belongings strewn across the grounds. By the open kitchen doors of the house, three books fluttered in the gusting breeze like wounded birds. He snatched one up, checked the cover. A piece of mid-20th century literature a girlfriend had once swooned over and pressed him to read. Elliot had found it mopey, and had told her so after a cursory skim. The beginning of the end of yet another short-lived hook-up.

Blood spotted the book's pages. A little smeared the side of his index finger—an identical shade of red to the blood on Radler's arm when he'd had to pick that up and bag it. Radler's arm, Eames' boot with the foot inside, McGovern's face—

He lost time, maybe a second, maybe a minute, maybe more. He came to himself with hands on thighs, bent over and sucking air. He slowed it, inhaled for five seconds, held it five, released it for five. Rinse, lather, repeat. He'd been here before; it would pass. Through the white haze, he counted pebbles in the garden beside him, noting the varying shades of green and grey and orange and brown, calming as those colors grew vivid.

Inhale. Five, four, three, two, one. Hold. Five, four, three, two, one. Exhale. Five, four, three, two, one.

It took a couple of minutes before he could look at the blood-dappled novel and then at the carnage without seeing flashes of light, without his blood pressure wanting to pop holes in his neck and temples. He channeled the energy of it into that deep reservoir of cold anger within him, storing it for a better time.

There came a tinkle of metal. The woman's bracelet. The crows had settled on her again, one on the arm, one on the head, taking it in turns to peck or watch him for further barrages. He straightened and swung away from the bodies, the flies, the birds. There was shit to do, things to assess.

He gave the rest of the grounds a careful recon. Most useful things had been looted—vegetables ripped from the ground, chicken pens empty.

He considered burying the bodies, or burning them, but neither action was worth it. The dead couple were no longer people. They were detritus, "damages", ended, anonymous. And this was the brutal nature of earth's history. *Blood, blood, blood.* The planet had always bathed in it. Survivors were the ones who made peace with that fact and worked with evolution's thuggish mandate: *of the fittest.*

These folk simply hadn't been enough.

A single brass casing caught the sunlight on a gravel path. Whoever they were, the bastards who'd ended them were armed and numbered nine or more. Elliot could only pray they wouldn't return. After burning through his ammunition in the first week of the collapse, his SIG P226 had been a dead weight in his bag. Every farmhouse he'd been, other people had beaten him to the firearms. He owned one looted piton hammer shoved through his belt, one 6-inch tanto knife hanging beside it, and one Schrade lock-blade folded inside the left cargo pocket of his combat pants. His entire armory.

The inside of the house was as trashed as the outside. The bikers had urinated on the carpeted staircase for Christ knew what reason. He hurdled the stain and inspected the bedrooms upstairs, established a profile of the people who'd owned the retreat. Syrian husband. Anglo-Aussie wife. Interesting and unusual mix in whitebread Tasmania. Teenage son and daughter, unfortunately young enough to be taken as sex slaves by the animals that killed their folks. That van had no doubt carried them both away—he certainly hadn't found their bodies.

The girl featured in several family photos and a school yearbook; long black hair, green eyes, always with a large pandora bracelet on one tanned wrist. The bracelet identified her firmly with the dead mother outside who wore one also; both boasted among other charms a gold Orthodox cross. The same charm. Theirs had been a close relationship. In the boy's room, he found hand-drawn artwork, and a handmade Happy 13th Birthday card from the parents. A computer game sat on a shelf atop its wrapping paper. The birthday might have happened during the collapse, the useless gift sitting in a cupboard while the world broke. The kid hadn't found a use for a computer game in a world without power. And for all their apparent green-sensibilities, the Oussefs hadn't thought to install solar panels.

Elliot tossed the game and the card on the bed and thought, *Kid hell.* Lewis Oussef had been on the cusp of manhood. In this world, he should *be* a man. Other cultures had it so. At thirteen, Masai youths were herding cattle and preparing for circumcision *sans* anesthesia. Lakota youths were off on vision quests. Young men in the land of Lewis's father were taking up arms, strapping on suicide vests, or out hustling Westerners for cash. At least, they had been …

When he'd been thirteen, Elliot had been already fending for himself. And he was still doing it a quarter century later.

He returned downstairs, hoping to hell the teenagers had fled, and knowing they hadn't.

The kitchen cupboards were emptied of food. Which didn't matter anyway. Elliot had a reserve of muesli bars and protein bars in his pack, but he resisted processed food unless desperate. For all he knew, the virus or the catalyst or whatever the hell infected people was in that next tin of creamed corn or packet of rice or can of soda. Once he'd accepted that packaged goods were suspect, that they were the most sensible reason for the universality of the outbreak, his calorie count had dropped dramatically. Nibbling processed food meant a sixty minute wait, painfully counting the seconds until he could be sure he had no fever before eating the rest. He'd used bottled water twice, but had boiled it first.

He spent a good chunk of the remaining daylight cutting a leg from a horse, skinning and carving off meat which he cooked on the Oussefs' barbecue. He found some shiny yellow buttons in a sewing kit which he used to mark a path through the gardens back to the rear fence. Should he need to beat a hasty retreat back up the hills, they might help him better find his way in the dark. Rope would have been better, but he couldn't find any. He placed a horse blanket over the fence so he could navigate it without getting snagged on the wire. He took his SIG but left his pack where it sat against the far side of the fence. A ladder from a service shed went up against the parents' bedroom window on the side of the house facing his escape route.

He ate charred horse meat off a white plate while standing before a huge map of Tasmania in the father's den. A topographical map would have been better—and why were there no goddam military installations in this island-state?—but at least it was heavily detailed. Furthermore, six locations had been circled in red felt pen: an island off the east coast, a town in the far west, and lakes in the south-east and the west. One western lake was the destination Elliot had decided on while sheltering in a resort with sixteen dumbass people in the process of losing their minds and destroying their safe haven.

A regional map in the desk showed where he was now. The nearest town Harrietville was sixteen kilometers—ten miles—roughly north-east through farmland. And the map legend showed a police station there. He was headed west, but it was worth a diversion in the morning. If the only people left in the new world were dumbasses and murderous gangs, it was well past time Elliot got himself a firearm or two. Or ten.

After eating as much as was sensible, he practiced his bail plan twice. His stomach felt stretched to bursting point, despite his self-control. He shoved furniture in front of the exterior doors to barricade himself in. Because he couldn't face sleeping in any of the Oussef's beds, he went to the living room, piled couch cushions on the floor and lay down. Sleep was patchy and dawn a long time coming.

2

The town's founding fathers had deemed three holding cells plenty for a rough night in Harrietville; a similar town back home would have had ten. The police station was a 19th Century building with its iron-barred holding cells in an annex out back, lining a wall like zoo cages. Elliot could stand in the connecting doorway from the office and scope all three cells at one glance. He was glad the place was so old: more modern jail cells—the ones with a solid door, small viewing window and meals flap—would have made his job so much more difficult.

And this is gonna be difficult enough as is.

Two cells lay empty, doors ajar, cots made up with military precision and covered with dirt that had blown in through the high and narrow window at the farthest end. Elliot definitely wasn't so lucky that he'd find what he wanted in either of those. No, the thing he wanted was in the center one, the cell with the deader in it. A snuffling noise rolled out toward him, as if to underline his opinion on his luck. The cell's occupant had its back to him, head nodding like a psych-ward patient. Every ten or twenty seconds, another labored breath lifted its ribs.

Horse meat churned in Elliot's stomach. He'd wolfed down too much that morning, the stench in here making matters worse. Stepping down onto the cement floor, he pulled his black bandanna over his nose. "You'd think I'd get used to you bastards."

Whether the deader heard his comment or whether it smelled *him*, he couldn't know. But it chose that moment to whirl and reach for him in a desperate flounce that was one part spasmic dance, three parts animal savagery.

He flinched from the bars, kept out of reach as he studied the former-human, his heart thumping, tinnitus in his ears. "Long time dead, but ya still got rhythm." The joke wasn't funny, but it went a ways toward helping him keep control, and toward dispelling the electric buzz of anxiety vibrating his head.

Focus. Got a job to do. Get it done.

It had once been a *him* and he had once been a local cop, now pantsless and shoeless, shirt buttoned tight against his turkey neck, socks brown with undefinable muck, bare legs scabrous and slippery with body fluids. The only question, Elliot thought, trying to get a look behind the corpse, was whether the fluids were from its own body or someone else's. He squinted. In the back corner against the john, a crumpled mass resolved itself as another body, unchewed legs encased in denim, feet encased in workboots. It wore a polo-shirt like Elliot's but where Elliot's was black by design, its shirt was blackened with old blood. It lay with back to him, face and hands hidden by the curl of its body. A peaked cap sat nearby, as did the dead cop's pants and shoes. The cop's sidearm was missing from the holster, maybe under the cot or the other body, but a set of keys were visible on the belt and it was the keys he wanted.

Elliot fished out his pocket flashlight and focused the beam on the dead corpse's cap: the Shell logo matched the one on the truck outside. The tanker had taken out three parked cars and ended up in the middle of the Harrietville Council Chambers lawn. Elliot put it all together.

They toss the tanker driver in here DUI, only he's not DUI, he's Sick. It's early in the breakdown. Soon after, a bunch of deaders appear in town, all hell breaks loose and this cop locks himself in here with the driver, thinking he'll be safe 'cause he can protect the poor bastard from the cadaver hordes, except the driver is one of them and bites him. Cop shoots him in the head, but it's not too long before he gets Sick himself.

Elliot would never be able to ask the cop why he'd taken off his pants and shoes. Or why he didn't shoot himself when he realized his fate. Maybe he hadn't been as tough as he thought was.

Yeah, look who's talking. Quit stalling. Get it done.

"Well. The gun locker keys aren't anywhere in that office out there. Has to be them on your belt there. You hand 'em over and I'll let you live. Or whatever it is you're doing." He pulled his piton hammer out. "Your choice: hard way or easy way?"

The corpse snarled in response and tried to squeeze between the bars, dirty fingernails raking the air mere inches from Elliot's bandanna.

"Hard way it is." One swing of the hammer shattered the corpse's elbow so that it hung loose, dangling like ribbon. The next dented the skull, but not enough to kill it. The undead cop huffed and pulled away, broken

15

arm snagging on the crossbar. Elliot drew his tanto knife. He pinned the trapped arm with his chest, grabbed the shirt sleeve up higher, raised the knife and jerked the dead man closer. The deader's left eye met six inches of pointed steel coming the other way with a squelching sound and a squirt of black blood and yellowy vitreous fluid. It shivered a moment then went slack, slumping against the bars as Elliot yanked the blade free. The broken arm slipped loose of its moorings and Elliot let the body complete a graceless slide to the floor.

Beneath the bandanna, his nostrils flared at the fresh wave of stench. He held onto his breath and held onto his breakfast, carefully wiping the blade on the cop's shirt before going to find a broom handle to drag the man's pants over. The keyring remained unsoiled, a small mercy. He'd already gotten blood on his fingers once today.

With the thought of the Oussefs' blood, images and sound-bites snapped at the fringes of his consciousness, an ever-present swarm of memory and recrimination. The tinnitus was back. The knuckles of both hands wrapped tight around the broom handle and he swung it hard at the door to the office. It struck the jamb, snapped in two, the other half skittering off into the office. The shock of the blow sliced up his arms to his elbows like electricity. And the pain brought him back before he could vanish into flashback, it centered him.

He tossed the keys into the air, caught them, shoved them in his pocket. He saluted the dead cop with the jagged end of the stick, forcing a grin.

"Of the fittest, asshole," he said and turned back to the office with his arms buzzing and his head clear.

It took six keys before one fit the gunlocker. The steel cabinet stood by the rear door where the building had been extended past the cellblock.

"Bingo," Elliot said as the lock clicked open. He yanked on the door. The locker's emptiness mocked him. "Shit."

His head was pressed against the cool of the door when he heard engines. Two cars and a motorbike approaching at confident speed. He sidled up to a barred window. The vehicles came into view around the end of the tanker, brakes squealing as they slowed opposite the police station. A Harley. A red V8 with flame decals. A dirty white pickup. His hand went to his knife handle. His gut clenched. Three vehicles he'd seen leaving the health spa.

One guy in the pickup. The Harley rider was alone. The muscle car was past and parking nose-in before he could see through the window tinting. So anywhere up to five people.

The rider had dressed in leathers and denim, scalp wrapped in a black bandanna similar to Elliot's. His sleeveless jacket revealed thin and tattooed arms and sported a Celtic cross gang motif on the back. Elliot read *Death Druids* and would have laughed if the muscular guy getting out of the pickup hadn't been wearing the same clothes and carrying a Remington over/under shotgun. And if these guys hadn't committed multiple homicide the previous day.

The biker dismounted and stretched before reaching for something hanging off his saddle—a diver's spear gun. He also had a wood-handled .38 or .357 in a hip-holster. The V8's driver door squeaked open and a fat guy in Levi's and white singlet levered himself out. He reached back inside to retrieve an automatic rifle, an M4 from the looks. No one got out the passenger side. All three men were heavily bearded, the pickup driver with his long greying hair tied back in a ponytail while the fat guy had shaved his scalp. All had neck-tatts, arm tatts and gold ear-rings.

Perfect goddam timing.

Elliot padded to the back of the station house, checked the window between back door and gun locker. An enclosed courtyard lay beyond it with plastic picnic table and umbrella, plastic chairs, a mountain bike and washing line with rumpled handtowels still pegged to it. The brick wall was fifteen feet high to discourage late night visitors to the station perhaps; with enough time to shove the picnic table against it, he might have made it over, but raised voices approaching fast from out front made him abandon that strategy. He struck the window softly with his fist: there was only one option, unless he wanted to hide under a desk and hope they didn't notice his body odor above the background stink of rodent piss and zombie policeman. He padded back into the cell annex, pushed the door against the jamb as footfalls and scraped heels approached the stairs, raised the bandanna over his nose again and slid the most likely key into the cell door. The lock clicked and the door rolled sideways an inch before snagging on the dead cop's arm.

"Eyes open, bitches," a harsh voice commanded, and the station door creaked.

Elliot put his shoulder to the bars and shoved, snapping the arm off and sliding the body across the floor. He closed the door behind him and pocketed the keys. His backpack went beside the dead trucker—he wedged one end beneath the bunk, squashing it down. Then he took a deep breath he instantly regretted and lay on the floor, head toward the door, feet toward the trucker and cot. He reached for the cop and pulled him close. Even with his bandanna over the lower half of his face, it stunk to hell in here.

"Waxer, check what's through there. Ah, bullshit!—gun locker's empty."

"Course it is," replied a higher pitched male voice. "Told ya."

"Just check that back area," the first voice ordered.

"This is useless," said a third voice. "I'm checking out the town hall or whatever that council building is." The front door creaked again before boots pounded down the steps.

Elliot nestled up against the twice-dead policeman, pulled the uninjured arm across his face and turned his head toward the floor. Slime or blood or both leaked cold and gross across his cheek and down his jaw, under his ear and along his neck. The cellblock door was opened by someone with the rattly breath of a lifelong smoker. The guy with the high pitched voice— Waxer?—swore in a whisper, then raised his voice. "Nothin' here, Jeff. Just cells and bodies."

"They dead?" Jeff's voice came closer without entering the cell annex. Rustling and banging from the offices indicated he was searching drawers.

A scuff of feet on carpet as Waxer went back toward Jeff and announced, "One's arm's lying there on its own. None of 'em are moving. Should I pop 'em anyway?"

Elliot's blood turned to ice. Why the hell hadn't he stood to the side of the door, taken the guy out when he peeked inside? He'd given away control.

"You waste any more bullets, I'll gut ya," Jeff replied.

The slap of palm on scalp. Waxer grunted. He came back in, mumbling under his breath, feet shuffling right up to the cell. "This dead cop might have some ammo," he called. The cell door opened and the belt Elliot had tossed back in rasped across the floor as the intruder snatched it away.

The slime on Elliot's neck dripped, hit his collar. If he got out of this, he was definitely finding a new shirt. He couldn't see a thing, but imagined the sudden *crack* was the sound of Waxer kicking the door. The whiny prick swore loudly about the lack of gun or bullets in the belt. A moment later, Elliot was glad of the noise because the tanker driver's corpse twitched, its boots chucking against the steel frame of the cot.

Holy…

A bad day had just gone full nuclear fubar.

One of the corpses in the cell with Elliot wasn't fully dead.

3

"Nothin' here," Waxer said.

Something smashed into a wall, Jeff chucking a chair. Maybe a desk.

Another tremor shook the reanimated truck driver lying near Elliot's feet. The back straightened. The neck arched, the dead nose sniffing the air. Out in the office, Waxer and Jeff traded curses over where their next lot of ammo was coming from, though it sounded like they still had *some*—enough to put holes through both Elliot and the dead trucker if the trucker didn't stop squirming and smacking his gums. One dead hand spidered across the concrete floor, trying to gain enough purchase to push the driver up and over.

Struggling to keep his breathing even and slow, Elliot was faced with several choices. Kick the dead guy's head in and hope his skull was weak enough for a quick job—a noisy option. Use his boot to clamp the deader's head to the cot leg—again, noisy: an uncooperative pusbag was going to struggle. Finally, repeat his last move and stab it in the eye—probably best. The tanto blade was a little broad for the job, but it was the least noisy to draw.

The deader got his hand planted firmly enough to push up for just a moment. His head smacked dully against the floor when he lost purchase. Elliot had the tanto free. He drew his boots back toward his ass, bracing for the attack. If he moved too far out of position, he might be stranded when Waxer decided to come in again. A drawer squealed in the office as it was torn from the desk; it banged against something hard. The deader got his grip again, turned his milky eyes toward Elliot's knees.

"So what now?" Waxer asked. Boots stomped.

Elliot curled over, put the knife-handle to the side of his knee, angled the blade. The truck driver's mouth opened and closed, grey tongue flickering within the black maw. Elliot tensed, ready to spring.

The front door slammed, the bikers' yabbering picking up again outside and fading as they passed along the street.

Elliot shucked off his corpse-blanket and was on his feet with the blade sheathed in a second. He was closing the cell door by the time the trucker made it onto hands and knees. The deader swayed and sniffed, drooling bile onto the floor. His nose was a loose flap of putrefied skin, hanging loose, exposing bone.

"You look sick, pal." Elliot put the tanto away and ran sweaty palms down his pants legs. "Even for a dead guy."

He could have put the thing out of its misery—but why risk a bite? His backpack was under the bed, but he could fish that out with the broken broom, once the crisis passed. There was no need—he hoped—to ever go back inside that cell.

He snuck a look in the office. Nobody there, thank Christ. Maybe he'd get out of this one alive after all. The air was buzzing now; the bikers had let in plenty of flies. Elliot hated flies, and Australia was full of them. Holding the collar away from his hair, he pulled off the t-shirt, used a cleanish part to wipe his neck and face, bundled it and tossed it, untied the bandanna and repeated the process.

He crept out and sheltered behind the desks, close enough to retreat to the cells if necessary. He started searching drawers and office cupboards. Eventually he found a sealed fast food pack: paper napkin, plastic cutlery, alcohol wipe. He tore through plastic, wiped himself down with the wipe, repeated it with the napkin. When the Death Druids left, he'd find a shower or a water tank. He really needed a wash.

Sinking onto his ass, Elliot put his back against the desk. Towns were a risk and today proved it. There was little reward for the risk he'd taken here. No firearms. No ammunition—even outlaw bikers had been complaining about how hard that was to come by. There might be seeds in one of the outlying houses, a veggie garden, a chicken coop. Eggs. If the Druids didn't find it all. Hopefully there'd be some clean clothes that fit him too. It might be hot now, but he knew Tasmania played host to months of nasty cold weather mid-year. He'd need warm clothing, more knives for skinning and gutting, fishing line, a small tent maybe, certainly a more robust first aid kit than the IFAK in his pack.

An occasional shout traveled his way while he waited. No sounds of alarm or shots, no signs of undead combat or live resistance. That at least boded well for his later scavenging. After fifteen minutes, he was getting antsy. He crept to the front windows.

Nothing was visible in the street except the bikers' vehicles, the truck and the three cars it had totaled, plus a rusty old Holden hatchback someone had parked through the front window of a convenience store. That was maybe where the muscle-head pickup-driver went after checking the town hall; maybe the asshole was scarfing down all the processed foods he'd found there.

"Well, I ain't gonna fight ya for it."

After a meat dinner and breakfast, Elliot was a long way from needing to risk infection to eat. Beside, there was no way he was getting into a confrontation with three hostiles armed only with his climber's hammer and knife. Not over a little suspect packaged food. Not over anything.

Movement drew his eye back to the left. At the far end of the small town's shopping strip, on the corner of a narrow side street, sat one of the universals of Australian small towns: the pub. An old-world two-story white and brown building with fancier colonnades than it warranted. Two of the Druids—the fat one and the thinner of the two bike-riders, their voices identifying them as Jeff and Waxer—appeared from a side-entry lugging a steel keg between them. On the street they lowered it and the skinny one started rolling it toward the vehicles. Elliot knew the reflection of the sun off this window would keep him hidden from their view, so he watched, forcing down his impatience. Near the pickup, the rider stopped, straightened, rolled his shoulders, kneaded his back with fists while the fat guy Jeff laughed. Jeff lit up a reefer. They started talking crap, leaning on the car facing the pub, sharing the smoke with weapons slung over their backs.

Just move on, shitheads. Then I can restock and move on too.

He remained set on that far west wilderness where he could wait out the apocalypse until the undead all decayed and disappeared into the soil. A man with his training and experience could survive up there. Plenty of fishing spots and game. He did want to learn about those edible native fruits and berries though. Maybe the Council Chambers would have a library inside, or a tourist book store.

The gang duo flicked the butt away, left the keg where it was and wandered back towards the pub. Elliot thought about that pickup. Probably had a lot of supplies. Maybe they'd left the keys …

"Stop it," he muttered.

Keep your goddam head down.

There were other sources of food and resources. There'd be a farmhouse somewhere with weapons and ammo, seeds and books. Let these assholes have their beer and their cans of beans. When they'd gone, he'd scavenge Harrietville for leftovers, then start up that hatchback and take it as far across country as it would get him.

That was absolutely what he was going to do. Absolutely. It was the smart thing.

Then he noticed something swinging from Waxer's belt: the Oussef daughter's pandora bracelet. Even without field glasses, the various charms' colors and shapes were clear enough, clearest of all the gold Orthodox cross. It was the girl's all right, the one in all the photos of her. And this mouth-breathing sonofabitch was parading it as his trophy while elsewhere his buddies visited unthinkable abuses upon the girl .

A cold and familiar anger settled over him. His inner Unconventional Warfare Instructor said, *no, keep safe, keep low, stay out of it.*

But he wasn't going to do that. No, sir, he was not.

As he lived and breathed, Elliot was gonna teach these fuckers a lesson.

The third Druid who'd gone it alone was right where Elliot thought he'd be. Lying across the bench seat in the tanker's cab with his hands among the wires, trying to remember his elementary hot wiring. When Elliot whipped the driver's door open, the look of mild surprise on the upturned face was almost comical—and became pathetic as he saw his own death coming. With his hands busy and lying in an awkward position, the Death Druid knew there was nothing he could do to prevent it and simply froze. Elliot's right hand gripped the man's ear hard, wrenched his head around, plunged the knife into the base of the skull, twisted it. Brain stem severage. Lights out.

Door, head turn, knife plunge—this took Elliot about a second and a half. He slipped the blade out, spattering a little blood on his bare chest. At least he hadn't ruined another shirt.

He left the nameless Druid leaking fluid while he crouched at the front of the truck, surveying the street. He counted one-twenty, finally satisfied no one had seen his dash to the truck. He slipped around to the driver's door, confirmed the kill, grunted to himself.

The Remington over/under lay on the cab floor, out of reach of the creeping blood pool. Elliot drew it out, checked his surrounds again. Still no witnesses. The Druid had a bandoleer strapped diagonally across his chest. Avoiding a fuss with the buckle behind the dead guy's back, Elliot plucked out the thirteen remaining rounds and shoved them in his cargo pockets. Then he bolted back into the deadspace between the Council Chambers and a community toilet block. He wiped the barrels once more on a patch of weeds and checked the weapon over: loaded, oiled, good to go.

Unless they'd gone out a back door, Jeff and Waxer were still in the pub, maybe lightening their second keg a little before rolling it. Fine with Elliot: the drunker they were, the better.

The little park around the Council Chambers split the shopping district in two. Elliot jogged around the building and into a service alley behind the stores. The back half of the pub was visible at the far end. Running straight up the lane toward it would invite trouble: potential shooters would see him better from inside than he'd ever see them. He climbed the hood of a car to help scale the curbside fence and dropped into a timber yard. Jogging, he took a roundabout trip through yards of car parts, farming equipment, more timber, garden supplies with some plants long dead and others outgrowing their pots. The weeds in the garden supply business hid two bodies, who thankfully didn't move when he bolted past. He reached the side street the pub was on, crossing down the road where the Druids couldn't see him.

Seven houses sat between a football ground and the pub parking lot. Elliot hugged fences, pausing at the final house to crouch beside its hedge. The parking lot was an empty asphalt rectangle: no garden beds, no trees to break it up and no patrons' cars for cover. The building was still a hundred feet away.

The instructor voice said, *forget it, find an ambush point, let them come to you.* Elliot told it to shut the hell up and sprinted across the tarmac, keeping low until he reached a dumpster. It smelled like the dead but probably didn't host any. As if to prove it, a rat the size of a housecat poked its nose out the top, startling him. It squeaked once, dropped to the ground and scurried off, keeping to the curb the way Elliot had been keeping to property lines.

The sound of idiotic laughter meant his next two targets were close. A sign on the white door beyond the dumpster announced *Kitchen Entrance.* Empty plastic milk crates piled by the step up. The laughter was coming from behind that door which boasted an old-fashioned ornate knob. Hip and shoulder against the wall, he reached out, turned the knob, eased the door open.

The kitchen wasn't much larger than an average bedroom, stoves along one side, storage along another, interior and exterior doors front and back, a narrow steel-topped island-bench in the middle. A meth pipe smoked gently from the island-bench beside open bottles of bourbon and rum. The M4 and speargun lay on the top of the stoves. A steel cooler had been built into the storage wall beside the cupboards and shelves and the two Death Druids faced it with their backs turned to him.

Weapon ready, he would have fired if it weren't for the weirdness of the scene.

What in God's name?

Waxer leaned both hands on the cooler door as if being frisked, but he was giggling. Jeff—bald head shiny and fat arms jiggling—held a female zombie in soiled pajamas against a cupboard beside the coolroom, one hand clamped around her throat. The zombie arced her face toward Waxer's arm, jaws snapping while Jeff repeatedly poked her in the cheek with a steel skewer.

"Zom kebab!" Jeff cackled.

Waxer smacked his lips. "Stick her again, brother."

Two barrels, two dumb bastards, Elliot thought.

He steadied the shotgun against his shoulder. And something in the tiny movement got Waxer's attention. His eyes widened and as Elliot's aim shifted his way, he dived for cover behind the island bench. Elliot fired, regretting it instantly. The blast tore up wooden shelves, blew a set of pasta bowls to pieces, but missed his target. Jeff started turning, bringing the zombie with him. Elliot's second shot clawed a trench through the fat man's abdomen and a chunk from the deader's hip. Jeff huffed and toppled and the object of his deranged torture went with him, piling against the cupboard in a tangle of limbs.

Breaking the shottie open, Elliot dropped to one knee, expecting Waxer to pop up with his handgun. Instead, scurrying sounds from behind the food prep bench indicated the biker making for the door to the bar. Was he out of bullets? Elliot reached for fresh cartridges, freezing momentarily when the cooler door swung open to bang against Jeff and his wrestling partner. Elliot saw movement in the dark of the cooler, fumbled the first cartridge, dropped it. He pulled another out, but dead people poured toward him from the steel box, ignoring Jeff. The first one out was a big bastard, tall and broad-shouldered with hands the size of fry pans and dressed in what Elliot assumed was Australian football shorts and jersey.

Elliot backpedaled through the open door, determined to get his weapon loaded. He had the second shell in when the footballer hit him, moving faster than Elliot had anticipated. *Muscle-memory?* he wondered as giant hands closed around the shottie. He tried to use the weapon as leverage, to turn the big pusbag's weight against him, twisting and attempting a throw, but the weapon was wrenched from his hands and it was Elliot who lost balance, shoulder striking the dumpster. He pushed off and backwards as the zombie lunged again and cracked its knuckles and skull against the steel. It dropped to its knees and the others surged past. Two old women in knit sweaters and trackpants; two males of indeterminate age in shorts only; a woman in waitress uniform but no shoes; a bloated gentlemen in badly-soiled whites who may have been the cook.

Elliot turned and sprinted out onto the street in time to see Waxer vanish behind the corner store, headed for the vehicles. He either had no ammo or was simply a coward. But he might have more weapons in those vehicles and Elliot cursed himself for not taking time for a proper recon before he let his temper get the better of him. He had to get Jeff's assault rifle before Waxer returned with something similar.

The huddle of undead was on its way, the rattled footballer now in the rear, but Elliot had enough distance to keep ahead of them. His boots pounded down the asphalt and then pavement as he made for the pub's front doors, wide open after Waxer had crashed through them. He paused long enough to pull them shut and wove through a jungle of upturned chairs and tables back into the kitchen.

The cooler door had been knocked closed again by Jeff's struggles. Elliot blinked a moment at the spectacle of the big Druid holding in his innards with one hand and holding the dead woman's face away with the other. There wasn't a trace of fear or even pain on the big man's face, nothing but anger. His gaze swung Elliot's way and he swore, then coughed blood and returned his concentration to the dead woman.

A motorcycle roared. Elliot slung the M4 and scooped up the speargun from the stove, headed out into the parking lot again. He tossed the speargun in the curb where the rat had run, keeping it away from Jeff, then assessed the rifle as he raced out into the street, his focus still on stopping Waxer. He dropped the mag out, checked it, worked the action to clear the chamber, slapped the mag back in place and chambered a round. He selected single-fire, rather than wasting rounds on auto.

The dead were closing on the pub's front doors; the footballer had already reached them, scratching at the wood. Elliot took to the opposite sidewalk, aimed the rifle at the fast-diminishing dot at the other end of the shopping district, squeezed twice and lowered the weapon, swearing. He spun, got onto one knee, fired over and over until every member of the shabby crowd of pusbags dropped. He got up and stalked into the pub, kicking chairs out of his way until he stood by the food prep bench with the hot barrel aimed at fat Jeff's head. The Druid had defeated the dead woman. He slumped against the cooler door with a dripping knife in a shaking hand, needing the other hand to press on his guts. Blood was everywhere. Elliot was standing in it. He didn't care.

"What's his name? The one who got away? Waxer, right?"

Jeff answered by spitting blood his way and swearing hot rage.

"I only wanna know in case I run into him again. Then I can whisper it while I'm slitting his throat."

Jeff swore louder and tried to get up, but grimaced and fell back. The knife slipped from his hand.

"Death Druids? On your way to Stonehenge were you?"

This time Jeff said nothing, his eyes rolling, unfocusing.

"You butchered innocent people. You ..." No. There was no point in recounting the man's sins. Though he still panted shallow breaths, the blankness settling over his face meant he either couldn't hear or couldn't care. Safing his weapon and waiting it out, Elliot could only hope he still felt pain—pain that would extend into the next world and forever.

He retrieved the speargun and shottie and the cartridge he'd dropped. They fit snugly in a sports bag from a room upstairs, along with the two M4 magazines Jeff had in his back pockets. He searched a few rooms—got a shock when he found a suicide swinging from their belt in one. Another guest had left behind briefs, t-shirts, a couple of pullovers, socks, and a pair of torn joggers, all of it in Elliot's sizes, so he stuffed that in the bag too. He poured himself a double shot of bourbon and slammed it, sighed with the burn, left the glass on the bar. He collected the bandoleer from the truck—minimal blood; that was good—and slipped eleven shells back into it. He returned to the cellblock and dragged his pack out with a fresh and unbroken broom handle while the dead trucker mewled at him. The Shell peaked cap looked clean, so he scooped that out too, checked it over and jammed it on his head. He went into the police station bathroom and cleaned his chest with tap water and paper towels.

The sun felt like a mother's caress on his wet skin when he stepped back out into the street; he put the two bags down, held his arms out to the sides and soaked in rays for a count of two hundred. Then he carried the gear across to the pickup. Dumping it on the asphalt, he pulled up the pickup's tailgate, leaned in underneath …

His breath caught in his throat.

There, cowering in the fetal position between plastic tubs of supplies and three swags, his wrists and ankles trussed in fencing wire, his eyes puffed by tears and at least one fist, was Lewis Oussef.

4

Lewis sat on the gutter, arms around his knees, zoned out and vacant as a deader. Elliot had cut him free and helped him to the edge of the pick-up, carefully massaged some bloodflow into his calves and hands. The young man hadn't responded to conversation, staring into the middle distance. As blood returned to his extremities, he'd stumbled to that spot on the gutter and stayed there.

Elliot took ten minutes sorting through what he'd keep and what he wouldn't. The outlaw bikers' machetes, knives and pipes he slid down the storm drain opening, wanting to be rid of anything that might have been used on the Oussefs, wanting to deny the bastards their gear should they return. He didn't need their melee weapons anyway: so far, his tanto and hammer had served him fine. He found an open packet of lollipops, four left. He unwrapped one and stuck it in his mouth—strawberry; not bad—left another by Lewis and put the others in the pickup glove box. The logo for *Lonnie Cabinet Solutions* was emblazoned across the vehicle's sides and tailgate, but whatever carpentry tools *Lonnie Cabinet Solutions* might have once carried had been discarded by the bikers, which seemed immensely stupid to Elliot. At least they'd collected food and medical supplies. The V8's trunk had given up a tire iron, jack, screwdrivers and spanners, a jerry can of fuel and six bottles of engine oil. More importantly, there'd been a box of fifty full-metal jacket 9 mm rounds—completely useless for any of the Druids' weapons but perfect for Elliot's SIG. It was the only thing that day that brought him the slightest bit of joy. He bundled what he wanted into the plastic tubs in the back of the pickup, along with his pack and the duffel bag then took one of the Druid's first aid kits out to Lewis.

He placed it on the curb and inspected Lewis's face, wrists and legs again. The lollipop hadn't been touched. With more than a touch of irony, he murmured, "Sit still while I patch you."

Despite the warmth of the day, Lewis wore a red hoody pullover with a blue tee, a Pokémon character peeking through the hoody's collar opening. He wore shorts but no socks or shoes. He didn't flinch when Elliot touched an antiseptic swab to the cut above his left eyebrow and the scrape on his knee, or when Elliot pinched the face-cut closed with one hand and applied two butterfly plasters. Elliot dabbed the teenager's wrists with betadine and wrapped them in dry bandages. Then he sat back to admire the job. For a moment, he felt a familiar mental twinge: there was something about Lewis Oussef, something that nagged at him, something he couldn't put a finger on …

He pointed to the sticky sutures on the teenager's face. "Don't take these off for a couple weeks. Less of a scar that way." When the boy showed no signs of responding, Elliot attempted humor. "Although. Chicks do dig scars."

Still nothing. Well, he'd never been a guy to make others laugh. And he couldn't remember the last time he'd even spoken to a teenager.

"The bandages we'll change in a couple of days. Your wrists will heal ok."

A fly had settled on Lewis's knee, probing around the abrasion. Elliot glanced up and down the road to prevent surprises, waved the fly away and sat on the curb beside him.

"They touch you?" he asked.

The young man's head turned fractionally, his eyes tracked towards Elliot and a shallow furrow appeared between them.

"Those bikers, those asswads," Elliot clarified. "They … touch you?"

Lewis swallowed then pointed to his brow, and then the swelling under his right eye.

It was Elliot's turn to swallow. It wasn't easy to ask a guy about something like this. "I mean besides that? Did they …?"

The frown deepened a little and Lewis looked away, which told Elliot nothing. He let it go. In truth, he didn't want to know. The young guy's near-catatonia might be down to what his sister and parents suffered. And really, that was the loss that mattered in the longterm: Lewis was alone in the world.

Or was he?

"You have anybody you can stay with?" he said, remembering a bunch of places circled on that map. "Friends, family? Maybe your dad was waiting till things settled down before visiting someone."

After a moment, Lewis shrugged. Nothing more than that. His attention was back on the ground in front of him.

The rasp of shoe on asphalt brought Elliot to his feet. Sure enough, a new deader ambled their way from the direction of the pub. Probably hadn't seen or smelled them yet. Give it another fifty yards or so, and it would. He picked up the rifle, sighted on the corpse's head, then reconsidered, barrel dipping. The ammo was too valuable. He could take out the zombie with the hammer. Or he and Lewis could just leave. They should be moving anyway, he realized. If "Waxer" returned with friends …

"So," he murmured. "Where to?" Where in hell would Lewis—

"Minchenbridge," whispered Lewis.

"Huh?"

"Minchenbridge. Grandparents."

"Your grandparents live in Minchenbridge?"

A slow nod of the head. Down the road, the zombie lifted its own head, tasting the air.

"And where's that?" he asked, dropping his voice.

Lewis mumbled, "South of Launceston."

Elliot shut his eyes, pictured the maps: Hobart, where he'd landed, had been on the south-east coast and he'd traveled about sixty miles inland and north-west from there; the city of Launceston was up near the north coast, a hundred twenty miles away, maybe more.

Oh Christ. "How *much* south of Launceston?"

Lewis gave another languid shrug, said nothing.

Elliot squeezed the bridge of nose, teeth grinding. *Goddam.*

There'd be crowds around Launceston. Lots of undead. Lots.

And it was a long way from the remote wilds that Elliot was aiming for.

But what was he gonna do? Leave the kid here? The deader had their scent now, lumbering their way. He had maybe forty seconds until it reached them. Lewis wasn't even looking for it, much less aware of it.

Goddam hateful sonofabitch of a Universe.

"Minchenbridge, you say?"

The young man's twitch might have been a nod. Or just a twitch.

Use a car. All goes well, you'll be back here in twenty-four hours. A small detour, that's all.

Elliot sighed, lay the rifle down and took out his hammer. With other Death Druids out there, he wasn't going to get the chance to check the Harrietville Council Chambers building for books. Maybe Minchenbridge would have a library.

He checked the sun not far from the horizon now, considered the distance they'd have to cover, then offered Lewis his hand.

"Up you get, Cochise." Lewis stared at it a moment, then got himself upright without taking it. Elliot spun the hammer inside his fist. "That biker may be back soon, so we better find somewhere to camp the night, lay low. There were a couple farmhouses I saw just out of town. Thick woods nearby we can run to if need be. Then tomorrow we go find your grandparents."

"Farmhouses?" Lewis's tone was as dull as his eyes. He wrapped his arms around himself despite the latent heat of the day.

"Don't fancy driving in the dark. Besides," he added as he flexed his arm and pointed the hammer at the zombie closing in on them, "tonight we could both use a rest."

He chose to hide them in the long garage building off the side of one of the farms. The property was accessible only to someone investigating down a maze of dirt access roads as Elliot had. And raiders would check the house before the out-buildings. Also there was easy access to the high-grass paddocks out through the back door, so they could bail if needed. The owners had created a single-room apartment in the garage, with cheap ply walls and exposed insulation bats. He parked the pickup inside the garage proper, closed the door over it. He found seven eggs in the chicken coop which scrambled just fine, and he put half in front of Lewis. Lewis picked at it, which was a good sign, but any time Elliot made conversation, he would pull his hands back into his lap, drop his head and close down. Elliot gave it up. It wasn't like he enjoyed conversation anyway.

They wouldn't be staying long, so he didn't bother cleaning the fry pan or plates. He found a plastic garbage bag, put the used utensils, plates, pan and eggshells in it. His hand hesitated over a pile of dusty lottery tickets before shoving them too into the bag. He took it out into a patch of scrub behind the garage and shoved it beneath the bracken. That would discourage overnight rodents and ants, and distract the goddam flies. It would also hide the fact they'd been here from any Death Druid snoopers who might search later.

The low garden fence around the main house had a white paling gate. It was open, and this time when he looked, he saw a shoe, a sneaker with toe pointing at sky. Venturing closer revealed a leg, bare, a woman's. It wasn't moving. He risked an even closer look. She was young, mid-twenties, only days dead. Maybe even one day. Crows and foxes hadn't got to her, though the ants had. She'd cut her wrists, laid on her back under the bright Australian sky—maybe to let the sun warm her even as her body cooled, maybe because she liked the color blue as he did. He thought of burying her and decided not to. He'd let the Oussefs lie where he found them. He'd let a *lot* of bodies lie where he'd found them. Better to keep well away from the truly dead, avoid infection, disease. Better not to get involved.

He went back in to find that the teenager—he almost thought, *client*—had curled up on one of the two camp beds, face to the wall. Only half the eggs had been eaten. Elliot ate the rest, then took the plates to the trash too.

What the hell am I doing?

He thought this as he squatted by his stashed garbage, wiping his hands on the grass. He was doing what was right, that's what he was doing. What had to be done. Elliot might be an asshole, sure, but even an asshole could have a conscience. Once the teenager was at his grandfolks, he'd be off Elliot's hands.

Waving away flies, he checked on the car, brought all the weapons inside. He cleaned and oiled the firearms, did another inventory while loading bullets into the SIG magazines. M4: three mags, seventy-three rounds all told. Aimrite speargun: one spear loaded, two spares in rubber mounts on the side of the body. Shotgun: loaded, bandoleer holding eleven spare rounds. SIG, two loaded mags, thirty spare rounds.

He braced the door with a chair and groaned in weariness as he spread himself across the spare cot. An hour ago he felt like he could sleep on his feet. Now that he wanted it, sleep eluded him. One ear whined with tinnitus. He hurt all over. He contented himself with relaxing, resting, listening to the whir of a moth at the skylight and replaying moments from the day while the evening curdled into night around him.

In the other cot, Lewis snored.

In the small hours, he heard the growl of motorbikes, prowling. Distance was hard to tell in the night and he stood at the door, armed and ready. After some time, they faded. But even when he sat back down on his cot, even when he was *sure* they were gone, he could still hear them.

II

A Ghost in the Land of the Dead

5

They raced through farmland, sticking to back roads. It would add many hours to the trip north, but the strategy could help them get there alive.

Staying alive was all Elliot had to live for.

He didn't trust the main highways to be free of log jams of crashed traffic, of old police roadblocks, of crowds of the undead, of looters ambushing people. Of bikers. For weeks, Elliot had been happy to walk, avoiding anywhere he might find people. This was his first time driving an Australian vehicle, though he'd had experience with RHD vehicles at other times and places. At least he wasn't doing it in traffic; out here, he could and did drive down the center of the roadway.

In the back, canned goods and other crap rattled in the plastic tubs, while the rifle and shottie clacked against the back of the driver's seat. Lewis was a lump of pain in the seat beside him, curled against the door and window, eyelids hooded, breathing shallow, skin pallid, hair sweat-pasted over his forehead. And everytime Elliot glanced at him, he felt that same little psychic niggle, a fish nibbling at the back of his mind. There was something familiar …

The teenager had slept late, and Elliot had let him; it meant time for Elliot to use the home owner's shaving kit to scrape off days of irritating stubble, time for a little more scavenging. But it also meant they hadn't left until mid-afternoon.

The teenager's continued non-responsiveness was a concern. Elliot had the thought that the Druids' set of maps might prove helpful in more ways than one. He cleared his throat, asked Lewis to grab them out of the glovebox and do some navigating for him. It wouldn't matter whether he was any good at it or not, since Elliot had already memorized what he'd needed. But the ploy might work in prising the boy out of his malaise.

Activity: the best antidote for depression and the best inoculation against trauma.

His Southend Security supervisor's words upon induction. Elliot wasn't sure how many mental health experts would agree with that cauliflower-eared moron, but without a psychiatrist handy to step Lewis through the recovery process, activity was all Elliot could think of.

"C'mon, Cochise." He took his foot off the gas. "There's a crossroads ahead and I need to know whether to keep going or turn right."

Lewis' only response was to curl tighter. Elliot could only hope the grandparents had the juice to get the young guy through it.

A wallaby grazing the grass on the verge looked up at them, but held its ground as they passed. Elliot slowed further, considering the potential for fresh meat. But there'd be others and he was eager for Minchen-bridge.

Clumps of flowers—white, or yellow, some blue—punctuated the incessant greens of farmland and scrub.

Birds jinked and wheeled in a flock against the soft blue sky to his right. This was still a pretty world for the most part, but it wouldn't be one that Lewis Oussef would enjoy living in, even if he recovered from his loss, Perhaps it would have been kinder for those outlaw bikers to do him in along with his parents. Then again, they weren't in it for the kindness.

For a moment—and only a moment—Elliot considered telling Lewis that his sister was still alive, probably. But what kind of cheer would that be? *Hey, kid, your sister's a biker's bitch, a slave.*

He opened his mouth to try asking about the map again, then gave it up and sped up through the crossroad, still pointed roughly north.

To his left, a field——or paddock, as Australians called it——caught his eye where a dozen or more black and white cattle watched him pass. They appeared well-fed; the grass was plentiful and there were the remains of hay bales out in the middle of it. Behind their paddock, tin milking sheds or barns bounced the sunlight back at him. An orange tractor poked out from behind them, a quarter mile back from the road up the long dirt driveway, but no other vehicles were visible. He wondered if someone still lived in the single-story farmhouse near the sheds, someone protecting and feeding the cows, keeping marauders at bay. Keeping the undead at bay. If there was, he wished them luck, but he wouldn't be stopping in for a cup of tea and a hamburger. He reached between his legs into the mug full of blackberries he'd brought from the farm and shoved a couple in his mouth, wishing he hadn't gone and started thinking of burgers.

Two miles on, they had to squeeze past a pile-up—two cars and a tourist bus. The bus was on its side, one car a mashup of metal, the other poking out of a roadside ditch. He saw bodies but none of them moved. There was an arm on the asphalt by the bus's rear wheel. Elliot thought of Radler and IEDs for the second time in as many days.

Lewis pressed his head into the headrest, his hands in his hair, eyes glued to the scene, his normal dark skin dialed down a shade or two as the blood left it.

Elliot couldn't think of anything to say to make that mess seem better. There'd been nothing to say in Syria. Nothing to say in Jordan or Iraq. Nothing to say in Hobart.

Past the blockage, he could gun it again. A mile later, as they entered a clutch of bushland between properties where tall eucalypts competed with a line of power poles, a metallic whine started in the car's engine. Elliot frowned at the fuel gauge which indicated a three quarter full tank, then relaxed the pressure on the accelerator. The whine stopped momentarily before becoming a growl. He smelled burning rubber and the vehicle shuddered. He took his foot off the gas a little more, cursing. Lewis recoiled from the torrent of invective and Elliot wondered if it reminded him of the bikers. Right at this point in time, Elliot didn't give a shit if it did. The car jerked and spasmed. He planted his foot hard to force fuel into the motor and it stopped completely. He cussed even harder as the pickup coasted to a stop, engine dead and ticking.

Elliot stamped the clutch into the floor, turned the key and got nothing for his effort but a dull clicking from somewhere under the hood. He slapped the wheel, tried starting it again with the same result. He craned his neck both ways, checked the side mirrors—no pusbags around. Not yet, at least. He shouldered the door open, went round back, flipped open the cardboard box of tools he'd taken from the Druids' V8 and grabbed a flathead screwdriver, returned to his door.

"Lewis, I need you to…"

Lewis stared straight ahead. He'd taken his hoody off when they'd set out and now had it bunched like a teddy bear against his blue Pokemon t-shirt. Elliot swore again. This was making things harder. He'd seen plenty of guys shutting down after a skirmish—one guy *during*. Shutting down wasn't going to help either of them survive. Another fifty or sixty miles and Lewis could turn catatonic all he wanted in the arms of his grandparents while Elliot moved on to browner pastures.

Leaning in, Elliot shoved the screwdriver in a back pocket and snapped his fingers a couple of times by the kid's ear. "Hey! Lewis! I need you to get me the topmost map in the glove compartment."

"What," the teenager murmured.

"Get the map." He snapped his fingers again then went around the front of the utility, wrestling with the hood release. It finally popped and he shoved the heavy iron sheet upwards until the brace clunked into place to hold it there. The passenger door squeaked open and a moment later the map landed in the engine cavity and flared open in the light breeze. Elliot caught it before it could fly away, shoved it under one armpit.

"What the hell was that?" He grabbed Lewis's elbow before he could wander back to his seat. "Where you going? I need you on watch."

"What?" Lewis blinked at him, face like a mannequin.

"Sentry duty. Stop the deaders sneaking up on us. On me in particular, since I'll be the one with my head buried in the engine." The boy frowned blankly at him. Elliot hadn't actually needed the map, so he stomped back to the passenger door, stuffed it in the glove box and dug out the SIG. Returning, he showed it to Lewis. "You ever use one?"

Lewis' flinch was answer enough. He buried his hands in his jeans pockets, shoulders bunched.

Elliot fixed him with a hard look and rattled the SIG. "Well, you're using one now."

A stir of emotion on the boy's face for the first time, a flicker of something. "Mum and Dad say guns are wrong."

Bleeding heart bullshit. Just what we need.

"You're telling me your Dad never used a piece? You survived eight weeks without firing so much as a BB gun?"

Lewis gave a little shrug, turned away to study a yellow-wattle tree on the verge. When he spoke, his voice was dry and crisp like the rustling of the map in the cab. "Didn't need them. He kept us *away* from the gimps. He said brainpower was better than firepower."

With maybe five hours of daylight left, Elliot was in no mood to discuss the finer points of gun control. And he sure as shit didn't want to be stuck in this car all night waiting for the dead to come knocking. "Well, anyone with *half* a brain takes what they can get in this day and age. So you'll be taking this sidearm, getting over there where you can see down both sides of the truck and warn me if anything comes calling."

Lewis flushed, lips clamped together. For a horrible moment, Elliot was sure he'd cry. Then he reached for the pistol.

Elliot pulled it back. "Weapons training first. This is the safety. It's on. You want to shoot, you flick it this way, then back to put it back on when you're done. Very important you don't carry it around with the safety off." He held it at arm's length, aimed it at the bushland. "Maybe you played a computer game or two? Maybe you've seen some of this? Well, let's make sure. You grip it like this, line this rear site with the post here at the end of the barrel. *Squeeze* the trigger only when these two are lined up on the thing you want to die. Never ever point it at me. Or at your feet. Or at anything valuable you don't want messed up." He racked the slide and handed it sideways to Lewis. "There's now a round in the chamber."

Lewis took it lightly as if it would explode and stumped down the road a dozen yards where he planted his feet with his back to Elliot and shoulders hunched. One hand disappeared in a hoodie pocket. The pistol hung limply at his side.

"Don't use it unless you have to. And *don't fire near me.* Just warn me and I'll get out the way."

Lewis did not respond, but jammed the SIG in his jeans and folded his arms.

"Jesus, Mary and Joseph, spare me," Elliot muttered. "Probably shoot his pecker off."

He got busy inspecting the engine, laying the screwdriver on the battery for the moment. Apart from the tang of hot oil it smelled like burning wires in there. When he leaned right in and over, he could see a belt hanging off the engine block, connected but floppy, loose. God, he wished Uncle John had shown him this stuff when he was a kid. How could you be a trucker and raise a child without teaching them basic mechanics? He slapped at a fly, slapped again—stupid things never got the message. He leaned in again, ran the tips of his fingers along the belt: it was a little cracked in places and rough like skin calluses. What was it for, the alternator? He vaguely remembered something about that from motor pool guys talking shop at a bar once.

What the hell did he do now? Where was he gonna get another and how was he gonna fit the damn thing? In concert with the buzzing in his head, the drone of flies got louder; it sounded like a bunch of them flying sorties, triangulating his position, zeroing in on him. He hated the little bastards all the more for their timing.

Best he try to get the belt off, see if it had some writing on it to indicate what it was. He felt around for the screwdriver. Something clammy like damp vinyl fell on his fingers. Elliot jerked his hand free, looking up into the curdled-milk eyes of a corpse as it bit down on thin air, air where his fingers had been a half-second earlier. The deader's teeth clacked against the chassis. Flies droned around its head, others crawling in and of out the open wound on its neck.

Behind him, Lewis cried something inarticulate while Elliot backpedaled. The pusbag rounded the car towards him, a big guy in a farmer's coverall, in good condition all things told apart from his eyes and neck. Maybe recently turned. Elliot had left his weapons in the pickup. And the screwdriver was now beside the highly mobile corpse. The thought crossed his mind to jog back to Lewis, take back the pistol and pop this dead bastard, but his blood was up. He stepped *forward*, swiveling on his left foot and driving his right into the corpse's leg above the knee. With a satisfying crack, the joint gave. His opponent toppled while Elliot danced aside. He skipped back to the engine, snatched up the screwdriver. The zombie's head came around to seek him out and met the screwdriver coming the other way. Elliot left it sticking from the dead man's temple, as the corpse collapsed onto the asphalt and meet its second death with tremors and a sigh of escaping breath. Elliot stomped its head and stomped again until the point of the screwdriver punched through the back of the skull. He kicked it in the ribs.

Checking alongside the truck both sides to make sure nothing else nasty was coming, he shuffled backwards toward Lewis. "A little warning next time, huh?"

"S-sorry."

The boy was mannequin-still, the gun pointed at the tar and shaking in his trembling hand. Elliot reached down and plucked it away, turned it muzzle-down and checked the safety. Still on.

"You had my back, dammit. What the hell happened?"

"N-nothing. I … I was watching the bush."

"You have to watch everywhere! You—"

But Lewis was running. He hurdled the dead man, made it to the truck, wrenched the passenger door open and flung himself inside, slamming it after him.

Elliot stomped back to the body and kicked it three times in the hip.

"Sonofa*bitch*!" He wasn't sure if he meant the Universe, the dead guy or the boy. Any of them would do.

After another ten minutes of tinkering, Elliot gave it up. The sun was just above the trees. He needed another of whatever these belts were. Maybe there was something back on that farm with the cows. Or another pickup or truck they could use. It was probably two miles back to the driveway, but they could leg it overland, come up on the house from the side. Maybe they should spend the night there and fix this tomorrow.

He opened the tailgate, pulled the M4 strap over his shoulders and chest, did the same with the shottie. He shoved a couple of spare water bottles in his backpack. His hand hesitated over two tins of baked beans but he grabbed them too and slammed the gate. When he rounded the passenger side, Lewis had his head out the window, eyes wide with sudden alarm.

"Where you going?" Lewis said.

"Farmhouse. Be dark in a few hours and I need some parts to try 'n fix this."

"What about me?"

"What about you?"

"Can I come?"

"Can you…? You think I'm gonna leave you here?"

Lewis blinked.

"Shit."

He let his pack slip to the road and peeled back the sleeve of the green button-down shirt he'd found last night until the tattoo showed. Lewis pressed his lips together, concentrating.

"Leave no man behind," Elliot said. "Even if he did almost get me eaten."

The growing peace on the boy's face vanished, he blushed. Softly he said, "I didn't mean to."

Elliot grunted, picking up his stuff. "We got a hike. Grab your gear and that spear gun." He started off, heading up the verge, then paused halfway as his companion climbed backwards from the truck. "And grab the keys from the ignition."

There was no one home. Elliot felt the truth of it, because there were no dogs barking, no dogs tracking his incursion warily or waiting with wagging tails. Farms always had dogs, or rather farmers did.

Still, they approached carefully from the east, from the shelter of bushland and across an empty paddock, Lewis forty yards behind Elliot and a dozen to his left so as to offset them for any would-be snipers. The grass was only ankle height; grazing animals had been here recently.

Lewis labored under the burden of his swag. The huge bedroll had been stuffed with personal items looted from the garage apartment: toothbrush but no paste since Elliot didn't trust it; a full change of clothes slightly too big; a rain-jacket. His original personal items were all gone now, scattered around a different property neither of them would ever return to. Puffing and panting, he looked like he'd never done a minute's exercise in his life, despite his skinny physique.

The vicinity of the house boasted a stone drive and turnaround with a well-kept rose-bed as a centerpiece. Lavender plants along the near side of the building were not flowering which Elliot thanked God for—lavender put him in mind of old people for some reason. Apricot, plum and lemon trees had been spread around the drying yard behind the house, three of each, the stone fruit showing signs of bird raids, unsalvageable. A chicken coop marked the back boundary of the yard. Ducks lazed around a small dam on the near side of the paddock beyond the house where the cows were. The barn he'd seen had peeling walls, one door swinging open in the breeze. Steel fittings in the other structure indicated it probably was a milking shed. The orange tractor had a flat-tire; the shoulder of an old 70s model car poked from behind it. A gas barbecue and home-made workbench furnished the back porch, while the front one had a bench seat and pot plants on it.

Elliot entered the house first, leaving the SIG and shotgun with Lewis who lay in the paddock. He moved from room to room on the balls of his feet with the M4 at the ready. No one was there. He found a General Motors Holden key hanging on a *See Tasmania* keytag by the back door. He pocketed it, hoping it belonged to the old car behind the sheds. The two bedrooms reeked with a history of bed farts and unwashed linen; one belonged to a single parent or a couple with only one partner making their side of the bed. The child's room was wallpapered with bad crayon and pencil drawings of princesses, dinosaurs, cats, trees, people; the bed was also unmade. School notices and bills addressed to Mrs Emily Wilson clung to the fridge beneath magnets along with a photo of a small girl in school uniform. In the kitchen, a heavy traffic of ants ran between a crack in the wall and a single dirty bowl on the counter crusted with the remnants of cereal and UHT milk. An empty UHT carton had been rinsed and left to drain on the sideboard. Everything was dry.

Elliot returned to the back door, whistled loud and waved a hand. A head popped up followed by the rest of the body and Lewis loped awkwardly toward the house while Elliot returned to scour a kitchen stripped almost clean of food stuffs. He scratched at a mosquito bite as the backdoor squeaked shut. Maybe the chickens had lain recently.

Lewis slid the weapons on the small dining table, then pitched his swag on an armchair and slouched onto a couch that desperately needed re-springing. He put his feet up on the coffee table, his head back against the cushion.

Elliot returned to the girl's room, gathered up a handful of crayons, a notebook, a rubiks cube and jigsaw puzzle box and placed them on the table by Lewis's feet, inviting him to keep his mind busy. Anything to prevent a return to his earlier malaise.

Lewis's eyebrows rose. "Where'd you get these?"

He said, "In the bedroom back there."

Lewis got up and headed that way.

Elliot figured he'd be okay for a while and shoved one of the armchairs against the front door. He exited out the back, checking the outside of the house and the area around the sheds. No sign of deaders. He did find plenty of empty cans, bottles and string. He used these to create noise-makers and strung them around the house as hidden as he could, creating tripwires and an early-warning system. The key by the back door started the old car—a gold, rust-spotted "Torana"—without any trouble. Just over half a tank of fuel. He revved it a couple of times to blow out the pipes and switched it off, pocketed the key.

The chickens pressed around him as he raided the chicken coop. He retrieved six good sized eggs which he carried back to the house in a plastic icecream container. He thought maybe they hadn't been fed for a while and considered doing it. Later. He'd do it later.

Back in the living room, he eased himself into the spare armchair, closed his eyes for a moment's rest. Images swam around his mind's eye, most of them unpleasant. No peace there. He leaned forward to inspect Lewis's artwork instead. The shapes and swirls on Lewis's page were subtle but they were all in black. Depressing. Maybe the cauliflower-eared idiot at Southend Security had been right. What the hell was he thinking giving the young guy pencils? There was work to do and he needed to be busy.

"Time you fixed dinner," he said.

Lewis took a purple pencil, placed the pointed lead inside a thick black line he'd outlined and started shading it. "Can I do it later?"

For Christ's sake. The picture was unsettling, like Lewis was drawing some kind of voodoo spell. The dark colors, the shapes, they messed with Elliot's head, made him want to kick the table over.

"It's called helping, man," he said. "Doing your part."

"Can I do breakfast instead?" The question was asked in a polite tone, if distracted, Lewis' focus entirely on the page. He put the pencil to his lips, considering his next move.

Elliot had to clench his jaw and remind himself of what Lewis had been through. Through gritted teeth, he said, "I'm securing the place, in case you hadn't been paying attention. Making sure we don't have visitors— and if we do, we're aware of them well before they're aware of us. And getting these." He shook the plastic container, rattling the eggs. "I need you to do your part, making dinner."

Lewis scribbled harder. "I'm not hungry."

Elliot put a hand over his jaw, rubbed hard—then flashed back to Uncle John doing the same thing, on all the occasions where he was about to become truly mad. He dropped the hand. "I am."

Lewis kept drawing. Elliot leaner closer still, studied him and couldn't tell if the young guy was even aware of him, he seemed so engrossed in what he was doing.

Elliot let a few options run through his mind and chose to stomp into the kitchen and get himself a fry pan, spatula and cooking oil. Out on the back porch, he used the barbecue to cook himself a meal of three fried eggs which he ate from the pan with the spatula. He washed and dried the pan and spatula in the kitchen where the water still ran clean and strong. He placed the container with the remaining eggs on the table in front of Lewis.

"In case you get hungry."

Lewis didn't respond. The picture was looking like a human figure. A woman maybe, in blouse and skirt.

Elliot sighed and selected a book from a nearby shelf on Australian history to spend the last of the useful daylight reading it by a window, occasionally glancing outside and down the driveway. When the light became too bad to read by, he got up, found all the useful stuff he could in the house and started piling it on the floor near Lewis's swag.

He came back into the living area with a blanket to find Lewis flicking a switch up and down without result.

"Do you have a torch?" Lewis asked him.

"A flashlight? I do, but we're not using it."

"Why?"

"Anyone outside, they'll see it. They see it, they'll come for us."

Lewis checked the windows, scratched his ear with the back of a pencil. "How do we see at night then?"

"We don't. We sleep. We do things when it's sun up."

"It's … it's too early to go to bed."

"Your family stayed up all night?"

Lewis winced but said nothing. After a moment, he went back to the table and hunched closer over his sketchpad, his coloring frantic.

Elliot lifted the blanket and nailed it over the window. He pointed to the pile on the floor, said, "Too late to cook eggs. You can eat from there if you're hungry." There wasn't much: some old muesli bars, a plastic packet of raisins and a few UHT milk cartons. All labeled *Australian produce* which he could only hope meant *uninfected.* "Better you don't touch this and eat the eggs tomorrow. But if you have to take something from here, let me know what you eat. It's important."

Lewis didn't look up.

Elliot took a plastic jug of tap-water into the parents' room. He put it on the bedside table, cleared the surface of lace doily and reading lamp. He leaned the shotgun and rifle against the wall by the door, unbuckled his belt and lay it over the table, the piton hammer and SIG clattering briefly. He hung his shirt on the back of a chair to air. He was running clean water over his toothbrush in the bathroom when Lewis appeared at the doorway.

"Where'm I sleeping?"

Elliot turned the tap off. "I got the main bedroom. You got the kid's one." He stuck the brush in his mouth and started scrubbing, *sans* toothpaste; he'd never been able to use it since he'd read about its chemicals doing damage to your man parts. And there was always the chance it was toothpaste bearing the agent that had created the deaders.

"Can't I drag the mattress into your room?"

Elliot spat into the sink, ran some water and continued brushing. "Nope," he said around the brush. "You snore."

The hallway floor creaked with Lewis's steps away, then he halted. "Do I use my swag or the bed?"

Elliot cleared his mouth again to answer. "Whatever you want. But you use the swag, you have to roll it up in the morning." He waited. After a moment, the floorboards started creaking again.

He finished brushing, washed his face. He considered the shower stall. The evening was still warm, the house stuffy. A cold shower would be better now than in the morning when the temperature had dropped—and he was weeks overdue for a full wash. But he was exhausted and he'd suffered worse things than cold showers in the cool of the morning.

"You showering now or in the morning?" he called.

There was no answer. Something—probably the swag—dragged across the bare boards of the hallway and into the child's bedroom. The door closed.

"In the morning, it is," Elliot said and rinsed his brush. He tapped out the excess water and left it there to dry overnight. With cupped hands, he scooped water into his mouth, swished it and spat, dried his hands on an old towel hanging over the shower. He took a piss in the toilet, flushed. He did another lap, checking the doors and the windows, except the one behind Lewis's closed door. He leaned against the wall and listened for any sounds coming from the room, but there were none. He stood there for five minutes, or maybe ten or twenty, angry at the universe for lumbering him with a teenager who could barely communicate, who seemed incapable of cooperating fully, of acting to survive, who kept folding in on himself internally. And wouldn't

Elliot love to do *that*, just curl up in the fetal position in a warm dark space and let the dark take him? Let it take him, all his memories, all the things he'd seen and done, the screw-ups, the carnage?

And yet.

And yet.

"A man don't give in. A real man don't give the world the satisfaction." John's words. John's legacy. The only Uncle John Advice that Elliot knew to be true, useful.

He went into his room, kicked off his boots and closed the door, checked his weapons. Then he lay on top of the bed, dragging a thin comforter up to his waist. And fell into a fragmented sleep, populated with meaningless dreams.

6

"What the hell …?"

Elliot rolled off the bed, kicking the comforter aside and scooping up his belt. Lewis's head popped out of his door the exact same time as Elliot's; the frantic lowing of cattle must have woken them simultaneously.

"What is that?" Lewis asked.

There was more cow noise, an abrupt surge of raw animal pain and panic that Elliot couldn't put words to. But the meaning was obvious.

"*What is it?*" the young man insisted.

"One guess," said Elliot.

Lewis's eyes popped wide. According to his own words the day before, he'd never come across deaders for himself. Sadistic bikers, sure, but not deaders.

Had to happen sooner or later.

Elliot buckled his belt, reached for the shotgun and padded barefoot into the living room. Lewis followed at his shoulder as he went to the west and north windows to peer outside. There were no pusbags anywhere along the driveway or around the house on those sides. He went into the kitchen on the south side where the paddock with the cows lay. The animals were pressing up one end of the field toward the milking shed. But he couldn't see clearly into the field, though he could imagine what was happening.

"You have to go and see."

He startled at that, forgetting Lewis was nearby. "A quick look maybe. We still need to go check those sheds for car parts. Here, you might need this." He handed Lewis the piton hammer which the kid took as if it were hot.

"I don't wanna go out there."

"But you want me to? We're in this together or not at all."

Lewis spun the handle a moment then shoved it through a belt-loop of his jeans where it wobbled precariously. He swallowed. "Okay."

"Better." Elliot grabbed his pack and extricated the torn sneakers he'd found near Harrietville. After weeks in boots, his feet were craving a change of footwear. "Go get the spear gun and your shoes. Careful with the speargun." He pointed down the hall. "We'll go out the back."

Three zombies were visible through the railings where Elliot and Lewis crouched. One lay trampled and unmoving, doubly dead. Two others had brought down a heifer, chowing down while their meal still shuddered and kicked.

"How in Christ did they do that?" Elliot wondered aloud. It seemed quite a feat for them to bring down an animal that size. "And where'd they get in?" He scanned the fenceline forty yards away, saw the narrow staff-gate ajar. He'd missed that yesterday, dammit.

"Can we save it?" Lewis whispered. His eyes were big and round, watery.

Elliot frowned at him. "Save it? I'm more worried about saving us. A couple aren't dangerous, but if there's more of them around—"

The heifer gave a wet moan, head lifting a moment before crashing back into the grass. One of the corpses pulled a string of tendon from its leg.

Lewis started to rise. "We *have* to help it!"

A zombie cocked an ear, listening. Gristle trailed from its mouth.

Elliot gripped his shoulder and pulled him back down. "It's a cow. Cows are food. *We* used to eat 'em, now *they* are." He grimaced as a waft of death-stink blew his way. His empty stomach churned. "Better the cow than you."

One of the dying animal's legs thrashed out, knocking a zombie over. The head lifted again, then crashed into the ground. It wasn't long for this world, but there was no doubt it was having a real bad time on its way out. When he turned back, Lewis was staring at him, those puppy-dog eyes wide and imploring.

Elliot's shoulders drooped.

"I take the deaders out, but you follow four yards behind me and four to my right just like yesterday. You don't fire, you just keep a lookout for any others sneaking or crawling around. You alert me if you see one."

The kid's face tightened a little and Elliot wondered if he thought Elliot was still sore about yesterday's near miss at the car.

Well, tough shit if he is. He tossed the shotgun through the railing, worming after it. When he was back in a crouch, he held out his hand for the spear gun. "You carry the shottie." Lewis passed it across and slipped through after it.

Elliot stood and slipped the two extra spears from their rubber fittings, kept them in his left hand with the weapon in his right. He started across the field wondering what the hell he was doing, putting their lives at risk to mercy-kill a cow. He glanced back and grunted satisfaction that at least the kid was learning to follow orders: he was exactly where Elliot had told him to be, head and gaze sweeping their surrounds.

He stepped in close and put spears through both pusbags' heads before either became aware of him. He reloaded the final spear and shifted around to the heifer's head, sighed and lowered the weapon.

Lewis came alongside, keeping some distance between himself and the carnage. "Why are you waiting?"

"It's dead."

"What?" The young man stayed where he was, but leaned toward the cow. The animal was still as a stone, eyes wide and bulging. Lewis made a little noise in his throat. It sounded like defeat.

Elliot retrieved the spears from the deaders' heads and wiped them clean on the cow's hide. He'd rinse them in kerosene or gasoline later. There weren't any other deaders around and shutting the gate over the other side would be simple. He studied the other dozen cows milling at the end of the field by the gate to the cattle run.

"You know, we could stay here a couple more days, get our strength up, and stock up. There's an older car back behind the milking shed that might work if we can't find parts for ours."

"Stock up? On what?"

Elliot nodded toward the animals. "Meat."

They spent forty-five back-straining minutes maneuvering two cows along the cattle run into the shed and hand-milking them. While the animals stood in their corral shuffling their feet, Elliot jogged back to the house and returned with two clean mugs which he dipped in the bucket they'd used. He handed one to Lewis who just watched him.

He took a long gulp of his own, felt the warm fluid filling in some cracks of his hunger. The more he thought of it, staying here might be good for both of them as long as the bikers didn't think of this place. Meat. Milk. Eggs. He might even put some weight back on and get some put on Lewis. And a new thought occurred to him, an entirely unwelcome one. What if Lewis had no grandparents, not anymore? What if they were dead or turned? The teenager was showing signs of life today. Perhaps he could be taught. Perhaps he could learn to do what he had to in order to survive. Perhaps in time, if Elliot couldn't find him a community to join, Lewis could watch Elliot's back; they could partner up if the kid could grow a pair.

Lewis sniffed at it, sipped and screwed up his face. "Yech!"

And perhaps not.

"You're citified, Lewis," he sighed. "This is way it's meant to taste."

"But the germs."

Elliot considered, thinking back on reading he'd done years ago while waiting for deployment. To be fair, it was a reasonable objection. There was the argument *for* unprocessed milk holding onto more vitamins and enzymes, while the argument *against* it echoed Lewis' very concerns about bacteria such as *E. coli* and *Listeria*.

"Well, the science says that the unprocessed milk humans have been drinking for millennia can protect you against gut conditions. But it can also cause gut conditions. Your guess is as good as mine. You wanna boil it first, go right ahead. If you think you know what you're doing." He gulped the rest of his and dropped the mug in a steel wash-trough.

"How do I boil it?" Lewis asked, swishing the liquid around his mug. "There's no power in the house."

"Gas-bottle-fed barbeque behind the house. Used it for the eggs. Fire it up but keep some gas for later."

Lewis' eyes flickered to one of the cows and back. "You didn't mean that, did you?"

"About fresh meat? Damn straight I did."

"But we have eggs. We've got tins and packets."

"Eggs are nearly gone. Tins are suspect. You're telling me you never ate a steak before? A roast chicken? Well. What's the difference?"

Lewis shrugged and considered his feet. "Seems cruel."

"Lewis, come over here." He led the young man to one of the cows, whose eye swiveled to study them.

Elliot lay a hand on its neck, stroked velvet. "This here is a domesticated animal. It was domesticated to provide milk and meat. That's its purpose in life. You think if we set them all free to wander the highways round here they'll live long and happy lives? Maybe they will. Maybe someone else will come across them and eat 'em. Maybe the owner will come back and do it. Maybe a herd of deaders will. Maybe they'll all get hit by cars." He stroked the neck again. "We're not going to hurt it. We'll kill it cleanly and then set about cutting it up, cooking some steaks and curing some for later. Might take a week, but I think your grandparents would be pretty damn happy if we showed up with real meat."

Lewis just blinked and avoided eye contact. He reached out a hand to pet the cow too. "I guess," he said in a small voice.

Elliot took out his SIG, grabbed a dirty towel from a nearby bench and wadded it over the muzzle to absorb some of the sound. He returned to the cow and grabbed Lewis' right hand, pressed the handgun into it, flicked off the safety and let go. He pointed to a spot on the animal's temple.

"One round, exactly here. She won't feel a thing."

Lewis' eyes grew round again and he stepped back, holding the gun away from his side. The towel slipped to the ground. "I'm not doing it."

"Why not?"

"I'm not killing it."

"You never killed anything?"

"N-no."

"Time to start then," he said.

"I'm not killing it." Lewis tried to hand the gun back but Elliot crossed his arms.

"Brave new world, Cochise."

"Wh-what about the cow out there? It's already dead. Eat that."

Elliot shuddered. "After the pusbags have been sucking on it? Not a fan of infection, Lewis. This cow is fresh and fresh is good."

"No way."

"Sooner or later, you have to kill something. May as well be sooner."

"No *way*!"

"You like eating?"

"I'll eat tins then."

"Tins don't grow on trees. Tins don't roam the fields or live in the bush."

"There's thousands of them around."

"And they won't last forever. And tins might be poisoned. You're thirteen. You want to live to thirty, you gotta kill meat."

"I'll … I'll eat vegetables. I can grow vegetables. And fruit. Mum and Dad did. I can too."

Good to know. Maybe you can teach me.

"You're an omnivore, Lewis, not a herbivore. You want to be big and strong—and you need to be big and strong these days—then you gotta eat meat. So shoot the cow."

Lewis had the presence of mind to squat and place the gun on the ground rather than toss it. Then he retreated from it until his ass was against the shed wall.

Flies buzzed around the milk bucket and cow patties. The air in the shed grew warm with the morning sun beating on metal walls. Magpies warbled somewhere outside. Elliot regarded Lewis a long time before stooping for the pistol and towel. He turned, popped one in the cow's temple and moved out of the way of the falling animal.

"What the hell!" Lewis cried.

Elliot waited for the kicking and trembling to stop, tossing away the ragged remnants of the makeshift silencer.

"Why'd you do that!"

"Told you—"

"You didn't have to do—!" The teenager whirled around, hand over mouth, retching and stormed out, his footsteps crunching gravel all the way up until the laundry room door slammed.

Elliot swiped sweat from his brow and flicked it away. He regarded the dead cow sullenly. He heaved a sigh and swore.

Stupid thing was, Lewis might be right: he really *didn't* have to do that. What the hell was he thinking, slaughtering a *cow*? Was he really going to hang around and butcher a carcass that big? How long did he want to stay on this farm, curing meat, inviting deaders to the party because of the smell, risking the return of the farmer or the bikers and an unnecessary confrontation?

He poked the wadded towel with his toe and scratched his neck. His stomach gurgled. And Elliot decided that hell, yeah, he wanted to cook up a big ass steak.

He used carving knives from the kitchen to fashion five long and thick slices of meat from the cow's haunches, regretting the waste. Properly gutted and hung up to drain, the animal might have offered up a couple hundred pounds of beef. With time to experiment, he'd have found a way to smoke it, make jerky, source solar panels and fire up a freezer for the rest of the meat. As it was …

He dragged the gas-barbecue inside the house for privacy and soon filled the air with the maddening aroma of frying meat. It was almost ready when Lewis finally appeared from his bedroom, where presumably he'd been drawing since the paper and pencils had disappeared from the table. He handed the teenager a plate and asked him to find some condiments. Lewis appeared flat again, not angry or anxious, just lifeless, like a blanket had been laid over his personality, his emotions. He dug a single red bottle from a pantry without comment, putting it on the kitchen table. Elliot turned off the gas, poked the steaks again and used tongs to drop two of them on a plate which he handed to Lewis. The young man got a knife and fork from a drawer for himself, smothered the steaks in ketchup and disappeared back into his room.

"You're welcome," Elliot called after him.

He left one of the remaining steaks on the hotplate where he hoped it would dry out enough to keep until night time for them to share. The other two went on his plate with a sprinkling of pepper since pepper should have been safe. He spent the next twenty minutes chewing slowly, savoring his meal and washing his early lunch down with a "stubbie" of Crown Lager he'd found sitting alone in a beer fridge in the shed. It was warm, but he didn't care. It complemented the meat perfectly. He was left with a protruding belly and a satisfied feeling. With midday approaching, it was one of those warm Australian days where the sun threatened tyranny and the best defence was a retreat into slackery. He easily could have taken a nap on the couch, flicked on the TV, watched a game …

Elliot forced himself up and took the rifle outside, checked around the house, then returned to the cattle run. He opened the gates at both ends wide and wedged them open with bricks. He left the shed door open and released the other cow still standing in the milking brackets. It scampered out of the building and halfway along the driveway towards the road before stopping to eye its sisters across the fence.

"Live long and stay away from deaders," he told it.

A flash of brown in his peripheral vision. He turned. A huge rat skulked at the far end of the milking shed. It lifted its nose to the air, whiskers twitching, and scurried in behind some wooden pallets.

"The rodents shall inherit the earth," Elliot muttered.

He gave the fly-covered carcass in the other stall a final look; he'd read enough about curing meat to know that without the proper nitrates and a good smoker, and without a working fridge, the results would be risky. They'd stay here tonight and head out early in the morning, take the farmer's car, get the rest of their gear from the pickup and head toward Minchenbridge. One more night in a nice soft bed sounded good, but he needed to get them back on the road.

He spent some time transferring useful items to the Torana, packing them tight against the sides of the trunk so he could fit things from the pickup in there too. Back in the house, he read some more of the history book, not sure he could believe its claim that Australia had fired the first shot of WW1, targeting a German ship in its waters. A travel agency catalog he picked from under the couch made him swear: probably wasn't much left of the places it advertised. And no one would ever be traveling for pleasure again, not in this world. There were two more eggs in the chicken coop, so he used them and the ones Lewis hadn't eaten—along with some fresh cow's milk—to make a scrappy omelet on the barbecue. He scraped it into two rough semicircles. He reheated the last steak, divided it and served it all up on two plates.

They ate together this time, slouched at opposite ends of the dining table, Lewis watching a large fly butting against a window, Elliot thinking about the wilds of western Tasmania and where he might find the survival information he needed. He was startled by a sob. Lewis dropped his knife and fork, burying his face in the crook of his elbow.

Elliot hesitated then asked, "What's wrong? You … crying about the cow? We needed the strength, Cochise."

"Not the cow."

"Is it what happened on the road yesterday? Look, man, crap happens—"

"I don't care about that!"

Elliot pressed his mouth shut and ran a hand over his jaw. *Well, I sure as hell care. I was the one nearly got his fingers bit off coz his squadmate was busy daydreaming…*

"They were screaming! All of them. Even Dad. I shut my eyes but I couldn't shut my ears and I heard it all and they had me tied up in the ute and one said he was saving me for later and—" Lewis threw himself onto the sofa, sobbing into a throw pillow.

Elliot knew it was the wrong thing to say, but in the absence of anything else, he told Lewis the only truth he knew from experience. "It gets better, man. Well, easier anyway. It won't always feel this bad."

The pillow dropped, the flushed face reappeared, eyebrows knit. Elliot recoiled from the fury burning there.

"Why did you bring me here?" Lewis said.

"I … I'm taking you to your grandparents."

"Why won't you let me see them?" Lewis said and sniffed a huge string of snot.

"What? Who?"

"My parents. My sister. I want to see them."

"Lewis, seriously, you don't."

"I do."

"You *don't*. Not after what those biker pricks did to them."

He swallowed, eyes darting around as if searching for a handhold. "But not my sister, not Alyssa."

"What do you mean, Cochise?"

"They took her." He blinked, doubt surfacing when Elliot didn't reply. "Didn't they?"

"You saw them put her in a car?"

"… no."

Elliot softened his expression. "Because they didn't. She ended up like your parents, Lewis." The lie came so easily, rolling off his tongue like honey off hot butter. It was for the best, this lie, this noble untruth. And Elliot felt like shit.

Lewis gaped at him, the little color he had left draining from his cheeks. He heaved a breath. "How do I *know* what happened?"

"Because I'm telling you. I came upon your house afterwards. Not long afterwards. And I saw the aftermath. Wish to God I didn't. Wish to God it hadn't happened. But it did. And I don't see any point in lying to you."

You lyin' prick.

There was a moment, a still moment when Elliot thought that Lewis would call him on it. But it passed, Lewis shooting to his feet and fleeing for the bedroom. The slamming of the door was like a gunshot.

Elliot finished his meal in silence, put the plate on the floor and went into the kitchen. He drained two full glasses of water, watching cows meander along the driveway in the golden afternoon light. Before retiring himself, Elliot spent two whole hours walking the darkening house, peering out each window in case Lewis's noise had drawn the dead. Or the living. He covered the remains of Lewis's meal with aluminum foil he found in a drawer in case the teenager got hungry again. He drummed his fingers on the table beside the plate.

The teenager wasn't going to make it. Not unless he hardened up. Grief or no grief, Lewis needed to learn about what it took to survive now. It wouldn't be long before it'd be him looking out for his grandparents, not the other way round. Drawing black and purple pictures might make him feel better, but it wasn't going to fill his stomach. It wasn't going to protect him when—

Elliot froze halfway across the living room as he suddenly realized what had been bothering him about Lewis.

He reminded him of Tommy Harrison.

"Well, don't that take the cake," he muttered in the dark. "Stuck with a ghost in the land of the dead."

7

The alien warble of magpies drew him from a shallow sleep. He'd been dreaming of some woman. Maybe he'd met her once; maybe she'd been an amalgam. Whatever the case, he was sorry the dream had evaporated with the approaching dawn.

Something was different in the house, a different quality of sound perhaps. He strained his senses, but nothing came to him and he gave it up as fatigue dicking around with his mind.

He lay on his back for maybe a half hour, listening to birdsong and wind in the eaves, debating how long they should sleep in before getting back on the road and how long he should just lie here. His bladder eventually made that decision for him. He crossed the hallway to the toilet, took a long and joyful piss, and washed his face and hands in the bathroom sink. In the mirror, he looked like himself, only older. The house stank of cooked meat and greasy hotplate. He returned to the bedroom, stuffed the green long-sleeve shirt in his pack and pulled a white t-shirt from the farmer's wardrobe. He headed down the hallway, planning breakfast. He knocked softly on Lewis's door before cracking it open. The sooner he got him to Minchen-bridge, the sooner he could get on with his own life. Such as it was.

Lewis wasn't in bed. The swag he'd taken from the Harrietville house wasn't there either.

One step into the living room and he knew both that the teenager was certainly gone *and* why the house had seemed different when he'd woken. The front door was ajar.

"Sonofa—" He shoved the door closed, locked it, leaned his head against it. The speargun was on the table, but the shotgun and bandolier were missing from the hallway where Elliot had left them. How had he gotten out without waking Elliot?

Am I slipping?

He let loose a sigh. Maybe this was a gift. His "package" was gone, his mission over, any onus on Elliot to escort the teenager further gone with him. And it would serve the little turd right: that was twice in forty-eight hours he'd put Elliot in danger, first by not paying attention on sentry duty and now by leaving the door unlocked while Elliot slept. The smart thing would be to accept the gift, put Lewis from his mind, start up that car and head west.

He tapped his forehead lightly against the door a couple times. "And I always do the smart thing."

He returned to the bedroom, zipped on his hoody over the shirt, put his SIG in the holster and buckled on his belt. He slung the M4 across his back and took the speargun on his way out.

The morning air was especially crisp outside. Elliot smelled rain, noting the clouds scooting across the western horizon. There'd been showers over that way somewhere but they weren't coming here. No, it'd be another warm one once the sun really got going.

Lewis would no doubt have gone toward the pickup because of the maps and supplies left there, but Elliot doubted he'd have taken the driveway to the road. They'd crossed country to get here and he'd probably take the way he knew. He shrugged off the idea of getting in the old "Torana", instead hunting around near the fences on the east side of the house where they'd come from. On one side of the wire fence, he found a vague shoe print in the dewy grass and fresh dirt kicked up on the other side. He climbed over, leery of the barbed wire along the top and started jogging. It was maybe two minutes later that a shotgun blast disturbed the quiet, scattering birds from gums along the border of the nearby bushland. He picked up his pace, adjusting his direction. It went off again before he reached the trees.

He smelled them before he saw them. Five pus-bags—no six!—shambling across his path from the right, twenty-five yards ahead. Farmhands, dressed in bloodied denim and flannelette, workboots too. His heart lurched. Lewis was down in the bracken, crawling away three-limbed, favoring his left arm, shottie abandoned. One butterfly plaster was flapping loose above his eyebrow. A zombie was also down, but the others would be on him in moments.

Elliot came to a stop, planted his feet, aimed the Aimrite and put a spear through the left ear of the one closest to him. Reloading was going to take too long so he ditched it and took out his hammer. He began dancing amongst the remaining ones, slashing and crashing. In seconds, they lay around him with crushed skulls, bleeding in black.

Despite the stench, the fresh air tasted good as he leaned one hand on a knee and wiped the hammer in the wet grass then dropped it there.

"Shit, pal," he huffed. "I don't need this much exercise this early."

He stepped over and held out a hand. After a moment, Lewis took it with his right and allowed Elliot to help him up, then he cradled his left arm with his good hand. There was blood soaking through a tear in the fabric.

Elliot took a step back. "You bit?"

Lewis's gaze traveled slowly to the tear. He shook his head. "Cut myself on a branch, running. They … they chased me from the road."

Elliot hawked and spat bile from the back of his mouth, hitting one of the deaders in the eye. "Show me."

He inspected Lewis's wound through the hole in the cloth without touching him. Elliot couldn't see teethmarks. Not too bad; the branch took a shallow chunk of flesh from just above the elbow.

"I'll tend it back at the house." He stooped and picked up the hammer, then the speargun. Sticks cracking drew his head up. There was movement in the trees forty yards away. More sticks cracked.

"Let's go," said Lewis.

Elliot wrenched the shaft from the first deader's brain pan. "Get your weapon." If there were too many of them, they could easily out distance the dead on foot. If not, this would make good practice, good training.

Lewis looked about to argue, then moved to obey, left arm clamped to his chest. Just before he reached the shotgun, Elliot stopped him with a noise.

"On second thoughts," he said and pulled his SIG. "Take this. Easier one handed. Just don't get blood on it."

Lewis took it without fear this time. "Can we go now?"

"Flick the safety off there like I showed you. No, don't pull the slide back. I already did that. It's live, so go easy."

"Can we go *now*?"

"Nope. Not yet. Looks like maybe three or four more coming. Not too hard to handle."

"But ... but the noise."

Elliot raised his eyebrows then went across and collected the shotgun, held it up. "I think that bridge got crossed." He came back over and took two shells from Lewis's bandoleer, reloaded it.

"We're going to fight them?"

Elliot pointed to two trees growing a couple of yards apart and started their way. The trunks were about as thick as he was. "You're going behind that tree. I'll be behind that one. They'll pass us by if we keep quiet, then you'll come out, close in to about twenty feet away—six meters."

"But—"

He stopped and spoke without turning. "No buts, Lewis. We do this. You think you're old enough to head out on your own. Well, that's good. Good to be confident. But you gotta have the experience to make it work. So. Let's get you some experience."

Lewis followed him to the trees where they took shelter, catching their breath. Elliot leaned the shotgun against the trunk, testing the speargun's load. The wet hiss of zombie-breath and the crackle of sticks and bracken grew closer.

"What do I do?" Lewis whispered.

Elliot mimed pointing the pistol and pulling the trigger one handed, then shrugged. "Pretty simple," he whispered back.

At that range anyway.

"I don't want to."

Elliot shrugged again. "You gotta learn this. Situations like this are normal now. And in situations like this, you're either moving or still, doing or not doing. It's binary, you understand me? On or off, living or dying, acting or being acted upon. There's simply no place for fear, just action."

Sure, a voice whispered, fear came later, in the cold dark night when a man had time to think back, remember how close he'd come, and what he'd had to do to keep on living.

He took a peek, saw three pusbags weaving their way through their dead comrades, snouts raised like that rat in the milking shed, tasting the air. It was as good a time as any. He caught Lewis's eye and nodded. The young man swallowed, then crept out from his hiding place in a crouch, aping movie versions of Navy SEALs. Elliot adjusted his grip on the Aimrite and followed to Lewis's right.

The teenager must have realized he couldn't shoot all hunched over like that, so he straightened and took aim. He was still a little too far away for Elliot's liking but he didn't interfere. Lewis's hand shook and when he fired first, the bullet went wide and high, scuffing bark from another tree, sending wattle pollen flying. Three heads swiveled his direction and the bodies wheeled around to follow. He took a couple of steps backwards but took aim again and fired, punched a hole into one of their heads. The zombie dropped and Lewis made a noise that might have been a laugh. He aimed again, but hit the next one in the chest. It stumbled but kept on.

Elliot could see the shaking begin again in Lewis's hand so he said, "Wait."

Lewis dropped his arm and backpedaled as Elliot came forward. He put the fishing spear through the left knee of the one with the chest wound, took the SIG out of Lewis's hands and plugged the last one through the eye.

Without turning, he asked, "So where were you headed?"

A pause, then Lewis replied, "Home."

"Why's that?"

Another pause. "I heard them. I heard them with my sister, with Alyssa, not far from the ute."

Ute? Elliot thought. *Oh, the pickup.*

Lewis continued, "I couldn't see, 'cause they put a pillow case over my head. Or a bag or something. But I could *hear* her."

Still facing the bodies, Elliot said, "And I turned up an hour or so later, Cochise. And I'm telling you, there's nothing back at that house you wanna see." Not a direct lie, not this time.

A long and labored breath, then: "Okay."

"Get the shottie," Elliot said, putting the safety back on the SIG and holstering it.

"Huh?"

"The shotgun."

"Oh."

Lewis scrambled back there and returned with it, held it pointing up by the barrel, offered it. Elliot shook his head. "You took it with you today. You must want it."

"Oh. All right." He blushed, lifted his right shoulder up and down. "Kind of hurt when I used it before. I think I sprained my shoulder."

"You didn't sprain it. Might be bruised. That's a mean weapon and you gotta learn how to respect it and use it properly. So let's teach you." Elliot indicated the last zombie, dragging itself across the earth with one leg a ruin. "She's yours."

Lewis winced but nodded.

"Your left hand okay?"

"I think so."

"Good. You're going to fire left-handed to protect that injured shoulder." He raised the empty speargun, pressed the back of it into his left shoulder, using it as a demo. "A lot of people watch movies, they think you gotta clamp a shotgun or rifle butt in hard against you. You're just gonna lean it against your shoulder like this, but grab up here forward with your supporting hand and keep tension on it, like you're pulling it off your shoulder. Okay?"

Lewis tried it. "So I'm kind of pulling one way and pulling the other at the same time?"

"Not pulling exactly, just keeping tension in the two directions. If your forward hand keeps that tension up like you're doing now, it'll cut a lot of the recoil, save you hurting your shoulder. Okay, that looks fine. Now lower it toward her and squeeze the trigger."

Nervous, Lewis swung the muzzle her way, hesitated.

"You've done this, Cochise. You're just doing it again."

The deader reached for the teenager as if anticipating the end. When he fired, he took two of her fingers and the right side of her skull. He swore under his breath and lowered the weapon, transfixed by the mess he'd made.

"Hurt as much as last time?"

Lewis actually smiled, tearing his gaze away from the gore. "No."

Elliot stepped in close, pulled his tanto. "Hold your weapon still for a sec." He made three scratches in the stock and put the dagger away.

Lewis examined the marks with a frown. "What's this?"

"Tally. You made your first kills today." He gave him a thumbs up. "Now, if it's okay with you, Cochise, let's get the hell back to the farm and our new wheels. Maybe you can learn to drive today too. I'm kind of tired."

After Elliot bandaged up the gouge on Lewis's arm, applied a fresh plaster to his brow, and they'd finished up the cereal, and after they'd loaded up the old Torana with their belongings and supplies, Lewis got behind the wheel. Under Elliot's tutelage, he managed to get the car back to where they'd left the pickup without completely stripping the gearbox, but it was a painful trip.

With the young man watching their surrounds carefully this time, Elliot transfered the useful stuff from the pickup to the Torana's trunk and got behind the wheel. Lewis slid in beside him and placed the shotgun carefully on the back seat, then dug his sketchpad and pencils out of his pack. He was subdued, his eyes troubled, but he seemed a little more centered than he had been.

He glanced up at Elliot and nodded as if reading his mind. "I'm okay."

"Very well then." Elliot slammed his door and started the motor. "Minchenbridge trip, take two."

They headed off again, making good time along a clear highway. At one point, Elliot slowed at a T-intersection where a sideroad branched off the main road between rows of cypress trees. A dead woman stood swaying there, standing just behind the white line. One of her eyes had been gouged out and a string of gore hung out on her cheek like a runner of snot. Her head followed them as they inched past. Lewis glanced up from his artwork, gave a shudder and returned to his drawing.

Elliot thought about leaning out and blowing the dead woman's head off, ending her brainless misery, but they'd wasted enough rounds today. As she took a faltering step toward them, he planted his foot, hurrying past.

III

Shitstorm

8

The train completely blocked the road ahead. A carnage of steel and wood filled much of the V where highway met railway between two hills. Elliot coasted to a halt a few hundred yards away. He cut the engine and eased the door open, used his hand as a sun-visor. From the looks of it, the damn locomotive had hit a semi and came off the rails.

"Shit. Hand me the map." He studied it, converted metric to imperial. Available detours were sixteen miles in one direction and twenty three in the other. "Shit," he repeated.

"We should check it out," said Lewis.

Elliot hopped down onto the road and tossed the map on the back seat. "You want to check a crash site? What's there?"

"Maybe more food we can gather up. Weapons."

"Well, it's good you're thinking of those things, but there won't be weapons there. Might be dead people though."

"If they died in the crash, then they're just normal dead. Not … what do you call em?"

"Deaders."

"I like what Dad called them: *ghuls*."

"Whatever we call 'em, I don't like this."

"You don't want more supplies?"

Elliot ran his hand through his hair, chewed his lip, then nodded. The car was pretty full, but they could squeeze more in. And it might be wise to do so if the pickings were good.

"Grab your pack and the Aimrite." He opened the back door and reached for his pack and the M4.

"My swag? I'm not taking my swag. It's heavy."

"And if the car's gone when we get back?" Elliot asked, straightening and slinging his pack on. He surveyed the raised ground above and around them. Anyone might be up there.

"It won't be."

"You know this how?"

Lewis groaned. "My swag's heavy."

It wasn't. Not by a long way, comprised of a bedroll wrapped around a change of clothes and toothbrush. He shook his head and said, "Get it and get the Aimrite."

When Lewis shoved the doors shut on his side, Elliot locked the car and then headed for the verge. The train track, like the road, had been cut through the hills to create a path of least resistance for both.

"Why are you going up there?" Lewis asked him. "Can't we just go along the road? It's, like, straight there?"

Ten feet up the siding, Elliot paused and jabbed the rifle at the accident, forcing patience. He pitched his voice low. "Could be people camping in it. Could be un-wild-life. Better to go up and over, take a look before we commit. Then we know what we're in for."

"Looks fine to me," said Lewis.

"Safety first."

Lewis dragged himself up the hill, short of breath. In the bushland atop the ridge, Elliot waited for him by a patch of young ferns and brambles. He was struck afresh by the strangeness of the bush. A tree close by had white bark peeling like the rotting skin of a deader. Its dense foliage carried raised bumps like glands or blisters, again putting him in mind of the dead. At least it didn't smell that way; in fact the competing scents of its flowers, the dry leaf litter and eucalyptus hung heavy enough in the still air to make him drowsy, wooing him towards sleep. He was weary… so goddam weary. There'd been weeks of running and hiding and stalking and avoiding and hiking, with little food and even less sleep.

He shook it off as Lewis came to a panting halt nearby. "The other thing we're doing up here is hiding this gear." He'd located a relatively snag-free pocket within the brambles and slid his pack there, realized then that Lewis hadn't bothered bringing his. He swore and shoved the spear gun and M4 in there. "Anyone comes across the car, at least they won't get our weapons. Plus, we'll go in light so we can carry more stuff back if we need to. Just the Remington and the SIG." He kept the shotgun and bandoleer, Lewis the 9-mil.

They slipped through the bush toward the cut-through until they were regarding the wreck from above. To their left, it was more obvious up close that the train's engine had hit the semi dead in the middle, forcing it along the tracks westwards. The engine and first two goods cars had come off the rail, tipping. The last ten cars were still upright. Most carried what looked like rocks or ore in open trays. Four were enclosed carriages and two had their doors open already; he'd take one, Lewis the other. There was no sign of life, no noise apart from birds fussing and insects buzzing.

He slapped at a fly. "God, I hate trains."

Lewis stared at him. "What? Why?"

Elliot shook it off, slapped at the fly again and started down the siding. "Let's just get this over with."

They went into their separate train cars. Elliot was instantly disappointed. Open on both sides, it contained crates of untreated wool—it might have been useful as insulation for clothing, but they were better off to simply loot the finished product. Groceries, dry goods, weapons beyond the occasional piece of iron: *nada*. He peered out the door on the other side, sighing. Now he was here, it'd be worth climbing the northern siding to get a look at the way ahead, see if there were clues to what kind of journey awaited them once they found a way around the blockage. He slung the shottie and climbed down the short ladder with his back to the siding, found his footing on the shale of thick stones around the tracks. And whirled at the sound of a cocked rifle.

Three women stood along the top of the siding, spaced at ten foot intervals, two brunettes, one blond, all in their late thirties. They were thin to the point of malnutrition, their clothing and skin smudged with dirt. The blond was tall, long limbed, wearing jogger gear with a wet-weather poncho tied around her waist; she bore the rifle and had it aimed steadily at Elliot's chest.

The brunettes were short—about Lewis's height—and so alike they could have been sisters, both in t-shirts and cargo shorts, their knees scabbed and freshly bruised. One had a handcuff dangling from her left wrist, her cheeks peppered with cuts and the yellow stains of old bruising. More bruising ringed her throat. The other brunette had bruising around her left eye and along the bone of her right forearm and the bicep above it; her hair was piled up beneath a sunhat. She had a carving knife, gripped so tight her knuckles were white. The police revolver in her hatless sister's hands shook, the handcuff rattling against the grip.

The blond said, "This is our train."

He had his balance now, but there was no point going for the Remington. He'd only get one at best. He kept his hands lifted a little from his sides. But he couldn't help asking, "Your name on it?"

Ignoring the question, Sunhat said, "Where's your friend?"

"Don't have any." That much was true. He hadn't had a friend since Tommy. And a goddammed train was the perfect way to remind him of that fact.

He did have a Lewis, though. And if Lewis had any brains at all, he'd be climbing out the other side of the train right now and running.

"Wait, don't kill him!" The squeaky voice came out of the next carriage.

"Shit," Elliot sighed. *No brains.*

Lewis showed his hands from the door, empty, *sans* SIG. He clambered down the ladder and approached slowly, his footing unsteady on the stones beside the track.

"Stop there, kid," said the blond when he'd travelled a dozen feet. "First thing you both do is put your guns at the bottom of the hill here."

"I don't have one," said Lewis with an apologetic smile. Elliot looked away before his partner could make eye contact and blush or something. But the young guy's smile had been winsome and guileless—maybe the one he'd used on his mom and sis to get his own way.

Not so dumb after all. There was hope for him yet.

"Lift your shirt," she said. She waited while Lewis swiveled awkwardly, shirt held high. "Now your pants legs: show me what's in your socks."

She grunted when there were no hidden weapons beneath his denim.

"Your turn," she told Elliot.

"How do I know yours are even loaded?" he asked.

She smiled a harsh smile, said nothing.

"Trust us, they are," said Handcuffs. Her gaze kept flicking to Lewis, Elliot noted, brow crinkled with concern. He nodded to himself: at least one of them was a little conflicted over this. He might be able to use that.

"I could prove it by shooting you in the leg," said the blond. "Course I might miss and hit something else." He took a better look at her—yeah, she *did* remind him of that chick at the sanctuary outside Hobart. The one who'd started the trouble there, ruined the place, turning the men against each other.

Just looking like that chick was almost enough to make him shoot her.

He shifted attention to Handcuffs, got eye contact, told her, "I'm just a guy trying to survive out here. Can you cut me a break?"

She looked away, found something on the train's roof to study. The pistol still shook in her hand.

The blond adjusted her aim from his stomach to his forehead. "I'd say you haven't got much choice."

None-too-happy about it, he complied, unbuckling his belt and laying it at the bottom of the slope. He felt a pang of grief: that hammer and that knife, they'd been allies, team mates. The tanto especially—there wasn't much of his original PMC kit left.

He added the shotgun and bandoleer with almost as much grief.

"Same as the kid," she said. "Show us what's under your shirt, your pants legs."

He turned slowly with shirt lifted. "Like what you see?"

She snorted without smiling.

"I just threw up in my mouth a little," added Sunhat, but her voice had a tremor.

He flashed ankle and the blond grunted. "Where's the gun from that holster?"

He winced theatrically. "Lost it."

"You lost a gun?"

"Big fight. Lots of zombies and running and tripping. You really want all the details?"

"No," she said. "We heard a car, so we'll have the keys too."

"Come on," he tried but she shook her head. He added the keys to the pile.

She grunted and gestured with the rifle in the opposite direction to the crossing. "Now you get walking down the tracks that way, so we can keep an eye on you as you go."

"Or we could go that way." He nodded at the crossing.

She shook her head.

"Look, we could get back in our car and go around," Elliot said, reaching a hand toward the keys.

She waggled her rifle. It was small caliber, maybe .22, but it would still sting if she shot him in the nuts, which is where the barrel was pointed. "You can walk."

"Look, me I can understand you not wanting around. But Lewis here." He focused his attention on the woman with the handcuffs, using Lewis's name to personalize him. "He's lost his folks, his sister. He just needs to get to Minchenbridge."

"So?" snapped Sunhat.

"Well, I mean, Lewis is a young guy. Just lost his family, all of them. It's a win-win, isn't it? He can take you to sanctuary; you can give him the female attention he needs."

Sunhat actually took a step forward at that, right onto the edge of the slope, brandished the knife though she was too far away to use it. "Female attention?"

"Nurturing. I mean, nurturing. Not … the other."

Her eyes were wide now, face flushed. Elliot had made a tactical error and he could only be glad she didn't have her sister's pistol. "That's all women are good for, huh? Nurturing. And *the other.*"

"*I didn't say that.*"

The blond cleared her throat to take over. "Well, we're not his mummies so forget it. Get walking."

Elliot almost replied that he wasn't Lewis' dad either, but for once he had the presence of mind not to say the insensitive thing. *Chalk one up for ol' Elliot. Looks like someone else is the asshole this time.*

"Lewis needs to get to Minchenbridge," Elliot tried again. "I need the car to get him there."

The woman with the pistol let it droop, the crease between her eyebrows deepening. "Where's Minchenbridge?"

"Not far from Lonnie," said the blond with no wavering of her weapon.

"Shit," she said. "You don't want to go that way."

"Shutup," said Sunhat.

"But—"

"They're lucky we're letting them live at all. They can go wherever they want, as long as it's not near us." She gestured to her left with the knife. "Off you go. And let's hope we don't cross paths again."

They trudged a good three hundred yards before Elliot stopped and dumped himself on the siding with a huff. He cracked a strip of dry bark between his fingers. It had last rained a week ago; the ground was dry as toast, like being in Africa, the Kalihari. Dry twigs. Dry leaves. Even living grass crackled under foot. Shit, what if there was wildfire while they were out here? He hadn't thought of that. Would the higher terrain out west be wetter, less prone to it?

"What do we do?" Lewis asked, nudging shale with his toe.

"Wait ten minutes. Go back and get the 9-mil. I didn't see them check the carriage you were in, which shows how smart they are." They'd come down the slope one at a time, covering him and Lewis. Collected his belt and headed back to the crossing along the tracks, carrying his shotgun, his piton hammer, his tanto. And they were no longer in sight.

"What about after we get the gun?"

"It's not a gun; it's a weapon." Elliot picked up a clod of dirt and tossed it hard at the opposite bank. It exploded against an exposed tree root with a dull puff. "We go get the gear we hid and then I guess we walk to Minchenbridge. Unless we find another vehicle on a road nearby. Although ..." He turned another clod over in his hands. One side was hot from the sun, the other cool like death. "The one with the pistol didn't seem too keen on us heading that way. I wonder how bad it is up there."

Agitated, Lewis shoved his hands in his pockets. "It's bad everywhere. My grandparents are there. I wanna go there."

Elliot lifted a hand in placation. "Of course. Yeah."

"You wanted to dump me."

"What? No, I was just—I was trying to get inside their heads. You know. Appeal to their feminine instincts."

"Feminine instincts?"

"Yeah, compassion, empathy. Bitches didn't seem to have much of either though," he added and threw the clod.

"Don't call them that."

"Bitches? Why not?" He glanced back down the track. By now they were probably starting up the car, though he couldn't hear it. His car. With his stuff. "They are."

"You shouldn't talk about women that way."

"Seriously? Those three? Christ, they couldn't take pity on a young guy who needed their help and that doesn't bother you?"

Lewis thought a moment. "Yeah. I guess. Bothers me that you wanted to get rid of me too."

"Jesus, Tommy, I told you I was trying to get on their good sides."

"Tommy? Who's Tommy?"

"I said Lewis."

"You called me Tommy."

"Bullshit."

"Well, it didn't work."

"What didn't work?"

"Getting on their good sides."

"Duh it didn't work and now I'm pretty sure this conversation is going round in circles."

There was silence then Lewis came and sat beside him, not too close. He tossed a few dirt balls of his own.

Had he really called him Tommy?

From the distance came the stressed crunch of someone with little aptitude operating a clutch and gear shifter.

Our car, goddammit.

He strained his ears but heard nothing else, not the scrape of tire on asphalt nor the revving on an engine.

Were they idling, waiting to see whether the men would return? Had they themselves been ambushed? Or had they left already, the noise masked by the screech of parrots and hum of bushland insects? He'd give it some time before he found out.

Five minutes into their wait, Lewis said, "So you didn't want to get rid of me?"

"No," Elliot lied.

Another long pause, then: "Thanks."

Elliot plucked his sweaty shirt away from his chest, let some air in. God, it was hot today and the breeze wasn't reaching down into the cut-through. "Don't thank me; pay it forward or something."

"Pay what?"

"You never saw that movie?"

"Don't think so."

"Oh."

"Why?"

"Just seems the kind of old movie your parents would get you to watch. Had kind of a good message."

"What message?"

Elliot shrugged. "Paying it forward."

"Which is what?"

"Which is I do nice for you and instead of paying me back, you do nice for someone else who needs it."

"That does sound cool."

"Plus the main character was about your age."

"Nice. So what happened to him."

"He died." Elliot winced. "Maybe. I can't remember. I think it's time to go get our stuff."

Lewis stood back while Elliot retrieved the gear, updating his inventory of their earthly goods. One backpack with spare clothes, a modest first aid kit, some muesli bars, cooking oil, gun oil and a carton of UHT milk he'd taken from the farm house. One hoody for if the weather turned, but zero wet weather gear. His rig for distilling water. The assault rifle, the speargun and 9 mil, but no hand-to-hand weapons unless he wanted to use a short blade Shrade or his pocket flashlight. Then again, the bush was full of deadwood they could use as clubs and spears. His canteen had a little water, but Lewis's had of course had been left in the car along with Lewis's pencils and sketchbook; fortunately the young guy seemed to have forgotten *them*.

"Some basic medicine, a little food, one canteen, no sleeping gear. Goddam them."

Lewis fumbled the Aimrite, twisting the strap as he tried to get it on his back, making a meal of it. "Why were you so mean to them?" he asked.

"The bitches?"

Lewis took a deep breath and blew it out hard.

Disapproval. From a thirteen year old. Maybe he really was an asshole. Maybe it *was* wrong to think of them that way. They looked like they'd been through hell and they were trying to survive, like he was.

He sighed. "And just how was I mean to those women, Lewis?"

"You were kind of a smart alec with them."

"*I* was a …! Who was threatening to shoot who in the yam bag?"

"Maybe using some manners would have made them change their mind."

"I was nice to them. At the start. Goddam it. Okay, so using manners is not my first instinct, you got me. But this isn't a world for manners. " He looked Lewis over from his perfectly tied laces, to the way he held the elbow of his injured arm with the opposite hand, to the way he stood with one hip out. "You've been feminized, Lewis. In a soft and safe middle-class world, that's fine. Manners are fine. In that world, you can brew your herbal teas, attend your inspirational seminars, practice mindfulness, color in mandalas. But in this world? This world right here?" Still crouched, he dug a finger into the dirt. "This world is more like the old world, the world humans had to survive in for a hundred thousand years. It's harsh and bloody and goddam dangerous. And you will not survive it by being nice to people. Men—real men—they use this—" he flexed a bicep though it was hidden within his sleeve, then brandished the rifle, standing "—and this. To make their point. To establish their bona fides and their place in the pecking order. The Death Druids weren't stopped by manners. And neither were those chicks back there, the ones currently driving our car south when we should be using it to circle around and head north. Speaking of which, let's quit the meaningful conversation, huh? And do what men do best. Getting on with it. "

Lewis was studying the nearby paperbark. He walked to it and peeled some bark, crumpled it in his hand and said, "You're a jerk. Which way are we going? Coz after all your crap, I *want* to 'get on with it'."

Elliot hadn't realized how great it had felt to drive again until he was forced to walk again. Forest detritus, dry and constantly cracking under foot. The occasional screen of bracken and scrub they were forced to detour around. The flies. The sun burning through the sparse shade afforded by eucalypts.

It would take them days now to reach Minchen-bridge.

They could have followed the road north of course but with no guarantee of viable vehicles or lack of further roadblocks, without recourse against sun-on-scalp since his Shell cap was in the stolen car, and because he knew the road they'd been on eventually arced around to the north west away from the direction of Lewis's grandparents, Elliot had decided that overland was the better choice despite the terrain. Also, it would be easier to find quick cover this way rather than out on an open highway.

A half hour into their walk, he was forced to rest while Lewis emptied dirt from a sneaker. Elliot rested his back against a towering gum as black ants came to investigate his boot.

"Why did she have a handcuff on?" Lewis asked.

"Don't want to think about that," Elliot replied. He shifted his foot to keep the ants at a distance. These were big bastards with cruel looking pincers. No telling what kind of pain they'd inflict.

"Kinda weird. Maybe they were criminals. Maybe you were …" Lewis was going to say right, Elliot was sure of it.

He moved across to another tree, losing the ants' attentions. "They weren't criminals, Cochise." It wasn't police custody they'd escaped from.

Lewis sat, wrestling his shoe on. "Then how'd she get a handcuff?"

Shit. You had almost a day with the Druids and you don't know? I'm truly happy for you.

"Cut the chatter," he said and pushed away from the tree. "Let's move."

Grumbling, Lewis stood and followed him.

In the next gully, in the middle of a curtain of new growth, sat a car. Elliot gestured for Lewis to stay where he was and descended carefully, weapon up, checking the ground for traps and stepping around a few scummy puddles and the surrounding spongy soil. Mosquitoes lifted and came to inspect him. He slapped at a couple, got up close to the car. No tires. No rear bumper and plates. Some trash littered the weeds and bracken. All the windows were up and no one was inside. The ground was blackened near the trunk in the middle of a circle of rocks, but weeds were sprouting through the fireplace's remains. No one had been here for a while. He signaled Lewis to come down and keep an eye out, then set to work inspecting the back seat, the trunk, the glove box. Nothing came of his troubles but a few candy wrappers. Nothing useful—not even a tire iron—had been left behind.

He climbed out and wiped sweat from his face, ran his hands down his shirt.

"We could sleep here," Lewis said.

Elliot frowned at him.

"We could," Lewis insisted.

"Lewis, it's not even midday."

"I'm tired."

"We've been walking less than an hour."

"Why couldn't we walk up the road again?"

"Like I told you: too hard to find cover in a hurry, and this is more direct."

"But it's harder."

"Harder ain't always worser."

"My legs are sore."

"You were happy to walk home this morning."

Lewis scratched at his nose and thought about that. "What if we get lost?"

"I won't get lost."

"How do you know?"

Elliot tapped his head. "Map's in here."

"People get lost in the wilderness all the time."

"Dumb people, sure."

"That's not fair. Smart people too. University professors and stuff."

"University professors. Jesus, Mary and Joseph. See that tree there?" He pointed up the far side of the gully where a sapling had sprouted. "Get moving and use that to pull yourself up to the top."

Once they were up out of the gully, Lewis said, "If there was someone in the car, would you rob them?"

Elliot started walking, ignored it.

"Would you?" Lewis insisted.

"No."

"What if we didn't have anything? No weapons or food. Would you do it then?"

Goddammit, if he wasn't wishing the kid would turn catatonic again.

"No," he said. "Yes, probably. I'd take a little of their gear. Even it out. Make it fair."

"So—"

Elliot sensed exactly where the logic would take him, so he interrupted loudly. "Geez, will you shut up! Got enough to think about without this crap."

A few minutes later, Lewis spoke again. "You're not actually mad at me, are you?"

"I'm not mad at all."

"Yes, you are. You're mad at those ladies."

"Hell, yes, I'm mad at those ladies."

"They had nothing and we had something. So they were just surviving."

"And as far as they knew, they took everything we had; they left us with nothing to survive. That's not right."

"Maybe they'd had a hard time."

"They'd had a *hard time*?"

"They had bruises everywhere."

"That doesn't give 'em a right to leave us up shit creek without a paddle." *We all got scars, kid.*

"Dad said you always have to walk in other people's shoes. You always have to try to see it from their point of view."

"Dad walk in the Death Druids' shoes?"

A pause then: "Don't talk about the Death Druids."

"I won't if you won't talk about those women anymore. In fact," he turned a triumphant smartass grin on Lewis, "I agree to not talk at all if you agree to the same thing."

Lewis turned away and tried to walk faster. He began to draw ahead of Elliot but soon had to look back to check he was going the right way.

"Want me to carry the pack?" he asked as Elliot passed him.

"What for?"

"Give you a rest?"

"I'm fine," Elliot replied and scowled as he had to hurdle a dead animal, a feral cat from the looks, a mess of corrupted meat and fur and claws.

"My fault we left the car," Lewis said quietly.

Elliot shook his head. "Not your fault."

"It was my idea."

"Forget it."

"I can't. We're walking because of me."

"I said forget it."

"You want me to grow up, so I am. Dad said growing up was about taking responsibility." He scratched his scalp for a moment. "He actually said that you know you're a man when you're taking responsibility for yourself *and* for other people."

A woman with a baby in her arm, bawling in Arabic. Radler's arm, Eames' boot with the foot inside, McGovern's face. Tommy's face, crestfallen—

"You can't take responsibility for everyone," he muttered. "Have to look after yourself first and foremost."

"You're looking after me."

"Pretty sure I told you to shut up about five minutes ago. That order still stands."

"Order?"

"Keep. Quiet. Bad enough you giving me a head-ache, but I don't want any unfriendlies out there hearing you at it."

"Unf—? Oh."

And thankfully, Lewis fell silent. And even better, as far as Elliot was concerned, he stayed that way for a long time.

9

Lewis only started speaking again when they both stepped out of the woods and into a shallow valley carpeted with knee-high grass and heath. "Thank God," he said, his voice husky from a dry throat.

The bush had gotten thicker for the past four hours. While providing better shade, it had also thrown up plenty of barriers created by screens of side-growing trees, complicated by blackberry bushes and other runners, forcing frequent detours. Bracken had regularly snatched at their ankles even when the going was clearer.

"There's a creek over there," Lewis added, pointing north where a silver twinkling line split the forested hills that cupped the northern and western edges of the valley. "I'm dying for a drink."

Elliot followed his gesture, then froze, put a hand across Lewis's chest to halt his progress, swore under his breath. A thousand yards away, at the northern tree line, stood a man, two women and two children, tweens by the size of them. All had stopped dead like he had. One woman had a small blob against her chest, a baby or toddler in a sling. A small child sat on the other woman's shoulders. Even at that distance, Elliot could make out the huge backpack doubling the man's bulk. The three adults carried poles or broom handles, but nothing resembling a firearm. The older children clutched bags.

Lewis raised his hand in greeting but the group backed up, blended into the bushland behind them.

"Huh?" said Lewis.

"Wait!' Elliot called. They had kids. They looked organized and fit, a group of clean and decent people; they'd been smart enough to survive two months of hell-on-earth. He'd jogged a few yards before realizing he'd moved—and realizing that the family had been coming toward them, heading *away* from Lewis's grandparents. There was absolutely no point in chasing them even if they were cool since they wouldn't be traveling with them.

"Were they...?" Lewis left the question unfinished. Perhaps he didn't even know *how* to finish it.

"We're better off alone," Elliot said and hitched his pack onto a better position on his shoulders. "And they'll be gone by the time we get over there." He dropped a hand to his side, drew reassurance from the cold steel of his sidearm just the same.

They were out in the open when they heard an engine. With hands shielding their eyes against the retina-searing blue sky, they watched the little Cessna appear above the trees where the family had vanished.

"A bloody plane," Lewis said, stating the obvious. He'd stopped forty feet behind Elliot.

It dipped low, buzzing them from a hundred feet up, tipping perhaps to give the occupants a better look at them.

"Yeah, but it's headed south," he replied.

A quarter mile past them, the Cessna banked and wheeled about in a lazy turn.

"Or not," Lewis replied. "Do you reckon he'll land?"

Elliot shrugged but he hoped so. Despite recent experiences, if there was a chance of a Good Samaritan giving them a ride north, he'd take it. They might after all be flying sorties from a safe haven, somewhere he'd feel comfortable leaving the teenager.

Even so, he unclasped his hip holster. He thumbed the safety while his hand was there, then slipped off his pack and M4, let them slip to the ground, raised his hands in a friendly wave as the Cessna cut back on a diagonal line across the valley. Lewis joined him in the wave. After it passed them, the pilot dipped his wings one way, then the other. Good sign, Elliot figured and stuck his thumbs through his belt to await what would happen next.

"Will he land?" Lewis repeated louder.

"I'm not deaf. I don't know, is all."

"They might take us to Minchenbridge."

"Sure."

Lewis took a few eager steps forward. "Or somewhere near there."

"They might, Lewis." He gripped his belt harder.

The Cessna banked again and came in from the far end of the valley, angling toward the most even terrain.

"They are landing!" Lewis laughed.

"Looks that way. Let's hope they're … nice."

Suspicion was stupid, he thought. No one was risking a landing here to shoot a couple of hikers, then take off. Only reason to land was to help.

Or ask for help.

Three hundred yards away, the Cessna cut speed, dropped low. Seventy feet off the deck. Fifty. Twenty.

Birds erupted from the heath in front of it. The plane flinched, jinked. Elliot dropped, sensing what was coming. One wing clipped the ground and the plane flipped, cart wheeling while pieces shot off in all directions.

"Holy Christ."

Something—a chunk of propeller maybe—whizzed past. He snapped his head around to follow it, watched it miss Lewis by a couple of feet. The teenager didn't seem to notice, frozen on his feet, mesmerized by the unfolding accident.

"Get down!" he shouted, but the crash was over, the body of the plane coming to rest belly down in the grass. Some debris still rolled and bounced and skidded but none of it near them. The plane sighed as if in pain, fuselage ripped but intact.

He expelled the breath he'd been holding. He and Lewis must have both had the same thought because after one more frozen moment, they sprinted as one for the wreck, abandoning their belongings.

There was no fire, no apparent sign of impending explosion; nevertheless he wasn't leaving anyone inside. The pilot was the only visible occupant—an indistinct figure pressed against a kaleidoscope mess of the side window. Lewis showed no fear, running right up to the door alongside Elliot, though he let the more experienced man reach for it. Elliot yanked the latch and the door came loose in a rush. He braced himself to catch the pilot, but the woman didn't tumble. Rather she flopped halfway with a soft moan; if he hadn't grabbed at her, the angle might have caused her spinal damage. If she didn't already have it. Her forehead pissed blood into her closed eyes. There was no time to debate moving her. The fuel reek was heady enough to make him dizzy. Lewis had his T-shirt up over his nose. Maneuvering himself to a better position, he did a quick check inside the cabin—no one there—and told Lewis to get under her legs and slide them free. He swore loud, making Lewis wince: she could have broken bones, she could have internal injuries, but he had to get her away from the plane.

Once her legs were free, he got himself under her then straightened, lugging her away in a fireman's carry. Lewis kept pace at his side as he hurried away. She cried out against his back as his foot caught a divot in the ground, but then she was silent again. Halfway back to the gear, he got Lewis to hold her head straight while he lay her down as gentle as possible. He checked her over while Lewis paced around them in a circle, face white. The slash across her forehead near the hairline still poured blood. There was more in her mouth. She was breathing, but it was shallow. Her eyes fluttered open, her mouth formed an O … and then she was out again. The fire around the plane's engine housing guttered low, so he didn't see the need to move her further away.

"Lewis," he snapped making the teenager blink. "Keep an eye out."

Lewis nodded, turned a three-sixty.

Elliot ran his hands up the pilot's arms then her legs, feeling for breaks, but couldn't find any. She flinched when he passed across her hips onto her ribs and she gasped, waking. He pulled away.

"Ah, shit!" She made to sit up, but barely got her head off the ground before she fell back. "Okay, that hurts. God."

A hanky poked from one of her jeans pockets. He tugged it out and pressed it to the gash on her head. She hissed, but held still, blinking up at him, focusing for the first time, then her face contorted and she swept her gaze around them and head turning. He assumed she was checking for the undead. It was habit now. Even for the badly injured.

He grabbed her head, held it firmly, pressed the hanky back. "You gotta hold still. Where are you hurting?"

"Where...?"

"Where does it hurt?"

She regarded him through squinted eyes for a moment before swallowing blood and attempting a laugh. "Everywhere, ya dumb bastard." She closed her eyes and bared her lips over gritted teeth.

"Where is it the worst?" he insisted.

She grunted, trying in vain to lift her head again, eyes fluttering open. "My head. My...shoulders where the harness was. My ribs where you pushed them, thanks very much. My hand here." She held it up to check it out, wiggled the pinky finger. "I musta banged it on something, the knuckle here hurts like crazy. But I'm ... I think I'm okay."

He moved a cautious hand onto her belly again and she raised an eyebrow. "I'm okay there," she said.

"You've got blood in your mouth."

She grunted. "Bit my cheek."

"Lewis, get the IFAK, the first aid kit. And my hoody to put under her head." The teenager shot off toward the pack without comment. "Get you some pain killers."

"Hope they're good ones," she said and tried to smile, licked blood off her teeth.

"They're not."

"Tequila shots?"

He shook his head, rueful. "If I'd had anything that good, it'd be long gone by now."

"I hear ya," she said and closed her eyes.

"Hey. Hey!"

She frowned a little, eyes still shut. "I'm not sleeping. Hurt too much to sleep." She opened them a little, focused on him. "You any good at medical stuff?"

"Some battlefield experience."

"The way you looked when you touched my gut. It's okay, honest. I think I just cracked my head, you know. Maybe a little concussion. My neck hurts too." She opened her eyes. "Not broken though. Can't be broken, if I can move it, can it?"

He shrugged his eyebrows. He was pretty sure it could be. He checked on Lewis who was still rummaging in the pack for the IFAK. "If we had a hospital, hell, we could run x-rays, but…" He let go of the hanky which stuck to the blood on her head, rubbed sweat from his eyes, then felt something brush his boot: her hand.

"Thanks."

"Thanks? I'm guessing you stopped to pick us up? Should be thanking you."

"Yeah, there's that."

"This goddammed world."

"This goddammed world," she agreed.

Lewis was on his way back now. Sensibly, he'd grabbed the canteen as well.

"Idiot," she croaked. "I thought I could do it."

"Land?"

"Land."

"Awful nice of you to try. Awful trusting too."

"Can't stand being alone, I guess. Haven't seen real people—real, *good* people—in maybe ten days. You look like … like good people."

"The young fella maybe," he joked.

She grunted. "An hour ago I got away from Launceston. I got to the airport and I … I got *away*. And now I've crashed my fucking plane and cracked my rib and maybe my neck? Out in the middle of nowhere." She squeezed her eyes shut a moment. "This goddammed world."

She lifted her head as Lewis drew near, then her shoulders.

"No you don't," Elliot started.

"Not a baby, think I can sit up," she growled at him. She did. Slowly. In a couple of stages. Completed the move without losing consciousness, though she gasped and swore several times along the way, apologizing to Lewis for the language. "Okay. Definitely fractured a rib. Hurts to breathe." She flexed the injured left hand, but with little range. "Mighta sprained this too."

Elliot took bandages from the IFAK, wound one tight around the hanky on her head.

"They'll catch us if they smell that," she said. "The blood."

"Maybe." He clipped it and dabbed iodine at a smaller cut on her cheek and one at the base of her injured pinky. The knuckle there was swelling. "What's your name?"

"Birdy."

He exchanged a glance with Lewis. "Your parents named you Birdy?"

"No. *They* named me something horrible, so when I got this nickname in high school I stuck with it. Shit," she added and twisted carefully toward the wreck. Flames flickered along the fuselage, but it hadn't exploded. "Fire. I knew it. I've got a lot of stuff in there."

"We're not going in for it."

"Course not. Just—pisses me off."

While she used her good hand to tug a sock up from inside a boot, he looked her over. She was a few years older than him, trace-lines of wrinkles along her cheeks and forehead, beside her eyes. She was also tiny, a sparrow of a woman, a full foot shorter than him and half his width and weight. The nickname made sense.

"Gonna tell me your names?" She pitched it at Lewis.

He smiled. "Lewis. Elliot."

"Which one are you?"

"Lewis," he laughed.

"Where you both headed, Lewis?"

"Minchenbridge."

"Don't know it, but I'm originally from Wollongong, so …" She made a *duh* face.

"Never heard of Wollongong," Elliot ventured.

"You haven't lived if you haven't been to the Gong," she joked. "Near Sydney. Long, long way from here. It's a good place, then, Minchenbridge? What's there? Food?"

"I think so," Lewis shrugged.

"His grandparents."

"Oh." She watched him checking out her hand, said, "Well, if we're going, we better drop the clutch or we'll wind up someone's dinner."

Lewis offered her the canteen and Elliot got painkillers from the IFAK. They weren't much, codeine and paracetamol. He still had two morphine syrettes in there, but morphine would only slow her down once they got moving again. And it was too valuable for her injuries.

He showed her the four pills. "Party time."

"Gimme," she said. He tipped them in her mouth. She sipped and swallowed. "Don't do drugs," she told Lewis. "What are we gonna do when there's no more of these? When all the millions of 'em left in people's medicine drawers are out of date?"

"We'll think of something."

"Willow bark," said Lewis. They frowned at him. He shrugged. "That's where aspirin came from in the first place."

"*Willow bark?*" Birdy asked.

He shrugged again. "You just boil it."

Elliot stared at him a moment longer. Where the hell had that little gem of knowledge come from?

"Okay," Birdy said. "I'm okay. Not great. But definitely okay. And we've gotta move, fellas. I saw a tower…a fire tower." She turned her head toward east. "Maybe three kays that way … If we can find it and hide, they should pass by."

Elliot exchanged a look with Lewis. "Who exactly should pass by?"

She gave a long shuddering sigh, it caught at a spasm from her rib. Elliot grabbed her hand and she squeezed it until the pain subsided.

"Not good news, I'm afraid," she grated. "Reason I landed? The direction you were headed in's a big mistake. There's a shitstorm on its way. I flew over it. Clusters of eaters. Like … thousands. Coming south. Maybe all the mainland refugees who got to Launceston and Davenport before everyone got infected. Lots of people came by boat, thousands and thousands. Lots came up from the midlands, other towns, trying to get *away* by boat. Then they … died and rose again. They're like a massive exodus, herds of the things all coming down here." She peered north.

"Shit. Okay. Shit." He thought a moment. "We'll go round it."

"No. No you won't. I could see 'em stretching out for twenty kilometers. More. Twenty kays wide and at least that deep. We're in the middle of the wave front here."

"Then we'll … we'll wait it out in this fire tower."

"Elliot. That's your name right? Elliot. You want to go near Launceston? Don't. You know Hurricane Katrina, in your country?"

"Long, long time ago, but yeah."

He'd got the message already but she added, "Ten times worse. Even if you keep away from the eaters.

Rape … s-saw people killing each other over a truck full of cat food. Enough for all of them, but they—"

A tear cut a line through the red on her face. She handed Lewis the canteen. He shook it and Elliot heard little water left, enough for a sip each maybe.

Twenty kilometers was close to twelve miles. She was right: they weren't going round herds of pusbags stretching out that far and they weren't going through them if they stretched that far back. Made sense now why the three women, the family and now the plane had been headed south. There'd be more refugees coming their way, keeping ahead of the wave. Maybe they'd be trustworthy like Birdy. Maybe not.

"How close?" he asked. "The dead?"

"I dunno. Three hours away. Four. Five. Not sure how fast they all move."

"Goddammit."

"Fire tower's on a hill," she said. "Sticks out of the bush. Can't miss it. That way." She jerked her head and must have triggered a big spasm. She groaned, clamped a hand to her chest.

Lewis shuffled backwards, clasping the aid kit to his own chest, attention torn between her and the trees to the far north of the valley. There was nothing there. Yet.

She clutched at Elliot's boot. "Gotta. Get. Going."

"Cochise, get our gear," Elliot said, then when he didn't respond, barked, "Over there! Get the gear! Bring it here! *Move!*"

Lewis stumbled backwards then ran for the weapons and pack.

He asked her, "Can you stand?"

"Can you give a lady a boost?"

He took her elbow, let her hold his arm with her good hand. She got up, eyes narrowed, jaws tight. She was as light as a child.

"We can do this," he told her.

"My hubbie used to say that. Whenever things were at their worst." She lost focus for a moment, sinking into a memory, her smile sad. Then she blinked and said in a whisper, "Not very reassuring."

"Maybe he made me do it, let you know he's still around," he tried.

She nodded. "That's a nice thought. But he might still be alive, far as I know. Back in Wollongong."

He chuckled. "Oh." Then she had a story for being on the island too. Birds of a feather. He experimented with letting her stand alone. "Okay?"

"Fine. Thank you. For letting me come with you. Really don't want to face the shitstorm alone."

"Thank *you*," he said. "You just saved our lives."

"They're not safe yet, mate."

When Lewis returned, Elliot swapped the M4 for the SIG. He made Lewis shoulder the backpack while he got his map out.

Birdy frowned down at it for a while then tapped a spot. "There."

He told Lewis, "We're headed here. Those deaders come, we get caught in it, you run, you hear. Don't wait for us and don't come back for us if we go down."

Lewis swallowed, nodding as Elliot shoved the spare 9-mil mags in the pack with the map. Then the teenager turned east, striding ahead of them.

Elliot slung the rifle and spear gun, waved Birdy ahead of him and followed watching her unsteady gait, his mind swarming with nightmare images of an oncoming storm.

10

The bushland was harder going the other side of the valley: rutted gullies snaking through small hillocks; pools of stagnant, mosquito-ridden water; slippery rocks poking randomly from the topsoil; screens of intertwined saplings to detour around.

Within twenty minutes, Lewis was well out in front, scouting easier pathways while Elliot stayed back with Birdy. Her breath came hard in the still warm air, her face pale, eyes narrow. But each time Elliot would go to ask her how she was doing, she'd brush off his concern before he got the words out, suck in a deep breath and push herself harder for a minute or two.

As they waited while Lewis checked the other side of a rise, Elliot asked her, "So you got stranded here too?" He kept checking the rise, wondering if he should have gone himself, leave Lewis back here with Birdy.

Ah, shit, he has to learn sometime.

Leaning on a eucalypt trunk, she replied "Not exactly." She closed her eyes.

Eager to keep her sharp, and eager to keep her distracted, he said, "You wishing you were back in Wollygong?"

"*Wollongong.*" She opened her eyes. They were moist. "So a little personal information then? Real reason I stopped for you two? I thought you looked a lot like my husband and my son. I thought since I can't be with *them*, maybe I could give another father and son some assistance. Like, join-another-family kind of thing." She made a face. "Sad, huh?"

He shook his head, but added, "I'm not his dad."

"Obviously. I can see that now. But I couldn't from the air."

"So … You're here and they're … in that unpronounceable town near Sydney. You were working here?"

"No. Not exactly."

"You keep saying that."

"Pssst!" called Lewis. He waved them forward from the top of the rise and ducked over it. Elliot shook his head, wishing the teenager would stay in sight.

He gestured. "After you."

"A gentleman," she said and stumbled on. "And if you are a true gentleman, you might end up giving me a piggy back soon."

A plain black and white plaque proclaimed the tower to be ten meters high and sixty years old, constructed as a fire lookout. The fire tower sat atop Mount Terror: the *Terror* part struck Elliot as appropriate under the circumstances, though *Mount* was a little overstated— the bald hill poking a couple hundred feet above the eucalypt forest around it was more like a bump. Then again, that too may have originated in the Australian love for irony.

It consisted of a white aluminum-and-glass box the size of a bedroom atop a steel-mesh platform and supported by four pillars. The pillars were braced by diagonal steel crisscrosses. Various connotations of radio and cell phone aerials sprouted at all angles from the box and its legs; Elliot counted nine of them. Four flights of steel stairs led up the exposed middle of the structure. The construct sat inside a ten foot high chain link fence in a grassy area maybe fifteen by fifteen yards. A row of solar panels inside the fence promised power—maybe some clever park ranger had left an electric razor and a well-stocked beer fridge up there. Well, he thought as he tested the lock on the gate, a fella could dream.

"We'll have to climb over," he said, grateful for no barbed wire. But this was going to be tough on Birdy who had paused halfway up the hill behind them to gaze up at the tower and suck air.

Lewis pointed to a slim brick building nestled against the outside of the fence on the opposite side. He'd been looking at it longingly the whole time they'd approached. "I need to use the dunny."

Dunny?

Oh.

"Me too," Elliot agreed, acknowledging the pressure in his bowel. Packing away all that steak and eggs …

He glanced down into the shadows between trees, cocked an ear to listen to the approach of a murderous horde above the trilling and hooting of forest birds. Nothing. If what Birdy said was accurate, they had hours yet. And maybe, if Lady Luck decided to shine on them just this once, the sea of undead would wash past elsewhere, missing them entirely.

"You first," he told Lewis. "Just don't stink it up too much."

The teenager flashed him a dirty look as he stalked away.

The sun was touching the trees that surrounded the bald hill he stood on. Fantails and parrots swooped and chirruped, catching last meals of the day, or vying for places to rest for the night. A black beetle whirred up to him, considered alighting on his shirt, changed its mind and passed through the chain link. He leaned his head against one of the fence uprights, the steel frame as cold as river stone in contrast to the harsh sunshine and high humidity. He smacked his lips, wishing he hadn't imagined beer fridges, and grudgingly pushed himself away from the fence to wander around to a rainwater tank on the side of the toilet block where he'd spied a spigot. He placed his canteen beneath it, turned it on. The dull notes of trickling water comprised the best music he'd heard in years.

"Can I have some privacy?" Lewis complained from within.

After a beat, Elliot replied, "No" and took a long swig from the canteen. The water was warm and plasticky. But it would be clean enough, safe enough. He swallowed, wiped his mouth, took another. He topped up the canteen, screwed the cap back on, crouched by the spigot. He flipped it open again and stuck his head under it, scrubbed at his face and hands, turned it off, wiped his hands on the dry grass around him.

Birdy was trudging the last few steps up to the gate. He watched her try the lock and lean her head where he'd leaned his. Yep, getting over there in her condition was going to hurt.

He patted the tank.

"Quit it! What are you doing?"

"Relax, Cochise."

It was half full. If the cabin above had food, they could stay here a couple of weeks. More if they got some good rain. It might give them space to let things cool down. *If* there was food. There wasn't much left in the backpack.

The run of a toilet paper holder made him stand. "About friggin' time."

"Shut up."

"Leave some of that paper for me."

"All right! God!"

"No, my name's Elliot."

"Geez!"

He chuckled and lay the canteen on the ground. "Water out here if you want some." There was a flush and Lewis struggled with the latch a moment before appearing, blushing and angry, the first time he'd seen the young man that stirred up. That was fine with Elliot—*anger keeps you alive.*

He kicked the canteen across the grass. "That's for drinking, but wash your hands under the tap first."

"I'm not an idiot.""

"Good to know. I'll be out in ten."

"And I'll stand here and annoy you."

"Whatever floats your boat, Cochise."

He closed the door with another chuckle and got ready to drop some kids off at the pool.

Getting Birdy over the fence with a cracked rib and a banged up hand was never going to happen. They used a shovel leaning against the toilet block to clear enough dirt from under the fence for her to lie on her back and use her legs to push herself through. Elliot and Lewis climbed, then filled the hole in enough to stop the undead from following Birdy's lead.

The tower cabin was more cramped than he'd expected. Barely three feet between any wall and the metal table occupying the centre. The table was spread with maps, a clipboard, an aging portable DVD player, and a scattering of biros. Elliot added his pack and weapons to the detritus there. Lots of gritty dust. A sagging cardboard box beneath contained an eclectic stockpile: Wiggles and Seinfeld DVDs with covers so faded he could barely read them; insect repellent; sunscreen; a cloth sunhat; a packet of plastic forks; half a box of Kleenex; dry crackers two months past their use-by date; a tupperware container with a fistful of trail mix; a pack of Styrofoam cups; a pair of field glasses; a large first aid kit; a spare roll of toilet paper; a leather satchel with shoulder strap that could replace Lewis's pack. Some of this stuff was going in that satchel, he decided; the sunhat could replace his Shell cap left in the Torana along with the other gear those witches had stolen from him.

A steel roadcase big enough for a bass amp had been installed as a storage cabinet in one corner.

Someone had screwed a landline telephone to the side. A CB radio sat on top beside a small pile of paperback novels and a forty page printout titled FIRE MANAGEMENT. Post-it notes with phone numbers and a child's sketching of a koala had outflanked the telephone. Two camp chairs had been folded up in the opposite corner.

No beer fridge.

But there were two desk fans screwed into the roof upside down. If there was a God, the solar panels were connected and functioning. He tried a fan and to his pleasure it hummed to life, sending a stream of delicious moving air across his scalp.

"Oh, *yeah*."

He lay the rifle on the table and Lewis did the same with the speargun. Birdy rattled one of the folding chairs until Lewis helped her unfold it. She settled into it gingerly and groaned with relief.

"Any more painkillers?"

Elliot put his pack on the table and rummaged for codeine. Lewis tried the phone, made a disappointed sound when there was no dial tone. Then he flicked the radio on. "You should try to reach someone."

"I should?" Elliot said, handing another pill to Birdy. There were only four left in the packet. "That will have to do for the moment."

Lewis sighed theatrically. "Okay, *I* will." He lifted the mic and thumbed the button, spoke meaningless innocences into it. There was no reply. "Is this tuned in?"

"You have to try different frequencies, Lewis," Birdy said.

"But what are you gonna do if someone answers?" added Elliot.

"Just, like, ask for help."

"Okay, Einstein. What kinda help you gonna request?"

"Like, evac. That kinda thing."

It was Elliot's turn to raise an eyebrow. "Evac. So you're Delta Force now?"

"You know what I mean."

"Mm."

Elliot stuffed the toilet roll, bug repellent and sunscreen in Lewis's new satchel and opened the crackers. Birdy closed her eyes, resting. Lewis pushed buttons, changing the frequencies and listening to various shades of static. Elliot chewed on stale biscuit. "And what if the guys answering aren't people you really want *evacking* you? What if those bikers hear you?"

"Bikers?" Birdy murmured. Her eyes stayed shut.

"It's not fair," Lewis muttered, but he put the mic back and went to the window to survey the forest.

They shared crackers and trail mix for dinner, washing it down with warm water. Elliot plugged in his recharger, slotted in the batteries from his beard trimmer and flashlight. The DVD player had charge, so Elliot slouched in the other camp chair and played two Seinfeld episodes, marveling at the high-waisted jeans and laughing his ass off, while Lewis used scrap paper and biros to commence a new sketch, seated in the lotus position near the door where the light was best. From her own camp chair, Birdy snored.

"That was stupid," the teenager said when the second ep was over.

"What was?" Birdy asked, stirring. She looked around confused for a moment before getting her bearings, smacked her lips.

"*That* was genius," Elliot told him and hit pause. He took out his battery charger and plugged in the DVD player in its stead. It would serve as a nightlight when night fell.

"Anyway, it doesn't feel like we should be laughing when people keep dying." He rotated the page, coloured in a patch heatedly.

"Sometimes that's the best time *to* laugh," Elliot replied. "Show the universe you're not letting it win."

Lewis chewed on a lip considering that. "Okay. But even the Wiggles would've been better than that crap."

"Four grown men dancing around in turtle-necks?" Birdy leaned forward and adjusted the bandage on her forehead. "I'd rather not."

"They were wearing worse than that in *his* video."

Elliot chuckled. "Must admit, I prefer a t-shirt and camo pants any day."

"Classy," Birdy told him. She stood, braced her thighs against the table and reached for the canteen. "Watcha drawing there?"

Elliot leaned closer to see too. It looked like the same kinds of swirls and curves Lewis had been playing with at the farmhouse and the car, but this time …

Lewis stopped shading and considered his image. He said quietly, "My sister."

Elliot suppressed a groan.

"Looks pretty good from here," Birdy commented.

"Probably shouldn't do that," Elliot said. When they turned to him, he explained, "Better to put our old lives behind us. Face forwards."

"Not sure that's true," said Birdy.

Elliot frowned at her, made a *quit it* gesture where Lewis couldn't see it. "I've always found it better not to dwell—"

Birdy turned her back on him, interrupting. "You go right ahead, Lew. Your sister would be proud you're remembering her this way."

You shitting me?

"Thanks," Lewis said in a small voice.

"She died?" Birdy's question was gentle.

"Yep."

"You see it?"

A pause then, "I heard it. Kinda."

"You ever want to talk about it, let me know."

"Okay."

Birdy gave Elliot a stern look over the top of the canteen as she drank. He shook his head and stood, slipping past her to stare out the windows at the darkening bush. He couldn't see much. Enough light in the sky to trace the shapes of clouds, the sillouettes of birds or maybe bats. The bush itself was a dark green blur.

There was a scrape of paper beneath the table behind him.

"Had enough?" Birdy asked.

Elliot turned to see Lewis disappear behind the table. "He told me we sleep when it's dark." A hand appeared above the table, pointed at the window. "Getting dark."

"I noticed." She regarded the floor with discomfort. There was no bedding and the floor was wood, marginally better in Elliot's opinion than lying on steel mesh. Sure he'd slept in worse places, but he wasn't getting any younger.

"If you want," he said, "we can break a few branches off those conifers down there. They'll be softer than this."

"I'm okay," Lewis replied.

Ignoring him, Elliot added, "How you feeling?"

"Like crap," Birdy said and drank more water. "Sure you got no booze? Pity."

He pushed off the window. "I'll cut those branches."

She stopped him with the heel of her injured hand against his chest. "I'll be fine. If you just drag me that roadcase to put my feet against, I'll sleep in the chair."

"That's not real good for the posture," he said.

"And the floor is? *Branches* are?"

"Have it your way. The chair it is." He dragged the roadcase closer to hers as requested, then folded his up and lay it across the table. He pulled a spare shirt from his pack for a pillow and draped another over Birdy's knees. She murmured thanks and braced her feet against the case.

Elliot rolled up his pillow and lay down on the opposite side of the table to Lewis. The young man lay with hands beneath head, watching the ceiling fan. "Should I keep watch?" he asked suddenly.

Elliot scratched his chin, considering the question. It was going to be full dark within an hour and the susurration of treetops below them was loud enough to mask the approach of anyone dead or alive. But there was nothing he could do about the light or the wind. There would be nothing for Lewis to hear or see. While he didn't think a zombie could scale a chain link fence without alerting him, people could. "I doubt I'll sleep well enough to let anything creep up on us. You get some rest."

Lewis grunted.

Elliot lay there tracking the dying of the day's light until it vanished completely. With cloud cover, there was no starlight, no moon, but the soft glow from the DVD player screen allowed him to keep most objects in the room in some kind of focus. If the potential for incursion didn't keep him on edge and awake, Birdy's occasional light snore and the whine of a single persistent bastard mosquito surely would. He had applied repellent as had Lewis, but it only seemed to keep the tiny insect circling him in a holding pattern.

Despite what he'd thought, he was drifting when a noise startled him back to full alert. The vicious growling-snarling of some hell-spawn sent his skin from hot to fully chilled in a moment. He rolled over and up, his hand snaking across the table for a weapon—then froze when Lewis started laughing.

"Shut the hell up," he whispered and when Lewis only giggled harder, he added, "What the hell's funny?"

"It's not gimps."

Elliot cocked an ear. It *was* a little more earnest than the average deader. But … "What the hell is it then?"

"Devils."

Despite himself, his blood cooled even more at that thought. "*Devils?*"

Lewis laughed again. "Not like Satan devils. Tazzie Devils. *Tasmanian* Devils."

"Say again?"

"Tasmanian Devils. You know."

"Will you guys shut up?" Birdy complained and shifted positions, pulling the shirt up over her shoulders.

Elliot ignored her, asking, "What is this, an Aboriginal myth?"

"Seriously?" Lewis said. "You don't know what they are? They're an animal, a marsupial. A mammal."

"Wait." Elliot remembered something then. A tornado of cartoon fur, growling not dissimilar to this. He lay back down, adjusted the shirt beneath his head. "Sure. The Tasmanian Devil like in the cartoon."

"What cartoon?"

He hummed a few bars of theme music.

"Huh?"

"Looney Toons," Birdy yawned.

"What's that?"

"Shit, Lewis," Elliot growled. "Daffy Duck? Porky Pig? B'deh b'deh, that's all folks?"

"You're weird."

"You don't know Porky Pig?"

"Nuh."

"Bugs Bunny?"

"I know *him*." There was a moment's silence. "Pretty lame."

"Lame? Shee-it. First you diss Seinfeld and now a classic like Looney Toons. You have no culture."

"Really? That boring old crap is culture?"

"Well, what's good TV to you?"

"Nothing. TV is crap. The best stuff's online."

"Right. Like pranking videos. Guys scaring the hell out of people in elevators and thinking it's funny."

Lewis laughed. "It's better than that. There's also like Japanese anime shows. A Norwegian stunt show. Gaming clips." The laughter died in his voice. "Or there was."

"Yeah. Was. Sad thing is, pal, we want entertainment in the future we might have to start reading novels."

Lewis groaned. "Or playing board games."

"Or whittling."

"Or banjo playing."

"If you can find a banjo."

"Spoons?"

"Yeah, spoons-playing."

"Or ... talking."

They both made throwing up noises and laughed.

"Nothing wrong with talking," Birdy said.

Neither male could find a response to that, falling silent.

"Or I could be wrong," she said.

After a while, Lewis said, "I'll be okay, as long as I can still get pencils and paper."

Elliot shifted on the hard floor, hoped Birdy's even breathing meant she was asleep again. "Yeah, you got a talent there. Not sure it's a useful one these days. Let's face it: there won't be much time for entertainment for any of us."

"I guess."

"Survival comes first."

"… I guess."

They kept quiet for a time while the Devils continued whatever the hell they were doing and the mosquito flew sorties.

Lewis cleared his throat and asked, "Were you a cop?"

"Private military contractor."

"What's that?"

Elliot half-smiled to himself. "Security guards, basically. For big business and big businessmen."

"Oh," said Lewis, but the tone suggested he didn't get it.

Elliot waved at where the mosquito might have been and added, "Protected staff of an oil and mining company when they went into the middle-east and Asia."

And before that is none of your business.

"So you would know stuff. About the gimps, I mean."

Elliot sniffed. "Not much more than anyone else. We did hear things on military channels though. We had tech wizards who could tune into it. Why? "

"Well, I mean, how does it work, being dead but moving around like they do?"

"I got nothin' but theories there, based on stuff I heard from smarter folk than me."

"That'll do."

"Well. First theory is they aren't technically dead. They did die from the virus—or caught it while another deader snuffed them—and then they were reanimated, with their organs mostly working. Organ strikes *will* kill 'em: if they can't breathe or pump blood, they die like a normal person would. Gut wounds, et cetera—that only slows them down.

"But they are rotting. And their brain function is as primitive as it can be and still animate them. So, yeah, zombies is a good enough name for 'em."

"Then you should call them livers not deaders."

"I think that word has been taken," said Birdy. "Livers."

Still awake then.

"Will they live forever?" Lewis asked.

He mulled it over, unable to answer.It had been weeks since he considered such questions. Early on—in the hotel room in Hobart while they still had sat phone access and the internet still worked—conversation had inevitably turned to the chicken-and-egg conundrum of the new world: what came first, the *idea* of the zombies inheriting Earth or the means to bring it about? Did Romero catch wind of something already cooking in a government lab or did the pocket-protector brigade watch "Dawn of the Dead" and think *What a great idea for a weaponized virus?*

However it had happened, *someone* had made a decision to break the world. *Someone* had ruined it for good. You couldn't unbreak a world anymore than you could unbreak a jar or a promise.

"Try to live a long life and I guess you'll find out," he replied to Lewis's question.

They nose-breathed for a while in the gloom. Lewis waved his hand at a grey blur circling his head, a moth maybe.

Better than a mosquito.

"How big are these devils anyways?" he asked.

"Oh, two metres long," Lewis said. He turned on his side, raised himself on one elbow, warming to the subject. "A lady got killed by a three meter one about fifty years ago. They've been keeping them in wildlife parks since then so they don't kill people or pets. These ones must have escaped since the world went bad."

Why hadn't he heard of these things? There were bear-sized predators prowling the bush around them and Lewis only thought to mention it now? He knew Australia had crocs way up north and lots of snakes and spiders all over, but this was never on the tourist videos. He fidgeted, adjusting the shirt behind his head. "Can they climb?"

"No, not really. As long as we stay up here, we'll be fine. As long as they're outside the fence."

Elliot lay there, picturing something like the Looney Toons drone but real. Something with a mouth half the size of its body, chewing through the fence and circling the bottom of the tower waiting for them to come down, salivating and grinning.

Until Lewis snorted.

"You sonofabitch." He kicked out at Lewis but the teenager sensed it, drew his legs out the way.

"Gotcha!"

Birdy joined in the laughter, a hissing-snorting kind of chuckle.

"You punked me, you rat bastard." He laughed too. Wasn't often that happened—the laughter *nor* the punking.

Lewis clapped his hands. "If I had a camera, I could've put it online."

When the laughter faded, Elliot asked him, "How come you know about them? And how big are they actually, for real this time?"

"They're like the size of really big cats, but chunky. And, I dunno, I'm into animals and stuff."

"Into animals?"

"Well, like, everyone in Australia knows about Tazzie Devils. But yeah, animals are interesting. Did you know we were making around a thousand species extinct per year before all this happened? Did you know that octopus DNA isn't like anything else on earth and some scientists think they're actually aliens?"

Yeah, that's real useful, Cochise.

"You know a lot about Tasmanian fauna?" Elliot asked.

"Sure."

"There's kangaroos here?"

"You haven't seen any?"

"No."

"Huh. There's heaps. Eastern greys they're called. Pretty big. We'll get to see some sometime. Wallabies too, but they're smaller."

"Wallabies? That's good."

"You like wallabies?"

"Won't know till I try one."

"Ew!"

"Hey, man, the original peoples around here would've eaten them, no worries. Can't argue with that."

"He's right," Birdy chimed in. "Gotta take what you can get."

"I guess. Seems mean though."

"You're not hungry enough yet, Cochise."

"I *am* hungry. I'm starving."

"Young man your age, course you are. And you need meat, along with the chicken food we been eating today."

"I guess."

"So I might have to catch us a wallaby."

"When the muesli bars run out."

"This is what I was trying to tell you back at the farm. About the cattle."

A pause then, "I know. Sorry I was such a douche."

"No worries. You're a guy: being a douche comes with the territory."

Birdy said, "Amen."

They shared a chuckle again.

"So, Lewis. You seem to know about flora too, huh?"

"Huh?"

"Plants."

"Oh. A little. Mum taught me a lot. I did a lot of gardening when I was a kid, but I've been getting kind of bored with it lately. Plants don't really do anything interesting."

Elliot replayed in his mind some grabs from a Discovery Channel documentary on pitcher plants and corpse flowers and those plants that looked like stones, but he didn't feel like arguing.

"Your mom was a naturopath?"

"Really?" Birdy said. "She ever make dandelion tea? Stuff like that?"

"*That* was disgusting," said Lewis.

"Sure. But good for digestion and your liver, I've read."

"I'd rather get something from the chemist."

"You mean the drugstore?" Elliot said. "No such thing anymore."

"Yeah, there is."

"Okay, they're still there, but what isn't looted ain't gonna last too long. Medicine's like food: has its own shelf-life." Lewis didn't reply to that and Elliot asked him, "You know about willow bark. You remember any more of your mom's knowledge of plants?"

"Sure. Bits."

"And you can read pretty well?"

"Of course. Why?"

"Just curious, Cochise." *And I think we found your usefulness in this new world.*

Next time they were wandering through mile after mile of dense bushland, Elliot would ask him if he recognized any edible bush foods—and hope he could tell the good stuff from the poison.

Concentrate on meat, on calories, his inner warfare instructor told him.

Yeah, and I'd like to concentrate on avoiding colon cancer thanks, he told it back.

He was about to tell Lewis they should stop talking. But he found he didn't need to; the conversation had reached a natural impasse. Eventually, light snores came from both his companions' positions. If Lewis could sleep on a hardwood floor, maybe Elliot could make a soldier out of him after all.

He lay awake, but slowed his heart rate, making peace with the fact he could sleep another day, like a good soldier himself. He passed the hours shifting his legs and occasionally getting up to stretch without waking the others.

He'd just checked the clock on the DVD player—5.32—when someone screamed in the distance. It lasted only a couple of seconds and it was a long way off, but it was a scream none-the-less. Straining his ears in the aftermath, he caught it then: that weird contorted growling of the undead, not so different to Lewis's cartoon marsupials, but much much worse in its way. Maybe that sound had been there for some time, but he'd unconsciously passed it off as local wildlife, as jungle hum.

He crouched by a window, squinting north. There was another spike of screaming—terror rather than pain. "Oh, no, no, no."

"Mm? What is it?" Lewis had obviously been asleep but he woke fast.

"Trouble."

Dawn smeared the eastern horizon, taking the edge off the darkness. He could make out Lewis, sitting up, hugging his knees. And he heard people now—living people—calling each other, two distinct voices, male and female, maybe a half mile west. Lewis shot to his feet and came to join him, shoulder pressed to Elliot's arm. Elliot shuffled sideways to break contact. Birdy stirred and mumbled a question.

"There's people out there," Lewis said.

A gunshot.

"Sure is," Elliot replied.

"Maybe we can join them."

Elliot threw him his best *wtf* look though it was lost in the gloom. He said, "We're not joining them." He scraped the camp chair across the table, unfolded it and faced it to the window, sat with his knees pressed to the wall. He reached back and slid the M4 closer across the table, then gripped Lewis's sleeve and pulled him lower until the teenager was forced to kneel. "They're armed. Let's give them as little to see here as possible."

"But … "

"You remember any of the last week? Your home? Harrietville? The train? People with guns aren't friendly."

Lewis swallowed and folded his arms across the narrow window sill, lay his chin on them. Birdy's chair scraped closer until she could touch Elliot's shoulder.

"You see anything?" she whispered.

"Not yet."

Her hand dropped away. "Is this a bad time to tell you I need to pee?"

The shouting stopped. Something moved down at the base of the slope. Squinting, he made out a couple of smudges, moving in typical jerk-ass fashion. He nudged Lewis, said softly, "Not just people out there."

Birdy cursed under her breath.

They waited and watched until the sun was halfway above the trees, and Lewis clutched at Elliot's chair and pointed west. The tower's height gave them a view over the trees and into a patch of dry creek bed before it curved away and into the trees again. In that clearing, twenty-odd people milled. They looked like they were collecting themselves, waiting in the basin while others emerged from the trees to join them, swelling their ranks to thirty or more. Half were women, some men, a few kids and teenagers.

"They look normal," Lewis murmured. "Like those people in the valley. There's kids there. I can't see many guns."

"Too many people, too big a target. We join them and we can't move quickly or quietly enough. Besides—" He handed him the binoculars they'd found in the box beneath the table. "—check 'em out, they're not running for sport."

Lewis stuck the glasses to his face and swore mildly. Even without them, Elliot could see the panic. People milled. The faint noise of the children crying filtered up the nexus of hills, the women bent over them trying to keep them quiet. Dread settled in his gut like lead. He took the glasses back, turned them five hundred yards north-west and echoed Lewis's curses before handing them to Birdy. A patch of open ground along the face of a hill to the northwest—a firebreak?—showed a ragged mass of undead.

There was a shout and he swung the binoculars back to the creek. A handful more people emerged from the bush fast, one falling down the slope. Tumbling after him came two undead, rolling over and over as the man righted himself and his group screamed and they all broke for the far bank like spooked sheep. Lewis shot to his feet to see better. Elliot pulled him down and retrieved the glasses for him; he himself could see well enough to make out what was happening. The people didn't get far, suddenly backpedalling down the bank they'd headed for, flanked now by deaders and heading downstream away from the tower's position. Moments ago, the creek bed had been a haven, but now it swarmed with undead in pursuit of the living.

Elliot shifted his attention to the hill below them. Sure enough, movement. Torn shirts and torn flesh. Stumbling, shambling masses, weaving in and out of trees, tripping in ferns and brambles, going down and scrambling forward, some with keener hearing veering toward the screams from the creek, others heading straight on and around the hill, a stream of living death breaking around a large rock, following the path of least resistance.

Lewis wrenched the binoculars from his face. "We have to help them."

"Can't."

"Oh, God," Birdy moaned.

Elliot turned back to the plight of the refugees in time to see two stragglers go down, vanishing into a frenzy. The figures were smaller than peas from this distance, but the activity was familiar enough from experience to know what was happening.

Lewis cried out, dropped the glasses and pressed against the window. Heads turned their way from the bush below. Elliot tackled him, dragging him onto the floor, clamping one arm and both legs around the teenager as he thrashed, pressing his other hand over Lewis's mouth. Lewis screamed against his hand.

"Stop it," Elliot hissed. "Goddamit! You're gonna get us killed."

Lewis thrashed and moaned, but Elliot wasn't letting a thirteen year old best him. He looked to Birdy who had pressed her nose and forehead to the window above the sill. She gestured that they were okay, the undead were moving on; he hoped that would continue. Eventually the young man began to relax and sob. Elliot tried lifting the hand and when Lewis only sniffed snot, he let him go. Lewis scrambled under the table before Elliot could grab him and around Birdy's chair. She shifted her chair in time for him to bury his face in her shoulder and though she flinched and grunted in pain, she held him without complaining, without pulling away, her back to Elliot. Lewis's shoulders rose and fell in great sobs. Birdy murmured reassurances in a loop. Elliot crawled to the far side of the tower, retrieved the binoculars, caught a glimpse of mother and child pulled from the scrub, dropped them and folded into the corner with the ringing of tinnitus in his ear from a nearby detonation, the smell of copper, Radler's screams as he bled out. It might have been a minute or ten that he'd lost. When he came back to the tower, it was still gloomy and Lewis was still sobbing.

More screams came from the creek bed. Elliot— clenching his jaw to force away the swirling lights at the edge of his vision—could only hope that the corpses below the hill became more interested in that than in the small noises coming from the shiny tower above them. He hated himself for thinking it.

Birdy and Lewis stayed in their embrace way for an hour more before Lewis's sobbing sighed away, and he slid away to face the wall, putting his arms over his ears.

The screams from the refugees had long since abated—either they were all dead or had fled out of earshot. But the noises of the undead had grown to a drone as if the tower were pitched in the middle of a football crowd. Elliot risked a peek over the window sill, and wished he hadn't. The bush was choked with them, staggering, bumping each other, sniffing the air. Two scrabbled side-by-side in the dirt halfway up the hill for Christ knew what. He duck-walked around all sides of the tower, checking windows. A tide of undead, a steady stream stretching in both directions, along a rough east-west line and headed south.

He sipped from the canteen, offered it to Lewis who refused, remaining in his half-fetal position. He passed it to Birdy and she received it without expression or comment.

The swarm thinned out by noon and the noise with it until only the occasional shambler was visible or audible meandering through the bush. He and Birdy ate a little trail mix and coaxed Lewis into sitting up against the wall and sipping water. But the teenager refused the last of the seeds and nuts, turning his head away. Elliot replaced the lid, kept it for later. He gave Birdy the last of the painkillers, checked her bandage. The cut looked clean, uninfected, a neat scab forming.

Between two and four o'clock, another smaller wave came and went, splashing against and around Mount Terror. As sun hit horizon, more pockets of undead became audible out there in the forest, though he couldn't see them. Lewis finally spoke then, needing to piss. Birdy echoed this, saying she couldn't wait any longer. Elliot handed him a foam cup and her an icecream container he found in the cardboard box. "No one's going outside," he said when Lewis refused to take it. "Not even for this."

Lewis took it dully and shuffled away on his knees, did his business with great awkwardness. When he was done, he and Elliot turned their back while Birdy followed suit. Then Elliot made them leave the containers in the corner rather than place them outside on the platform where the wind could blow them over, the odor alerting deaders.

This time Birdy got Lewis to eat the last of the trail mix.

In the soft orange of the sunset, Elliot caught his eye across the table and tapped the spot on the map he'd spread earlier, awaiting his opportunity for this conversation.

"We're going here."

"What?" Lewis said, voice still thick, emotionless.

"We're not going to Minchenbridge."

Lewis came to life then, face screwing up. "What! Yes we are!"

Elliot jerked a thumb over his shoulder. "We're not facing *that*. We're not getting caught between that and another wave behind it. If that's indicative of how many deaders are still wandering around north of here—"

"I'm going north!"

"Lewis," Birdy started, but Elliot kept going.

"The north is a washout. You heard her. People fighting over cat food?"

"My grandparents—"

"Maybe in a year or two, you can go looking for them. Maybe they'll still be alive and the plague will be gone by then. Maybe all the stupid people will have killed each other off. Right now, survival is the top priority … like I've told you a dozen times before."

"I'm *going* to my grandparents."

"You're going to survive long enough to see them. And so am I."

Birdy tried again, waving a hand between their two faces. "Elliot …"

"Dad wanted—"

Elliot squared his shoulders, got his angry Sergeant voice on: "Your *dad* wanted you to *live*, man. You are going to respect his wishes, you hear me?"

Lewis slumped in his chair, crossing his arms. "Sir, yes *sir*."

"Damn straight, siryessir. Now look at this." His fingers tapped the map again.

Birdy's good hand fell on top of his. "Give him some room, Elliot."

He pulled his hand away. "The hell I will." When she withdrew hers, he tapped the map again. "Look where I'm pointing."

Lewis turned away. "You look where you're pointing."

"On the map I saw in your house, your dad had Barnabas Island here marked. What is this?"

"Screw you," Lewis whispered, face still averted.

"Jesus, man, you can't even swear right?"

"Fuck you then!"

"That's better."

"Jesus," Birdy hissed and retreated to her chair.

Elliot said, "Tell me what this is."

Lewis jerked forward and studied it for a good ten seconds then threw himself back again. The chair squeaked alarmingly. Plastic cracked. "It's an island."

"No shit, genius. That why it's surrounded by water? What's its significance?"

"I don't know."

"Yeah, you do."

"I'm not going that way."

"Lewis," Birdy said, "we can't go north. Elliot's right," she added, but she didn't sound happy about that.

Great, another ally alienated.

"What's there?" he repeated.

"Veggie farms, berry farms, pigs, sheep, stuff like that and I don't want to go there. Understand?"

"Neither do I. Neither do we," he corrected himself, glancing at Birdy. She wasn't looking at him. "But we're going. So listen: Mom and Dad musta talked about it seriously for you to remember all that. No one else would've thought of this place?"

"How would I know?"

"How'd your parents plan on getting there? This is, what, a mile off shore, in the middle of a bay. What are the tides like, the currents, the waves?"

"I don't know."

"Did they know someone there or on the coast? Did they plan on finding a speedboat, a dinghy, a ferry, what?"

"I don't know! I don't care about bloody islands and stuff. Like, thirty people just died out there! Why don't you think about that?"

"Voice down, Lewis," Birdy muttered.

"I am thinking about it," Elliot said, having trouble keeping his own volume under control. "I don't want us to be thirty one and thirty two and thirty three. Now tell me what your dad had planned. This is an island: how'd he plan on getting to it and how's he know you'd be welcome there? You have family there? Friends? "

The fire departed Lewis as suddenly as it had flared. He slid down on a wall until only his eyes showed above the table. They were turned upon his knees. "No. I don't know. I don't think so."

Elliot consulted the map and its legend, tried to catch Birdy's eye and failed. He said, "It's a sixty kilometer hike from here to the coast. Barnabas Island is south east of Mount Terror, so if there's another deader wave coming, that heading might keep us from going through it. No food here. Dangerous to hunt. We need to leave and I vote going that way."

"Yep," she said.

The dying rays of the sun caught one side of Lewis's face, casting the other in deep shadow. He looked like a demon as one glowing eye glared at Elliot above the tabletop. "You're an arsehole," he said and turned his head.

Elliot gathered the map and folded it carefully, slipped it into the leather satchel. "So they tell me, pal. So they tell me."

11

In the morning, there wasn't a zombie to be seen or heard. While Elliot silently packed the bags as tight as he could get them, Birdy went onto the decking outside the door. When Elliot noticed her heaving shoulders, he sighed and lay his pack down. "Stay here a minute, Cochise."

Lewis—who seemed to have lost whatever ire he'd felt the night before— followed his gaze and simply said, "Sure."

He shut the door quickly behind him. Birdy's tears were silent and the shaking stopped the moment she heard him coming. She kept her back to him.

He said, "I'm not really good at saying sorry. But I'm saying sorry."

She snorted. "I'm not crying about you." That surprised him. Enough to have nothing to say back. She sniffed, dabbing her eyes with her sleeve. "I'm not the one you should apologize to anyway." His gaze slid off, caught Lewis's through the window. Elliot broke contact first. "Not gonna happen," he murmured.

"Feel like you ride him too hard." She turned a little, glanced at him, looked away.

"I disagree."

"He's lost family, yeah? He just witnessed a shit-load more people torn apart. He's lost the chance to connect with his family up north. And he's probably thinking they're dead too, since I opened my big mouth about it yesterday. He needs a little TLC, ya know?"

Elliot moved to the rail and leaned there beside her, studying the forest. Still no sign of un-life. Didn't mean they weren't out there. "TLC ain't gonna save his ass or yours. TLC can wait til the pusbags are long rotted into the ground and he's safely in the middle of some walled and civilized community. Until then, hurtin' or not, he needs to man up like the rest of us."

"Man up?" She nudged him with a shoulder. "What century you from?"

He sighed. "Same as you, darlin'. The one where humanity returned to the Stone Age in a few short decades. And all of Doomsday's children got to ride it out."

"You have a flair for the dramatic," she said after a beat.

He shrugged. "Too much cable."

"I need to pee again,"

He placed a hand against his own belly, but not too hard. "Me too. We'll use the amenities downstairs there. One person inside, one person outside on *each* side." He tried a smile and she returned it as he said, "Flair for wordplay too."

"Shakespeare, you're not, mate."

He pointed to the forest. "Think you can do this? Helluva walk ahead of us."

"Like you said," she sighed, picking up the spear-gun she'd leaned against the railing; "we all gotta man up."

The motor home's wheels were hidden behind a carpet of weeds, baby ferns and bracken. Above the forest canopy, the sky had clouded over, threatening but not producing rain. The humid air around them was heavy with cannabis—someone had been growing it around here before the outbreak. The ganga certainly explained why someone might stick a Winnebago in the back of a state forest. Far worse than the pot, the air was also thick with wattle. Elliot was coming to hate wattle. The little yellow flowers—nothing more than puffy pollen-balls—made his nose and eyes itch.

"You think anyone's in there?" Birdy asked him softly.

The vehicle was about twenty feet long with the driver's compartment and engine separate from the trailer and a single access to the living quarters opening off the passenger side. They were crouching thirty yards from the motor home's ass-end, behind a low thatch of blackberries, avoiding the thorns. A thick patch of cannabis provided shelter to the north. A maze of paperbarks, wattles and some kind of needle-leafed shrub lay behind and south of them. Lewis reached through the brambles to pick three underripe berries and popped them in his mouth, grimaced. Obviously sour.

Elliot answered, "Yeah, I think someone's in there. Or coming back here. Too good a foxhole to give up, this one." The real question was about whether or not to risk it. There'd been plenty of evidence that this forest wasn't uninhabited: several small collections of tents—all abandoned perhaps because of the oncoming dead—indicated strongly that many people had retreated here at some point. No living people though. Ten or so deadheads had made traveling interesting since leaving the tower. Six and a half hours of running and walking and ducking behind trees—and once, luckily just once, having to hack at a couple of moldering heads with the sharp end of a broken stick like some kind of caveman.

He had memorized the most salient features of the map: there were two small towns in different directions they could make before nightfall if they hurried and if all went well. A couple more within a five hour hard hike from there the following day, along with farming land rather than forest. They could hopscotch their way across the landscape this way for a week or two, using farmhouses and towns as stepping stones. Problem was, any kind of shelter might mean concentrations of living people as well as undead.

"Screwed if you don't; screwed if you do." He took a deep breath. "Okay, here's how we're going to approach it. I'll circle around to find a blind spot, somewhere people inside that cabin can't see me. Make my approach from there. Normally, I'd wait till dark, but I don't wanna be out here with the deaders then. Birdy, you're taking the Aimrite and heading back behind us fifty feet, watch for pusbags. Lewis, I get fired on," He pointed to the 9-mil in the young man's hand, "you fire a couple of rounds into the centre of the cabin, then you put safety on and crawl—and I mean *crawl*, keep low—back behind better cover toward Birdy where I can circle around and meet you later."

It looked like a game trail made a gap through the trees to his right. That might be the best route to take, staying low, taking his time.

"I can't do that," Lewis whispered.

Elliot leaned in. "What?"

"I can't do that. I can't shoot at people."

"You shot deaders."

"Not people."

"Lewis. You have to do things like this. Someone else's life might depend on it, not just yours."

"It's not me."

He gripped Lewis's sleeve. "This is what we do now."

Lewis pulled back. "A man is someone—"

"Yeah, I heard this yesterday, enough. I hate to say it. But comes a time like this one where responsibility is using this." He held up a fist, then touched the rifle with it. "And this."

"What if I kill someone?"

"What if you let me die?"

Lewis winced at that, face closing over. It cut close to the bone, Elliot knew: the young man might blame himself for not protecting his family. But he could get all the therapy he wanted once they got through this and he was safely enmeshed in a sheltered society.

He glanced at Birdy, but this time she was silent, tracking a finger along the cool lines of the spear gun, staying out of it.

He said, "This is the world now. This is what we do. I'm finding a way to sneak up on that motor home. With or without your help. But without your help, I could die. Now, I'm gonna get on with my day and leave it to you to decide what's—"

A stick cracked. Someone gasped. He spun on one heel, still in a crouch, aware of Lewis attempting the same but toppling sideways, aware of Birdy shooting to her feet and bringing her weapon up. A teenage boy had come out of the scrub, while four more spread out to flank him. Four young men, a year or two older than Lewis. One girl maybe twelve, small, like Birdy. She carried a short-handled shovel. The boys at the back held bloodstained and battered cricket bats.

The one at the front held a rifle.

Elliot watched and heard it happen in slowmo, color leaching from his vision …

The shock on the group's faces.

The reflexive raising of the boy's rifle.

The muzzle flare and sharp report.

The girl dropping her shovel and putting her hands to her mouth.

Birdy collapsing with an *oof* of breath.

The boys all swearing, one of them grabbing the shooter and pulling him backwards.

The rifle toppling into the dry grass while the group turned tail and fled.

Elliot threw himself on top of Birdy, while his own rifle fell away, while his lungs shrank to the size of golf balls, while his vision started strobing, while the ringing started. Something pulled on his shoulder: it might have been Lewis, it might have been a stray piece of shrapnel from the IED, it might have been a sniper up high above the wadi, it might have been a medic moving him aside.

He knew he was yelling but he couldn't hear it. He knew his hands were pressed against the bloody mess of a woman's chest, pumping so the heart would not give up, but he couldn't feel it. He could see her and she wasn't burning, but he smelled burning flesh, burned plastic. He knew—he knew something, but he didn't know what it was. Not until he was sitting on his ass with one sleeve caught up in a blackberry thornbush and one hand pressed into his mouth to stop him from screaming. Through the ringing, he heard birds. Then flies. And he knew. He knew he was sitting in the Australian bush with another dead friend behind him. And he knew she was a friend because friends always died.

And that meant …

"Lewis!" It came out hoarse, but he heard it, could hear his voice again.

Lewis was gone. Elliot staggered to his feet, tearing his sleeve as he ripped it from the brambles. Where the hell was he? The bush spun around him although he was standing still. The air swam with heat and marijuana and dust and pollen. Where was he? Where was Lewis?

"Here!"

A face—a tear-streaked face—appeared above a Pokémon tee shirt, coming around and through the needle-leafed bushes, that face unconcerned at the way the bushes snagged his clothing. Lewis ripped free as Elliot had done from the blackberries, the eyes locked on Elliot's. His gait was uneven. The SIG bobbed above the waistband of his jeans. He'd chased them.

Had he—?

"Did you …?" Elliot asked.

Lewis shook his head and stopped in front of him. He kept his eyes off Birdy, as did Elliot, their gazes locked together. Lewis's cheeks ran with tears but his voice was steady. "I chased them. I just chased them. I didn't even shoot. I should have."

Elliot shook his head, crouched and felt for his rifle without diverting his gaze. "You did good." *I'm the one who lost it.*

This wasn't happening.

This is happening. This just happened.

The other boy's rifle was gripped tight in Lewis's hand; Elliot hadn't noticed it until he squatted. As one hand found the M4, he reached out and took the bolt-action from Lewis, stood up straight. He handed the M4 to Lewis and worked the new weapon's bolt, ejected the casing. He pulled out the mag and checked it, then the breech. Nothing. The sonofabitch had been down to his last round. He raised his face to the sun streaming through the gum trees and laughed, laughed just one loud and sardonic bark. Then he sent the weapon spinning into the scrub.

He took back the M4, stalked around the blackberries, made it to passenger side wheel without getting shot, took a peek at the seats inside. No one there.

"What are you doing!" Lewis hissed behind him.

He edged forward beneath the first of the side windows where the curtains had been pulled aside then moved to the door. Moment of truth: compromising the safety of his own skull and he didn't give a shit. Anyone in there already knew he was out here.

"Let's get it over with," he said and wrenched the door open.

Unless they were in the shower cubicle at the far end, no one was home. He entered leading with the rifle-barrel. The air was cool. A fine layer of dust coated everything including the linoleum floor. No footprints. No one had gotten in that cubicle unless they levitated there. No one had been here in weeks. He checked the shower carefully anyway, found it empty, slumped against the wall in relief, kicked the opposite wall once twice three times.

"Birdy," he whispered.

Lewis followed him in, eyes wide, SIG at his side, taking in the state of the place, taking in Elliot's heaving chest and the dents in the wall. "What now?" he asked.

"Go get my pack." He'd left it near the berries.

"What about …? What about her?"

Spider webs clumped in corners like cotton candy, populated by spiders with tiny bodies and long gangly legs. Elliot wondered if these would inherit the earth when people had finished killing each other off. If in some distance future, would these things evolve a better society, a better world? Or would it they just enact more death?

"Elliot?"

"Get my pack. I'll think about it."

He blinked and Lewis was back, though a minute or two must have passed. He was still staring at the spiders when the teenager put the pack and the Aimrite on the table then closed the door and locked it.

"Daddy longlegs," Lewis muttered.

"Yuh. We got 'em too. My … uncle called 'em cellar spiders."

"Good name." He added his new leather shoulder satchel to the pile on the table, placed the SIG beside it and traced his finger over the stippling on the grip.

Elliot moved to the cupboard below the tiny kitchen sink. It held nine bottles of water, a six pack of James Boag beers, neat stacks of spaghetti tins, three bags of corn chips. No vegetables, not even beans.

If the agent or infection was in the cans, he no longer cared. He dragged the pack over, flipped it open and threw six tins and three water bottles in it. He fished out his toothbrush and said, "You take six more tins if you can fit them in." He handed over another water bottle. "Drink. You need to hydrate. Then use straight water to brush your teeth. I transferred my spare toothbrush from my pack to yours this morning." Lewis took the water bottle, but didn't open it, butt against the dining table. "We'll make the next town before nightfall, eat big then. Conserve the food. One big meal a day. Keep training our bodies to do more on less calories, like people did before the industrial age." He popped open another water bottle and wet the toothbrush bristles, put the bottle on the bench and stood. His brush paused halfway to his mouth. Lewis wasn't moving.

"Need to brush your teeth. I've only seen you do it once since … since Harrietville."

"Birdy?"

He jammed the brush in his mouth, started scrubbing. "No time."

"We have to bury her."

"We have to stay alive."

"You're brushing your teeth. We should be out there digging a hole."

Elliot snatched the bottle from his hands and twisted the lid. He reached over and banged the bottle on the table, splashing the surface. "Brush. You seriously don't want cavities in future."

Lewis looked away, said nothing, face tight, jaw working.

Elliot picked up a saucepan from the draining board, held it high and dropped it on Lewis's right sneaker.

"Ah! You *bastard*!" Lewis grabbed his foot in a standing yoga pose, withdrew along the cabin to put distance between them. "Why'd you do that!"

"That hurt?"

"Duh."

"Imagine that pain times twenty, all concentrated in your mouth and staying there 24-7-365. Imagine it getting so bad, you're screaming for someone to do anything they can to make it stop. Imagine me tying you down hard so you can't flinch and sticking a pair of needle-nose pliers in your mouth—without anesthetic, mind—and ripping the decaying tooth from your mouth before it can get infected and kill you. And all that because you wouldn't brush."

Lewis let go of his foot and swept the water bottle from the table to slam into the cabinets opposite.

They stayed in tableau for a long moment. Then Elliot spat in the sink and dropped his brush in his pack, locked the clasps. He lifted it, took the M4 and moved to the door.

"You coming?"

Lewis let go of a breath and picked up his satchel. He bent and squeezed three bottles of water, a pack of chips and a spaghetti tin into it. The spaghetti crushed the chips as he shouldered the bag. He checked the safety on the SIG and put it in his pants. Then he stepped up and reached past Elliot to unlock the door. He pushed it out and squeezed through, turning east.

Elliot leaned back and stamped down hard on a spider. He inspected the goo on the floor where it had been. It looked a lot like an exploded human corpse seen from the air.

The goddammed Oussefs had left him with a shit sandwich all right. He lurched outside and into the blazing sun. The growling, choking breaths of deaders came to him on the wind, drawn by the noise. In a minute or two they'd find her body and start in on it. That might buy him and Lewis enough time to avoid them altogether, keep ahead of them.

Lewis was already out of the clearing, a smudge of color amid the washed out greens. Elliot shouldered his pack and hurried after him, keen to get ahead and steer them right. Behind him came the frenzied sounds of the first deader finding Birdy.

Yep. A total shit sandwich.

A nest of boulders poking from the side of the hill gave them a place to rest along with a clear view of the town below. The map dot called Birns River Bridge was a meander of short streets housed with cottages and a penchant for European trees and gardens. It lay on the far side of the actual bridge beyond the shopping district that faced the river. Narrow parkland dressed both banks of the watercourse, the far side spotted with picnic tables and some kind of memorial stone. A blackened patch of grass resolved in the field glasses as some kind of funeral pyre, charred lumps resolving as skeletons. The black had spread across the grass, like ink running; sometime in the last two months, rain had smudged it, washing it inch by inch toward the river. Twenty storefronts made up the commerical strip, decades-old, some quaint, others merely aged. The river ran fast and shallow across fist-sized pebbles. The range of hills swept north, leaving the east as grassland: grazing property lay beyond the town as far as the eye could see, peppered with small stands of bushland. North-east of the town, river and highway cut a ravine through the hills creating pretty-looking bluffs either side. A stately two-storey home rose from one of the bluffs. Its front windows would have had a fine view along the ravine, while one side would get a glimpse of swathes of farmland leading east.

A mile beyond the town off a branch road by a river tributary sat a ten cabin motor inn with a gas station on the opposite side of the road. Those two structures seemed to be the only real industry in the area. And they promised cars. Through the binoculars, Elliot could make out the regular lines of an orchard in a farm close to the township—apple trees maybe.

For the first time in weeks, he didn't feel like eating but they should try the orchard; someone had told him Tasmania produced enough varieties of apple that one was always ripe for picking regardless of the time of year.

A speckle of grey-brown shapes on a field revealed themselves as kangaroos—a weird coincidence, given recent conversation. He considered commenting as much, but small talk felt wrong, as wrong as eating. There'd been no conversation since the motorhome other than the occasional grunt necessary for course corrections.

Whatever anger Lewis had felt back at the motor home had leached away as they'd clawed their way up and down hills and through barriers of vegetation. The teenager leaned on a boulder higher up the slope, rubbing his knuckles into his thighs. His face was as empty of emotion as Elliot's heart. They could both do with a few drinks and a long sleep in that motel down there.

Now that Elliot had leaned his ass against this big rock, now that he'd stopped, it was going to take an effort to get going again. He raised the field glasses, had to blink hard a couple times to get his focus back. The glasses caught no movement in the town anywhere except for two dogs traipsing side by side along one of the short sidestreets. No movement was real good. He pushed off the rock and started down the slope—a scree of loose stones, eucalypt bark and twigs—glanced back to get Lewis moving too and snagged his foot on a tree root. The rifle went flying. Elliot went down in a heap. His backpack caught, preventing him from rolling. His ankle flared in agony where he'd snagged it. He wrestled the backpack off, got himself untwisted and sitting upright, swearing as good as he knew how.

He straightened the leg, reached for his boot, and pulled back when the touch made him wince. He couldn't put weight on this.

Lewis was standing above him now, face blank but for the tiny crease he sometimes got between his eyebrows.

Elliot growled in pain and frustration. "Find me the IFAK."

Lewis ditched his satchel and Aimrite and rummaged through Elliot's pack. When he found the first aid kit, he pulled out a roll of bandages and some clips. "I'll have to take the boot off."

"I'll do it." It took Elliot over a minute of gritted teeth and further imprecations, but he got the shoe off. Rolling down his sock, he was relieved to see no purple and no swelling. With luck it'd only be a minor sprain. And the bandage would help brace it. He held his hand out for it.

"I can," Lewis said.

"Yeah right. Just gimme."

Lewis shuffled closer and inspected the joint with pursed lips. "Keep holding your pants leg back like that."

"*You're* gonna bandage my ankle?"

"It's easy."

Elliot cocked an eyebrow. "And you got your medical training where?"

"Mum taught me first aid."

Elliot was silent a while as Lewis got the bandage out and positioned it against the ankle. "She was a naturopath? They do first aid?"

But that was a stupid question. Lots of people did first aid. Store assistants. Office managers. Teenagers. Lewis's expression was understandably scathing.

"Okay," Elliot said, "make a start but I'm watching you."

To his surprise and relief, Elliot didn't once need to intervene. Lewis's hands were sure and the bandage was perfectly tensioned when he clipped it together. He sat back and admired his handiwork, then packed up the IFAK into Elliot's bag.

Elliot gently teased his sock up over the bandage. He rolled his right shoulder, testing it. The backpack straps had jarred it, but it was okay, just a little touchy. He searched around for a stray branch he could use to get up. "Guess I should thank you."

"For this too." A long thick stick landed beside him. Lewis came up beside him and lay the SIG on the ground. "Swap you this for the other two weapons."

Elliot resisted the urge to object; how would he wield a rifle one handed? He tied his boot to his pack by the laces, then got up, bracing himself with the stick. It'd hold him, but going the rest of the way downhill would be slow. Slow and sideways. What the hell was he going to do with his gear?

Following his gaze, Lewis slung the satchel across his back, strap across his chest. He slung the Aimrite the opposite way and tested the backpack's weight. He hefted the pack over the opposite shoulder to the satchel, carried the M4 in one hand with the barrel down and started downhill, picking his way carefully.

"Probably a pharmacy down there," he called back.

Elliot watched him a moment then picked his own way down—even more carefully than the teenager.

The river burbled below them as they crossed the bridge, cool and rippling with soft light, tempting Elliot. The cold water would have been good for his ankle if there weren't dead people soaking in it. He'd prefer the swollen ankle to disease. Lewis looked so sure of himself, walking twenty feet ahead of Elliot. So sure, that Elliot felt a sudden pang of doubt: what the hell made him think he could protect Lewis? He'd let those kids come up on them from behind. He'd let Birdy down, just like he'd let down … He'd twisted his goddammed ankle. What the hell was he playing at here?

Loser talk, Uncle John growled from the recesses of Elliot's mind. *Only losers talk loser talk.*

The dogs lifted cautious heads as he limped from the bridge and crossed into the town, growling in a perfunctory way before returning to their meal. Lewis lowered the pack onto a benchseat, swearing quietly at the animals because of what they were doing.

Elliot came to rest against telephone pole near Lewis, regarding the stores suspiciously, remembering why he hated towns. Too many vantage points. Too many potential sniper posts. Too many ways to surprise someone, the way his squad surprised those guys in Deir-al-Zour. Be ironic if someone played the same trick on him. The SIG was a comforting presence against his belly.

The pharmacy sign showed halfway along the stores toward the gorge. The dogs and bodies made a formidable barrier.

"Maybe I'll go around the back," Lewis said. He lowered the satchel to the sidewalk beside the bench.

Elliot pointed to their right toward the far end of the shopping district where a deader with skinny grey legs beneath a pink miniskirt shuffled toward them, arms twitching, bare feet dragging. "Might be more of them."

Lewis readied the Aimrite. "I can take her out."

"Might be other people too."

Lewis chewed that over a moment, then with forced bravado he said, "I'll be all right." He considered the dead woman inching toward them.

"She's not moving fast," Elliot told him. "Better we leave her where she is and both head round back."

Lewis said, "You'll slow me down" and jogged across the asphalt and into the east road that split the shopping district, Aimrite in his hands, rifle bouncing against his back.

Elliot swore—then swore a second time when the sound of a speeding car came from the south. Lewis skidded to a halt, hearing it too. With nowhere to hide and unable to run, Elliot waved at Lewis to stay back, get cover, then pulled the SIG and pressed himself against the post as a black SUV rounded the bend into town. He knew he stuck out like dog's balls, but there was nothing for it.

Ignoring his signal, Lewis walked to the corner, forcing a third curse to Elliot's lips.

Elliot sighted on the car, tracking its approach, as if a speargun would make much of a dent in that. The SUV swerved onto the wrong side of the road to clip the zombie woman, flinging her into the rendered wall of a storefront, then braked hard to a stop in the intersection of main road, bridge and east road.

The door cracked open. A fifty-something man poked his empty hands and the top of his head into the open. He eased out until he stood fully exposed with hands raised. The freshening breeze side-parted his shock of grey-white hair, ruffled his light blue business shirt and grey slacks. Thirty yards past him, the zombie woman twitched and wiggled, attempting without success to raise herself on shattered arms.

The man's smile was as open as his stance, teeth celebrity-white.

"G'day, fellas," he said. "Needing shelter?"

12

While Elliot and Lewis settled into the back seat, the older man slammed his door and twisted around to regard them with raised eyebrows and an easy smile. His teeth were flossed, the fingernails on the hand gripping the passenger seatback were manicured. The car smelled of pine air freshener and leather upholstery cleaner. The floors were clear of lint and trash.

"Bloody glad to see some friendly faces," he beamed. "Haven't lost the entire human race, then?"

"Not yet," Lewis replied seriously.

The man's eyes lit up. "Pretty good shot hitting that eater, eh? Had her dead in my sights." He waggled his brows until Lewis acknowledged the pun with a small snort.

"Okay, then. Not the time for jokes, huh? Look like you've both had rough time."

Rough time?

Elliot thought the guy must have a Doctorate in Understatement.

"You're on your way somewhere?" Elliot asked.

"Home." He eyed Elliot's bandages and stick, Lewis's cuts and scrapes, then nodded at the dogs. "The shop there, the pharmacy? That was mine. Still is, I s'pose. If you'd like, I can take a good look at that leg when we get home. Your abrasions too, young fella. Make sure there's no infection."

"We'd appreciate it," Elliot replied. "You don't need anything from your store while we're here?"

"Anything worth taking—" He faced forward, started the engine. "—I already have."

The man had a .303 rifle leaning against the passenger door arm rest. Elliot moved the M4 that stood between him and Lewis so it could move freely if needed. The safety was on, but he had a thumb near it. "And you're taking us where?"

The chemist pointed along the road to where it rose toward the bluffs. "The big house up there? *Mi casa su casa.*"

"Thank you, sir," Lewis offered.

The man chuckled and slipped the shifter into Drive. "Name's Jock, not Sir." He planted his foot, throwing Elliot into his seat back. The cargo space behind him was crammed with looted supplies, including three cages with chickens inside them. The birds squawked and scrabbled for purchase as the car shot up the road. In less than a minute, they were slowing at the high brick wall around the house on the bluff. "Get the gates, young fella?"

Lewis jumped from the car, stuck his hand through the bars of the gates and found the latch. While he dragged them aside and Jock eased the car between them, Elliot studied the weird curl in the back of the driver's hair, the gold watch on his wrist ... and his neat up-market clothing.

I didn't know this apocalypse was formal.

Jock's front yard had once been sculpted, land-scaped. Parts of it now were feral, rose and azalea beds going to weed like everything else in the world. However, a wide section of lawn had been turned over, the bare earth hinting at a vegetable garden. The rest of the property beyond the house was fenced off with a hotchpotch of iron sheeting, barbed wire and fence palings, and Elliot suspected more home produce there, vegetables, maybe more chickens. Maybe a pig.

Bacon and eggs.

His mouth should have watered at the thought. But he still wasn't hungry.

Birdy ...

Jock parked in front of the doors while Lewis shut the gates. Elliot waved off his offer of help out of the car.

"Who's here with you?" he asked Jock.

Jock's expression turned sad. "No one. Till now. Big house for one bloke. I could use the company. And the help, after you heal. Sure you don't want me to go get you a crutch? I have several upstairs."

"I'll manage." Using his stick and keeping the M4 in his free hand, Elliot hobbled to one of two colonnades framing the entrance and waited for Jock to get his key in the lock. He listened, but heard no pig. No bacon then. But there was a very real threat Jock had friends inside. The house boasted double front doors, the wood dark, lacquered. Barbed wire had been laid around the ground floor windows. No glimpse of the inside was possible through the scrim curtains. Elliot hopped up the single step while behind him, Lewis struggled uncomplaining with their gear. They entered in single file, Jock first, then Elliot, then Lewis with a mild "wow" which further fueled Jock's smile. No ambush. No people waiting. An empty house, warm and stuffy. The right half of the downstairs was one open living area including the kitchen at the rear. Bookcases. Three coffee tables. A two-seater and a four-seater couch. Three recliner armchairs. Home theater system. A staircase ran straight up the center of the house from in front of the entry. Open doors on the ground level beyond the stairs revealed a separate bathroom and laundry. Right inside the entry to Elliot's right—before the staircase started—another set of closed double doors hinted at a home office or library. The upper storey was large enough that it might host three bedrooms and another bath. The high ceilings were inset with downlights, all dark despite the gloom outside. The floor was lit by floor-to-ceiling windows set in the front and lefthand wall. Elliot could see smaller windows set above the kitchen benches out back. The lower half of these—as well as a glass sliding door to the yard—had been boarded up against intruders and peeping toms.

Once they were in, their bags settled against the lounge suite, and Lewis's speargun on the long hardwood coffee table that the lounge suite surrounded, Jock shoved five bolts into their catches to secure the front door. He'd carried in his hunting rifle and set it in an umbrella rack alongside a couple of ax-handles.

Thunder grumbled in the distance and Jock said, "About bloody time it rained. Good for the gardens," he added.

"Do you want your chickens?" Lewis asked. "I can go get them."

Jock waved the offer away. "We'll settle in first, then go get em. Want to have a look-see at your mate's leg." He ushered Elliot into a recliner and when his feet were up, took the bandage off. "Shame to take this off. You did a good job of this."

"Thanks," Lewis said. He was wandering the floor looking at knickknacks all cleaned and dusted.

Jock made an appreciative sound. "You know first aid?"

"A bit," Lewis replied and moved to a high book case set between two windows. He took a couple of volumes down and flipped through them while Jock felt Elliot's ankle.

"When'd you hurt this?"

Elliot opened his mouth to answer but Lewis beat him to it.

"Twenty minutes ago. He fell down a hill."

"Not all the way down," Elliot corrected.

Jock rocked back on his heels and considered. "Well. Not too many ultrasounds around these days to be certain, but I'd say it's a minor sprain. We'll get you some ice, alternate that with compression. You won't be dancing for a while, but give it some rest and you should be right in a day or two. Young fella, the freezer in the laundry room: down the left hand side are several icepacks. Fetch me one?"

Lewis replaced the books and trotted off in that direction.

Jock said, "Can't keep calling you blokes Young Fella and Bloke with a Sprained Ankle. You know my name. What're yours?"

"Lewis," the teenager called through the open laundry door.

"And Elliot."

"Welcome to my humble home, Lewis and Elliot."

Lewis returned with the icepack and handed it to Jock.

"Did you shut the freezer lid?" said Jock.

Lewis nodded.

"Sorry. Fussy, I know, but we must conserve what little power's left." The chemist arranged the icepack carefully on Elliot's ankle.

Elliot winced, leaned forward to adjust it himself while his eyes scanned the room. "You have power."

"Solar. Knew it'd pay off, just not like this."

"And you're here alone?"

Lewis, losing interest, returned to wandering.

Jock nodded and stood with a groan, hands on his knees. "Could do with young legs—and young backs too. To help me grow food, make this place more secure. Been converting my yards to veggie gardens, bringing in chickens. I built a coop. Even laid concrete for the first time in my life to keep the rats and foxes from burrowing under. My knees and my lumbar region have never felt so bloody sore." His laugh was self-deprecating, light-hearted. "I remember someone saying once that the only people who'd survive the end of the world were the working classes. They're the ones who know how to do things like this. Well, so far, I'm not doing too badly for a middle-class, middle-aged man."

Leafing through a book, Lewis murmured, "Birdy would have liked it here."

Elliot's gut twisted. He ran a hand over his chin, scratched his nose.

Smile wilting, Jock looked between them. "Birdy?"

"Never mind," Elliot said. "This is a good set up. Not sure I want to stay too long, though." He met Jock's eyes. "No offence."

"Got somewhere to be? There a party I wasn't invited to?" Jock grunted as he waved off his pisspoor joke. "Twenty-four hours and you might be okay to leave, though I'd suggest you take a car. I've got a couple more out back that I stole. Figured the eaters wouldn't want them."

Eaters. That's what Birdy had called them too. Elliot's gut twisted again.

Thunder rumbled again in the distance. Jock hummed. "Could be a wet couple of days anyway, so you might want to stay as long as possible. Think you will? Stay?"

"Depends…" Elliot started saying.

Lewis interrupted him. "Is this a basement or a cupboard?" He was standing at a door set into the side of the staircase, the books forgotten. There was a low set of free-standing shelves between it and the bathroom door, partly filled with paperbacks and partly with more knickknacks—golfing memorabilia, curios from Asian lands, fancy candlesticks.

"Cellar."

"Can I go down there?"

"Later." Jock started towards the kitchen, beckoned him. "You, Lewis, can help me prep some dinner while your friend rests. There's nothing down there but a lot of empty wine bottles and a box of potatoes anyway." He went around the island bench, bent to open cupboards and pull out broad pasta bowls. Past the benches and fridge, a boarded up glass sliding door led to the backyard, but Elliot could only see the grey sky through the glass at the top. "Elliot, you keep that foot elevated. Lewis, you'll find vegetables in a metal bin in the laundry by the freezer. They needed to be used soon, so you two are actually helping me out there. Water still runs here," he explained to Elliot. "I've been making the most of that. So I'll get Lewis to rinse and chop enough vegetables for a vegan stew. Might keep the eggs I've got for breakfast, if that's ok. No meat, sorry. I have some packet rice we can boil up though."

"I'll have mine without the rice," Elliot said, surprising himself. "Don't trust packet foods."

"Oh?" Jock thought a moment. "Maybe we'll all just stick with the stew. There'll be a fair bit anyway."

"Thank you very much," Elliot told Jock and forced a smile. This gent would be the type to appreciate manners. "Lewis and me, we've had a hard time of it. And your hospitality means the world to us."

Jock beamed as Lewis returned with arms filled.

"Just glad to be of help to someone again," Jock said, sliding a long carving knife from its wooden block. Elliot tensed, pulled the M4 in tighter beside his chair, finger on the trigger guard. But the older man only dragged potatoes onto a cutting board and started the blade on them. "And after dinner, you blokes can tell me a little about that hard time you've had."

13

Distant thunder and lightning played across the western skies while the three of them ate in the light of battery-powered storm lanterns. But the storm didn't break properly until Jock and Lewis were rinsing the plates. Wind thrashed the eucalypts outside as rain drummed against the windows.

"That'll fill up the water tanks," Jock said. "Tap water won't last forever." He'd kept up an unending river of prattle during the dinner, cracking dad jokes, telling what Lewis found to be funny anecdotes about dumb customers in his pharmacy, and describing minute details of things he'd learned in concreting a chicken pen and planting vegetables in his yards. As irritating as he found the old fart, Jock's banter seemed good therapy for Lewis, whose energy was returning. And he hadn't mentioned Birdy again.

As Elliot readjusted his third icepack of the evening, an overhead flash of lighting and immediate thunder clap made him jump and Lewis gasp, "Wow!"

He was goddam grateful they hadn't stayed in the motorhome. He could feel the temperature drop even sealed inside this house. Plus, Jock's house was also free of cobwebs and spiders. In fact, it was meticulously clean. No dust. No grit on the carpets other than what he and Lewis had walked in. The middle-aged pharmacist certainly was—in his own words—fussy. Then again, now they'd been sitting around talking crap while chowing down, he'd started to show signs of relaxing. He'd even kicked off his leather brogues.

"What's this on your arm?" Jock was asking Lewis.

Lewis considered the scrape he'd gotten back at the farm. "It's not bad. Do you need to put disinfectant on it?"

"Only if you're a floor. Antispectic for humans, matey." They shared a laugh. "I'll get some before you go to bed. Hasn't killed you so far."

Give the old coot a chance, Elliot told his suspicious self. Jock could have left them to die. He could have turned his car around at the end of town and fled, hoping they'd bypass his home, returning later. Instead, he'd helped them, despite the threat they posed. As Lewis and Jock worked side-by-side, trading puns and decades-old riddles, Elliot mused that despite *Homo sapiens'* deserved reputation as a flawed species, there always had been and therefore still were good people around. Like Lewis, whose instinct was always to help people and even cows.

Like Birdy.

That twisting of the gut again. That deep, dark well opening up inside him and wanting him, *urging* him to slip into it, to fall down and forget about trying, forget about life.

He straightened in his chair and told the deep dark well to go to hell.

Jock shook water from his fingers as Lewis picked up the forks to dry them. The older man wiped his hands on his pants and took two candles down from high shelves above the stove, lit them. "Think it's time we stopped working and relaxed for the evening. You blokes must be bushed."

"Totally," said Lewis, laying the forks in their place in a top drawer. He tossed the towel on a bench and leaned there.

"Come on in here," said Jock and moved into the living room. He set the candles on one of the coffee tables and went to a sideboard to turn off one of the four hurricane lanterns then opened a half-full scotch bottle.

Lewis took an arm chair, curling into it like a cat, eyes heavy but watching keenly.

Jock upturned two glasses and poured three fingers of the amber liquid in each. "Ice? Water?"

Elliot hadn't shifted from his recliner since arrival. The ankle still pulsed with the pain, but the icepacks and elevation had already made some difference. The booze would make more. He sat a little straighter and said, "It's fine the way God made it."

"Take this across to your mate," Jock said, handing the glass to Lewis. "You two *are* mates, I gather, not relatives?"

Lewis snorted. "Do we look alike?"

"No. I guess not."

Elliot took his glass, threw back a third of it. The sting on his tongue and throat was pleasant, welcome. Warmth seeped down the inside of his chest. His mouth filled with peaty aftertaste.

Jock bent down and retrieved a stubby glass bottle from a cupboard beneath the drink stand. "Heads up," he called and tossed it underhand to Lewis, who lurched forward to catch it. "Ginger beer, I'm afraid. Only drink I have for someone your age and probably a bit flat. Hope you like it."

The gravitas on Lewis's face said he'd certainly try to like it and he set about wringing off the twist top while Jock settled into another arm chair by a dark gas heater.

Elliot put the glass between his thighs and wriggled his toes. "You have a beautiful downstairs. What's upstairs?"

Jock sipped then swished his drink, admiring the color against a candle's glow. "Two bedrooms, a room I'm using for storage and a bathroom. Plus, a little reading area at the top of the stairs where I used to sit and watch the river. Still do sometimes. I'll show you how nice it is in the morning," he told Lewis who had curled back onto the two-seater couch. "Do you read, son?"

Lewis made a thinking face. "I like books on fauna." He took a sip of his ginger beer and almost hid his disappointment. He took another sip to cover it.

"A learner! That's excellent. I might have some like that in my study. I'll check later."

"How about books on what the traditional people ate in Tasmania?" Elliot asked.

"Bush tucker? Yes, I do have a book on that. Very interesting. I'll dig that out too."

"My mum grew some of that," offered Lewis. "Bush tucker."

I goddammed knew it, Elliot thought with a sigh, picturing what had seemed like untouched herb gardens at the health retreat.

"Why'd she grow that then?" Jock asked.

Lewis wriggled into a more comfortable position. "She grew a lot of stuff. She was a naturopath. We tried to eat as much unprocessed food as possible."

"Lewis picked up some of that knowledge from Mom apparently," Elliot said. If Jock could see value in the teenager, see him as an ally, someone to pass his own knowledge onto, it might make moving on easier. *Maybe there's safe haven for Lewis yet.*

He sipped his whisky to burn away another twinge in his guts. *Guilt. Shit.* The whole purpose of this mission had been transporting the young man to a safe haven where others more qualified could take over caring for him. Nothing wrong with that. And if he'd found that place, then he'd found it. Mission done.

"You did?" Jock asked Lewis, but he didn't look all that interested. Probably thought natural or alternative medicine was all voodoo. Let him change his mind when manufactured pharmaceuticals were long past their shelf life.

Elliot steered the conversation back to the older man. "So, married? Kids?"

The older man's even brow flickered, but he said calmly enough, "Long time since I've been married. She became a legal secretary when she turned forty and left me for a 'career'. Moved to Adelaide. I moved here. Never had kids." He raised his own glass to his lips.

"Big house for one man." Lewis frowned warning-ly at him and Elliot added, "I don't mean to be rude. I'm a curious bastard is all. You tell me if I'm asking too many questions."

"No. No. It's all right. We should get to know each other. I made a lot of money as a single man and figured this was a nice way to spend it. Space is the ultimate luxury. Also, I may not have family, but I do have friends." He winced theatrically. "Or I used to. I have a question for you, Elliot. Your accent: were you working in Tasmania when all this happened?"

"For about six hours, I was, yeah."

"Six hours? This started right as you got here? " Jock winked at Lewis. "So it's your fault."

Lewis didn't laugh.

Elliot ignored the dumb joke. He took a sip and leaned aside to place the glass on the coffee table between his seat and Lewis's. "I was a PMC. Private Military Contractor."

Lewis chimed in, "That's how he knows guns."

"Firearms, Cochise. Actually, I learned about them before that."

Jock put his head back on the headrest and his feet on a different coffee table. "Sounds like Lewis needs to get to know you better too."

"Well. It's a boring story, but I'll tell it if you like." He adjusted his foot with a wince. "Guess it counts literally as history now.

"Probably no surprise to Lewis here that I was never heading for a career in psychology or customer service, let alone diplomacy . Where I came from, there wasn't much opportunity anyway. Unless you liked driving trucks. I didn't. So I enlisted right out of high school. Army. US, obviously. Did my first tour in the Infantry. That was four years, done and dusted. Was coming to the end of it, just coasting, you know, no plans. Then this in-service recruiter came knocking, offered me a shot at promotion and further schooling if I signed on for another four years.

"So. I applied to Ranger School. Made it through and got assigned to a Ranger BAT—Ranger *Battalion*. Did the rest of my second tour with them and then— guess what?—retention specialist comes knocking."

He reached out for his drink, drew it back to his lap. "Never mind. I'm boring you fellas."

"No," Jock and Lewis said in unison.

"Like you said, it's history," Jock added. "Still want to know how you finished up over here. Not too many wars in Tassie."

"Is now," Lewis said.

"True."

"And there was the Black Wars."

Jock waved his hand in a circle to acknowledge the point, though Elliot had no idea what the Black Wars had been. Something to do with the Aborigines, he guessed.

He considered his whiskey. Less than a finger left. Maybe he'd ask for more. Maybe not. He'd been thinking only hours ago how nice it would be to get wasted, to stop his mind and conscience from chattering away in the background. But getting wasted would drop defences he couldn't afford to drop.

"Okay," he said, "so this time the recruiter offers a chance at another promotion if I apply to Special Forces. See I was already E-5. Basically that's a sergeant. To get to E-6, I was gonna have to leave the Rangers 'cause every second prick there's an E-5 or E-6."

"Every second bloke's a sergeant?" Jock asked, surprised.

"Not literally. But there's a shitload of them, an overabundance. So this guy tells me, 'Let's try Special Forces; they're always looking for young, experienced soldiers. You'll get your promotion to E-6 and most likely get out of the army an E-7 with a college degree while you're young enough to start a new career.' I had nothing better to do, so I said yeah, let's do this." When he told the story like this, it sounded clean, stripped of conflict with colleagues and superiors, stripped of all the crawling in dust, the long periods of mind-crushing boredom, the various kinds of pain, the blood, the horror, the mistakes. He sipped whisky.

"So I did my third tour. Was a six year commitment this time, but that was fine."

Fine until Syria. Fine until Libya. Fine until you're trying to convince a psych that you are *fine, that you're okay with being the last survivor of your unit, that you've been a lone survivor since you were a child.*

He almost smelled the desert, almost heard the choppers coming in to find him. He kept talking to stow it all away.

"I got out then. Thought I'd see what else there was. Worked warehouses while I applied to the Private Contracting world. Almost a year it took, but one firm picked me up. And I've done the last four years with them, ended up leading a team carrying out Executive Protection. Which is what I was doing when the shit hit the fan in Hobart."

Looking impressed, Jock asked, "Executive Protection?"

Elliot made a face. "Baby-sitting super-rich idiots. This one had come to the mainland for business. But wanted to try the oldest casino in Australia for kicks, even though it was way down here. 'Why,' we asked him. 'Because it's there,' he told us. Like I said, rich idiots. We saw our first deaders in that casino. And the rest of that story involves a lot of killing and running and hiding and scavenging. All the things we gotta be good at now. Luckily I was already practised at it."

"I don't doubt it."

"The others? The rest of your team?" Lewis asked.

Elliot expected judgment when he looked to the teenager, like Elliot had abandoned more people. All he saw was keen interest and maybe for the first time a little compassion. Elliot didn't want his compassion.

"Made dumb mistakes. *Dumb* mistakes. Got themselves killed. I been telling you, Cochise, no room for mistakes in this world."

Outside, the storm surged, tossing rain against the side of the house like a barrage of schrapnel.

"You know," Lewis said straightening in his seat, "we could plant a lot of little farms around here if we just had more seed. I think there's a lot of seed around that we could use for that."

The two adults exchanged glances.

"Where do you think this seed is?" Jock asked.

"My mum showed me an article once. We were talking about it for a while afterwards. Mum and Dad were pretty impressed by the idea."

"What idea?" Elliot asked, shortly. *Enough preamble, Cochise.*

"The article was about this survivalist guy who had a massive seedbank hidden underground on his property. Like, every vegetable and grain known to man. The guy denied it, which made the reporter more suspicious. The reporter reckoned there was a network of—crap, what was the word? what did he call them?— *curators*, that's it. A network of curators who were keeping seeds for the future."

Elliot and Jock exchanged another glance. Elliot knew of the project somewhere in Scandinavia, but he was never going to travel anywhere near that one.

"*I* never heard of this," Jock said.

"Was on a naturopathy website."

"Okay. Well. I never read them very often. Don't think many people did."

"Which means a lot of people may not know about this 'network'," Elliot said. "Where did the article say his seedbank was?"

Lewis screwed up his face remembering. "South maybe. Yeah, I think it was down south."

Elliot felt his shoulders drop along with his hope.

"Long way from here," Jock confirmed. "Maybe in a year or two people could go looking, but it's too dangerous right now."

"Guess so," Lewis said, losing interest in the idea. He tasted ginger ale and made a face like it wasn't that bad after all.

After Jock filled in some of the history of the town—in particular the bad times once the virus reached it—the conversation waned. Drinks were sipped until there weren't any. Elliot waved away the offer of a second. Lewis yawned, catlike. Jock caught it a moment later. And then Elliot.

Jock said, "Reckon it's bedtime. I'll re-wrap that ankle before I go."

"Lewis can do it. He did a fine job the first time." If this truly wasn't a world for mistakes, a man needed to know what he was doing, and competence meant practice.

Lewis blinked at him, blindsided by the compliment.

Jock shrugged. "Well. I'll take another look tomorrow."

Typical pharmacist, Elliot thought. *All frustrated doctors.* But truth be told, in this new world, a man with Jock's knowledge was as good as a doctor.

"Sure," said Elliot. He indicated the couches. "So I'll be sleeping down here. You too?" he asked Lewis.

The smile that had ghosted the teenager's face vanished. "No," he scoffed. "There's a bed upstairs. Isn't there?" he asked Jock.

"There's three actually. Two in the spare room which you can take your pick of. Usually my fishing and golfing buddies slept in there and they found them comfy enough."

"A real bed," Lewis said.

"I'll bring you back a pillow and blankets," Jock said, standing.

Elliot tugged his hoody from the backpack beside him and folded it. "Don't worry about the pillow. This'll be fine."

"You sure?"

"I've slept a helluva lot rougher than this."

"I bet you have. No worries. The blanket will be down shortly. Once I get the lad settled in."

Elliot watched them climb the stairs together, chatting about Tasmanian Devils. He shifted himself awkwardly over to the couch, with the speargun tucked under his arm. Once there he lay back with his hoody under his head and the Aimrite within reach on the floor.

Once I get the lad settled in? He's not a goddammed "lad". And it was true. In a single week, the "lad" had lost his family, his home and only hours earlier a new friend. And he was dealing with it. He was *getting on with it*. He was bandaging ankles, and carrying packs, and chasing off attackers and helping make dinner …

And Elliot was so goddammed tired, so sleep-deprived and undernourished that he was making mistakes. He needed to sleep. He should sleep. But sleep was dangerous. Birdy had paid the price for him dropping his guard. No one else would. Flurries of wind and rain continued to assault the house and the temperature was dropping further. Being a little cold was good. Being a little cold would keep him on edge, prevent him lapsing into unconsciousness. That and the bitch-pain in his ankle. He could sleep tomorrow. Staying awake tonight would stop the dead crashing through the defences, prevent the Death Druids or someone worse crashing the party.

Later, Jock came down lugging a folded blanket, crutches and a glass of water. He bent awkwardly to place the glass on the coffee table by the remnants of the scotch, lay the crutches on top of the Aimrite on the floor between the table and couch, and handed over the blanket which Elliot just bunched on his lap for the moment. It was soft, fleecy and smelled like lavender. Jock's hand probed inside his shirt pocket and brought out a single white chalky pill the size of Elliot's pinky nail. "This will help you sleep. And you need sleep."

Elliot screwed up his face the way Lewis might. "I'm not really a pill kinda guy. I sleep pretty well … pretty well anywhere."

"Humor an old fusspot."

He pointed with his chin at his empty glass. "A little scotch, a warm blanket, a flat surface and …" He made a hand signal "… I'm out."

Jock held out the pill. "You're sure?"

"I've been in more pain, trust me." Elliot jerked his chin toward the front door this time. "And if the dead come calling, I don't want to be too deeply asleep for action."

"Forgive me, mate, but with that leg, you're not exactly combat ready. Look, no one's getting through these doors or windows without waking the lot of us, trust *me*."

"I'm good," Elliot said with finality in his tone. A glass of booze he could handle. Pills—even a single valium—they were a slippery slope.

Jock folded his arms in resignation. "Fair enough. You know, you and the boy have been through hell and you need to recuperate, rejuvenate. You said over dinner you have your sights set on that island, but why not stay here a few weeks, relax, help me grow food. Help me *eat* the food."

"Sounds good, Jock. It does. But tell the truth, I don't do too well around people. Better off on my own."

Jock frowned. "Oh?"

"It's … Look, I'm not related to Lewis. He's a young man I met on the way who needed help. And I gave it. Anyone with half a conscience would. He's alive. But I'm heading into the wild until the pusbags all die off. That's no place for Lewis. I picked that island because his dad had thought of it and because I wanted him in a safe place. Maybe this is as far as he needs to come for the time being." He eyed Jock. "If that works for you?"

"You'd trust me to keep him alive?"

"You're as safe a bet as anything."

"Gee. Thanks."

"What I mean is, *you've* stayed alive. You have a rifle, ammunition, and I can leave Lewis the SIG, the pistol." That would hurt, but Elliot could live with it. "You have food. You're smart enough to put barbed wire around your windows. Maybe sometime you want to think about moving to a less conspicuous house, but yeah, I'd say Lewis would be relatively safe here."

Jock nodded, thinking and smiling. He moved into the kitchen and emptied the glass of water into the sink. "I'm honored you trust me, Elliot."

Elliot put his hands beneath his head. "Didn't say that."

Jock's smile frayed a little around the edges. He turned away, opened the fridge.

"Just promise me you'll teach him everything you know. Teach him to survive."

Retrieving a carton of UHT milk, Jock unscrewed the lid and started filling the glass. "I can promise you that."

"And that you'll learn what he knows about natural medicine. You won't talk him out of it."

"Sure. Fair enough." He replaced the lid, put the milk away and came over. "You know I have solar power."

"So you said."

"A solar powered hot water service."

"…Oh?"

"Hot showers in the morning. For all of us. At separate times of course." He arched his back and picked up the last live hurricane lantern, chuckling. "See you in the morning, Elliot."

Lantern in one hand, milk in the other, he climbed the stairs, the light bobbing and wavering.

At separate times? Good thing the guy was going to sleep. Christ Almighty, his jokes got worse the later the night got.

The only light Jock had left burning down here were the candles. Elliot lay back, watching phantasms play across the high ceiling above. Something about Jock bugged him and now he thought about it, it wasn't the lame sense of humor. Or his neat freak personality. It was that Jock was a father figure Elliot had never had—one that Elliot could never be. He had never wanted to be a father and the reasons were all about him being way too selfish and way too much like Uncle John, truth be told. Jock on the other hand had useful expertise, he had some of Elliot's resourcefulness but combined it with a Mister Rogers type of warmth and a generosity men like Elliot and John could never match. Against this Aussie pharmacist, Uncle John looked like Satan himself. In Jock's house, hospitality was a gift, assistance was a human right. In John's, your food and the roof above your head had to be earned. Constantly.

Happy voices burbled upstairs for thirty minutes or so, then a bedroom door closed. A heavy tread creaked floorboards above and another door closed. Both of them ensconced in their rooms.

Leaving Lewis here was a good solution. Elliot had taught him enough—wariness, firearms, stealth. But if he was trying to recreate himself in Lewis, the way John had tried to mould Elliot in his image, that was a terrible mistake. Here with Jock, Lewis would be taught further real world survival skills, and maybe he could heal from much of his trauma. Without turning into a hard-hearted asshole who left friends in the bush to be a deader's dinner.

And Elliot? Well, Elliot could go live from Uncle John's #1 maxim: *in the end, you're all you have.*

"Thanks a bunch, John. Thanks a whole bunch, you sonofabitch."

The candle on the drinks stand flickered in a draught. Another lantern sat cold and dark beside it, twelve feet from Elliot's position. His small flashlight was over in his pack. It was maybe nine p.m. The second candle was on a coffee table and both would gutter out about midnight leaving him in pitch darkness till dawn. The house might seem safe, but it made no sense to be without light in a strange place. If the river of undead changed direction, headed this way, smelled them...

He was exhausted and his foot throbbed. He could put it all out of his mind, let himself drift, worry about the darkness when the time came. Or when the deaders came calling.

With a groan, he tipped the folded blanket to the floor and sat up. He put on his hoody, got the speargun out from under the aluminum crutches and slung it over his back. He used a crutch to get up onto his good foot, got it under his armpit. He struggled over to his backpack where it slumped like an exhausted soldier by the recliner, ferreted out the flashlight and shoved it in the side trouser pocket holding his lockblade, moved to the drinks stand and blew out the candle, switched on the hurricane lamp to a low setting and made his way awkwardly to the front doors where he pressed an ear against them. The hiss of rain and shush of wind. The rattle of metal and wood. If a hundred or a hundred *thousand* undead were approaching, how in hell would he hear them over that? They'd be on the house with no warning. He sighed in resignation. Elliot was on sentry duty tonight.

He turned his shoulder against the doors and considered those of Jock's study. He had a light and he had hours to kill; Jock had a book in there on "bush tucker", maybe some others that would prove helpful. He used the crutch to move across to the study and opened the door. It met slight resistance with a crinkling sound and he stuck his head around it to find a plastic tarp bunched behind it. He raised the lantern. The room was large, lined with more book shelves plus a huge darkwood desk in the centre and a tall leather boardroom chair behind it. In contrast to the rest of the downstairs, the room was a mess. Three coffee mugs, an empty beer can and a plate with crumbs littered the desk. He could smell the beer from the door, along with a faint whiff of bleach. A pair of boots had been tossed on top of the tarp. There was a toolkit on its side beyond that, its contents spilling out. A plastic cooler bag had been tossed against the desk. Beside it an open cardboard box with soda cans and candy made a lie of Jock's earlier statement that he had no drinks for someone of Lewis's age. Jock's hospitality it seemed, only stretched so far. Elliot remembered then the subtle way he'd steered Lewis from the cellar door. Probably full to the brim with hoarded Coke and energy drinks. Not so much Mr Rogers then.

"Asshole."

He wouldn't be able to hide that lie from Lewis for long. Any teenager worth their acne was going to sniff out sugary snacks inside of a day.

A pile of books on the floor to his right appeared to have been swept from a shelf above. All the shelves were crammed with books, except for one holding Jock's degrees and diplomas and another hosting an eclectic mix of objects. This shelf—or more accurately its debris—jarred, even against the other mess in the room, and especially because Jock had said he didn't have kids.

Elliot came inside, kicking into a pair of dirty sneakers and releasing a faint whiff of smoke from them. This hobbling around like Long John Silver was going to drive him nuts. He tested his weight on the injured ankle. The pain jabbed at him, enough to let him know *I'm hurt here* but not too bad. Now he thought of it, the last time he'd checked it before the bandages went back on, it hadn't appeared swollen. Maybe he'd gotten off lucky here. Maybe he could do without the damn crutch. He let the metal strut fall back against the door with a light thud and hopped the last few feet to the book shelf, avoiding the litter of hardbacks, held up the lantern.

The clutter on the shelf was anachronistic. A tan teddy bear with matted fur along one arm. A supervillain action figure. A home-beading keychain. A plastic watch. Yellow headphones. A cricket ball. A foam dart gun. A die cast metal jetfighter. A folded navy t-shirt. A folded orange one.

And a home-printed poster poking from under the orange tee. Beneath the image of a smiling child, the poster read *MISSING! My boy. Adam. 8 years old.*

Dread settled like lead in his belly. Stomach acid burned his throat.

"He steered Lewis away from the cellar."

He hopped back to the door, took the crutch and made his way to the coffee table where Lewis had left the SIG. The steel of the grip was cool, the muzzle the same against his hips as he slid it in his waistband. He crutched his way to the cellar door. It had no lock. He placed the lantern on the floor, got out the small flashlight, turned it on and jammed it in his mouth, twisted the door handle and eased it open while waiting for a creak or crack that never came. A smell wafted up to him: dry earth, stale air … nothing foul, nothing sinister, though it was dark as death down there. He counted twelve steps in the flashlight beam; getting down them would be a sonofabitch. The enclosed stairs had a small square of earth at the base, a corner of the room, while the rest of whatever was down there stretched off to his left completely out of sight. Perfect place for an ambush. It made no sense that anyone or anything *would* be waiting there, but old habits died hard.

With the torchlight jagging and wobbling out in front of him, one hand on the wall and one on the crutch, he started. He got to step number four and wondered if it was worth it. At step seven he asked himself what he was thinking.

I'm a curious bastard is all.

Each of the last five steps put him within easy reach of the non-existent ambusher he fully expected lurked down there. He drew the 9-mil, flicked the safety. He stopped on each of the final stairs to listen. Nothing. But then if there was something or someone down here, surely the wavering flashlight would have already alerted them.

Finally he stepped onto the hardpacked dirt and swung flashlight and handgun to the left, checked the angles. Alone, thank Christ and all the saints. He leaned the crutch in the corner and took the torch from his mouth, wiping drool on a sleeve and working his jaw up and down. A few cobwebs ran along one side of the chamber, but frequent use seemed to have kept them at bay. The long rectangular room measured twelve feet wide, thirty feet deep and seven high; the low roof made it feel tighter than it was. Each wall boasted shelves running to a height of seven feet with small diamond alcoves for wine bottles. About half the alcoves were full. The shelving unit at the far end contained twenty bottles; Elliot played the light over it and saw only two had wine in them. He could see straight through the others to the backboard beyond them. Other shelves contained the occasional empty too.

Something moaned upstairs. He flinched and swung the SIG around. Just the wind. It had been so much quieter down here, the sudden gust had taken him by surprise. He sighed and gave the cellar one last look. There was nothing here but four walls covered in wine shelves. Sure, Jock had kept them from his cellar: he didn't want people stealing his good booze. There were no nefarious doings here; the items in his office weren't trophies; there was a reasonable explanation.

He ran a gritty hand over his tired face. *Maybe I shoulda taken the sleeping pill.* He hopped back to the crutch and slouched against the wall, summoning the energy to make the long struggle up the stairs. Best he lay down, got some shuteye and stopped suspecting eccentric and lonely middle-aged bachelors.

He had the support under his armpit when the thought froze him.

Backboard?

The farthest shelving unit was the only one to have board attached to the back. He could see the white of drywall behind the others, through them.

Jesus, Mary, Joseph.

He swung the beam around to the far end and then down to the floor. The dirt was disturbed like it'd been scuffed up then smoothed over with something like a broom. He hopped closer and inspected the shelves. There were discolored points on the paint on one side where the unit had been held, human skin oil and friction dulling the finish. He got in close, flashlight back in his mouth, tested the weight of the unit. Pretty light: wouldn't be hard to move it. Keeping his weight on one leg, he jiggled and lifted and dragged until the shelves were far enough from the wall for him to squeeze past and behind. Set in the drywall was a low door, steel, about five feet high. No lock, no knob, but a latch over a clasp. The iron looked as old as the concrete of the walls. No visible hinges, so it would open inwards.

A panic room?

Sure. Everyone keeps their panic room behind a wine shelf, in the cellar where they can't get to it in a hurry.

He took the flashlight from his mouth, massaged his jaw—*Welcome to Serial Killing 101, students*—and jammed it back in, got the 9-mil ready.

Not wanting to—truly not wanting to—he un-latched the door and shoved. Balancing on one leg made it difficult and he had to shove harder. It squeaked open a foot. A waft of stale farts hit him. He played the light in there, barely breathing, saw nothing but the edge of a desk and a heavy board wall. When nothing rushed out at him, he put the SIG in his pants, took the flashlight. He placed a shoulder against the door, shifting it another two feet, another forty-five degrees. He could see well enough now to wish he hadn't.

The wavering torchlight made it seem like the room was tipping as he recoiled, banging his head on the shelves behind him, fighting his gag reflex, heart hammering, acid in his mouth. He had seen enough that even with eyes closed, he had to mentally bat away the images trying to reassert themselves. A pinboard covered in photos. More photos on walls. A stack of them on the old desk. Some stuck to the ceiling.

And all of them containing children.

He lurched out of the tight spot. A spike of pain told him he was using both feet but he didn't care. The ankle was holding him and he'd just seen evidence there were worse things in life.

He only stopped moving when he'd backed all the way into the far wall at the bottom of the stairs. Shunning the crutch, he started up the stairs a lot faster than was prudent. Part of him knew adrenaline was masking some of the pain he was causing by putting a little weight on the bad ankle every second step or so. He did it anyway.

At the top, he flung the torch onto an armchair and got the lockblade from his pocket, unhinged it. He shifted the lantern to the first riser of the stairs to the next floor, left it there. The wind and rain were loud enough to cover his efforts climbing the staircase. Not so loud that he missed the snick of a bedroom door being opened above him. His heartrate—already high—spiked further.

Light peeked from above him, the solid glow of one of Jock's lanterns. He got himself to the top and checked his surrounds. Jock's reading room curled around to his left along the side of the staircase to a bay window. No one sat in the armchair there. A hallway stretched right and left, longer to the left with a door in each wall. The light leaked through one of them, left ajar. He hobbled fast on the sole of one foot and the ball of the other until he reached it. Readied the SIG. Through the crack, he could see a dresser with the hurricane lantern on it. Behind it a mirror gave him a good look at the rest of the room. Two low beds and Jock's back and shoulders as he stood above one.

He pressed at the door with finger tips and it swung in silently. He took a couple of steps forward.

Lewis was out cold, curled on his side. His face—visible past Jock's right hip—was a picture of childlike peace and innocence. That glass of milk Jock had brought him sat on the dresser under the lantern, half full.

Jock was dressed in pyjama shirt and boxers, his hands working at a camera. He hadn't heard the door.

"Game over, shitstain," Elliot said and raised the SIG.

14

Dawn was breaking as the black SUV arrived in the town named on the poster. A line of smoke almost invisible against the grey skies resolved itself as a house fire, the skeleton smoldering in the morning drizzle. Two bodies lay nearby, beheaded and of interest to the crows. Elliot blinked away the flashback to the health retreat and checked on Lewis: still out cold along the back seat. In the next block over, another body, burly, face-down in the storm water ditch along the verge. He slowed to check the insignia on the back of the leather jacket—sure enough, a Death Druid's symbol, this time with a bullet hole puncturing the second embroidered D. Whatever weapon he might have carried was nowhere to be seen. The rain had washed away any blood.

Elliot cut the engine, wound down the window and listened for several minutes. Nothing. No indication anyone was active nearby. Lewis snored lightly behind him. He started up and eased the car ahead.

It took a further twenty minutes of methodical driving to find the street he sought. Number fourteen was a white bungalow set in unkempt gardens behind a solid wooden fence, its lawn a jungle. A late model car sat with its hood up along the side driveway. The home's front door was wide open.

The SUV pipped twice when he locked it with the remote and he cringed at the sound. No deaders in the town, so far. Apart from birds and falling water, nothing was moving.

A cement path cut diagonally through the knee-high lawn to the porch and he limped along it with the M4 ready. Leaves piled up against the step up and the front walls. Some had blown onto the dark blue hallway carpet. He called the woman's name on the poster, said he was there about the boy, about "Adam". No response. The interior was all gloom and silence. The rifle's muzzle led the way inside. Three steps in, he lost what little hope he'd had at the sight of blood spatter up the righthand wall. The dots and squirts marred a couple of family photos and—having had enough of photos for a lifetime—he averted his gaze before the faces could register. He changed direction, entered the tiny living room. A TV and games console. Two arm chairs. A round coffee table with a photo album and a bottle of gin. There was a telephone on a corner table. Red pen and pink notepad beside it. Elliot took Adam's poster from the inside pocket of the waterproof jacket he'd taken from Jock's laundry. He unfolded the paper, wrote *I'm very sorry for your loss* beneath the boy's happy image and pinned the edge beneath the phone with the writing visible.

Adam's mom would never be back for it, of course. So the blood spatter said.

But at least the story had a conclusion.

A light sprinkling of rain persisted. The wipers beat a pleasant tattoo and Elliot fought to resist the draw of sleep, driving slow. Storm debris littered the highway, making progress possible but treacherous. Over that crest there might be a thick branch or a car wreck and he couldn't afford a moment's lapse. He cracked his window open, turned the vents his way and upped the fan speed. His ankle hurt, but it was dull pain. Maybe it would heal quicker than he'd thought, despite last night's rigors.

"Where are we?"

Elliot checked his mirror. In the back seat, Lewis's eyes were large, pupils dilated. His body was still covered with a red wool blanket.

Elliot referred to the odometer. "Twenty kays from the coast. Twelve or thirteen miles."

"Where's Jock?" One hand appeared from under the blanket and snatched at a handhold so Lewis could pull himself upright. He brushed his fringe to the side, squeezed his forehead, massaged it, stared back along the wet highway. "Wow, I'm spaced. What happened?"

Elliot ran a hand over his jaw stubble.

What happened? Jock slipped you a roofie is what happened. Jock was making ready to do you harm when I eventually left. Jock was already fantasizing about it. So I pointed my 9-mil at Jock's head and made Jock carry you down to the couch while he bitched the whole time, playing innocent. But when I marched good ol' Jock into his study and pointed to the trophy shelf, he turned to me with a face like the Devil himself and said "You don't know what you're missing." And I shot Jock in the throat and waited and watched while he thrashed and bled out on his floor.

That's what happened.

Elliot relaxed his deathgrip on the wheel and rolled his shoulders, his neck. "Nothing happened, Lewis. Jock took another car to visit farms in the next district so he could treat them. He's kind of like a doctor around these parts. And he said we could have this one."

"What? He left?"

"Sure. Helping people. You know. Doing his job. Nice 'bloke'."

"Well … why aren't we back there? There's other people around! We should stay. Like you said, he is nice."

"There'll be nice people at the island too. And it'll be safer."

I hope.

"That's no reason not to wait for him! I could have gone with him. Learned some stuff. He could've come to the island with us."

"My job is getting you to this island. Much much safer than that house with a guy past his prime. He ain't gonna protect ya from the swarms of deaders if they turn this way."

Lewis lashed out, slamming the passenger headrest with one fist. "You bastard, I never got to say goodbye!"

"Time's important. What if—?"

"I didn't get to say goodbye to Birdy."

"I'm sorry about that, but we had the same problem there too."

"I never get to say goodbye to *anyone!*"

Elliot did not reply. What could he possibly say that would make the young man feel any better about that?

"We should have gone to Minchenbridge."

Elliot sighed. A headache had started up above his right eye. "We couldn't go stomping our way through the Forest of Walking Corpses, Lewis. Be real about that. I'm trying to keep you safe, get you somewhere safe. Can't you see—?"

" You let those people die."

"Oh, I coulda saved them? I coulda kickboxed my way through a thousand zombies and piggybacked those people to the safety of our mighty tower?"

He struck the headrest. "You could've sniped at the ones chasing them!"

Elliot's fingers had curled tight around the wheel. "Lewis! It wasn't possible. This—" he was going to say *happens in war* "—is the way the world is now. I keep telling you. It's all tough choices now. Actually, no it isn't. They're only 'tough' choices if you're not sure whether you want to live or not. If you want to survive, you make the choice that makes it so."

Lewis twisted around in his chair, draping his arms over the back. A few moments, then he whispered, "You let Birdy die."

It had been a great many years since Elliot felt the need to explain himself. He'd been a child himself when he'd finally smartened up enough to learn not to. "That one's not on me, Lewis. You can't put that one on me."

He felt the ghost of a hand slapping the back of his head, heard Uncle John's words—*talking don't get it done, shitstain*—relaxed his grip on the wheel again, straightened in his seat.He hated to admit it, but sometimes John had been right. Lewis needed to get his mind on what needed doing, not what he'd lost. And Elliot needed some sleep. He snapped his fingers, watching the mirror, snapped them again but Lewis refused to meet his gaze.

"Hey. Cochise. Need you to drive here."

"Jock gave us his rifle too?" Lewis asked, his hand amongst the supplies in the cargo bay. "Or did you steal it?"

"He has five. Boxes of ammo. Was happy to help us out some more. Now, shut up about it. I'm pulling over so you can drive a ways."

It was lucky he'd taken his foot off the gas. The SUV crested a hill and if Elliot had been driving harder, there was no way he would have braked in time. The fallen gum tree was the size of a suburban house and completely blocked the road. Elliot slammed down the brake pedal and in the wet, the car slewed and skidded until it was side on to the blockage. *His* side on. Elliot sucked in a lungful of air and blew it out hard. It was a near miss. He could open the door and scrape the outlying leaves, he'd been so close.

He threw the automatic shifter into park and snatched at the map folded on the seat next to him, pressed it flat against the steering wheel, referred to the odometer.

"Sonofabitch." They were literally in the middle of nowhere. All the tight country roads that they'd crossed since leaving the town ran parallel to the coast or angled inland. He struck the dash with the meat of his fist.

"Sonofa*bitch*! They couldn't afford more roads round here?"

He struck the dash again and then once more, vaguely aware of Lewis rummaging in the cargo space. He wanted to be rid of him, just get it over with and get on with his own life. He checked the map again, adding distances as he traced a new route, then he threw it against the passenger door hard enough for one edge to tear. It was a forty-five mile detour from here, requiring him to return all the way to Jock's town and take the highway south before circling back to the coast.

A door opened: Lewis getting out. Well, let him. If deaders waited in the long grass behind the wire farm fences, it would give him a well-deserved scare.

The wipers squealed as they labored across the glass, dragging as the rain softened to a light drizzle. Jock had left a full-length raincoat in the car and Elliot had his parka snaffled from the laundry. But wet shoes and wet packs made for unpleasant travel. As well as rot and maybe fungus. Elliot wanted to keep these boots and his pack for years. He swore again. Forty-five miles. Still quicker than walking. If more trees hadn't blocked roads.

He put the car in reverse and started easing the tail around, craning his neck around to check behind. Lewis was doing something at the fence there, but it was hard to see through the rain-bubbled glass. He slammed it into park and opened his door, leaned out.

"What the hell?"

The young man had taken bolt cutters from the clutter of stuff Elliot had thrown into the SUV's cargo space and was working at the single strand of barbed wire along the top of the fence. It gave way with a dull *click* and he went to work on the straight wire below it. Inside of thirty seconds, Lewis had cut all four layers and started yanking them aside from the gap he'd made. When there was enough space for a car to fit through, he stood to the side, put the bolt cutters to one shoulder like a sentry and stared back at Elliot.

"Well? You gonna gawk at me all day or drive the car?"

He stalked through the gap he'd made and around the tree, readying the cutters.

"I'll be damned," said Elliot and closed his door against the rain. He maneuvered the car around, and bumped his way through the gap and through the grass to where Lewis was making a new gate on the far side of the tree.

After he'd tossed his tool in back, Lewis got in the passenger seat, sweeping the map onto the floor. He clipped his seatbelt on, put his head against the rest and closed his eyes. "You wanted to get to the island," he said. "Let's get to the island."

IV

River Crossing

15

The last deader in the pack was slow of foot, lagging behind his mates who crowded the bridge downhill. Because of this, he disappeared beneath the SUV as it slewed to a stop on the wet road.

Satisfied the crunch beneath his left front tire was the thing's head, Elliot reached back for his rifle and slid out the door. On the opposite side, Lewis followed, nursing the 9-mil Elliot had left in the console. The car's position was perfect for a firefight: the gentle slope below it overlooked the bridge with an open killing ground between them. The group of Asians occupying the narrow viaduct had it blocked each end, first with white camper vans and then with pallets and wooden beams and even a portable cement mixer—all presumably pilfered from a building site somewhere. The sandstone bridge was maybe thirty car lengths across and they'd pitched three tents in the middle held firm by what looked like small sandbags and gym weights. At the far end, two moms and two girl children about six or seven frantically stowed gear into the campervan there. Three men defended the end closest to the SUV, standing up on a pile of pallets, slashing and hacking with two shovels and a cricket bat.

Elliot aimed at the ones half-running down the hill toward the action, fired a round and another, pleased with the results. The rifle felt good—and all the better for ridding the world of more pusbags. "That's it, baby," he whispered and squeezed off another.

Three shots. Three deadheads had fallen between him and the makeshift barrier spread below. He glanced across the hood, grudgingly impressed with the way Lewis anchored himself in a spread legged posture and held his weapon the way Elliot had taught him. The young man fired, re-aimed and fired again, lowered it to assess the situation. Five shots and they'd taken out four between them, leaving fifteen harrying the Asians. He caught Lewis staring at him, challenging, the SIG forgotten.

"What?"

"You're gonna leave them, aren't you?" Lewis brushed his fringe from his eyes then lifted the handgun again.

Elliot made a quick decision. It was three hundred feet down to the bridge. Way too far for Lewis to fire accurately that close to friendlies. "Cease firing. Keep that for close encounters." He raised his own weapon, picking targets carefully. He kept catching glances from the men at the barrier, perhaps worried he was going to hit one of them. He concentrated on thinning out the pack from the back to the middle, leaving the closest to them. One of them disappeared from his post; at first Elliot worried that he'd hit him with a ricochet, but then he saw the spade swinging up and down from behind the van: evidently some of the dead had gotten the idea to crawl under.

With only three left and taking a battering from the bat and shovel, he got back in the car, placed the hot rifle behind Lewis's seat and eased the car down the slope. He parked it at the very edge of the mess of bodies, killed the engine and watched the end of the show. When the last zombie toppled and the three men stood panting on their precarious perch, he and Lewis opened the doors and stood on their running boards to avoid the mess on the ground.

"Hey," Lewis called to them. "How ya going?"

The three men nodded and lifted hands to shoulder height, up and down, quick, tired. They were dressed in almost identical tracksuit pants, sneakers and rain-jackets over black t-shirts. One had a baseball cap on. It had stopped raining. The sun peeking through the clouds was strong enough to make Elliot wish for his lost Shell cap.

"Thank you," they said in chorus.

The baseball capped one—the least wary looking of the trio—added, "You came along at a perfect time."

Up close, Elliot could see the people were southeast Asian, maybe Laotian or Cambodian, dark skinned with short shiny hair and strong wiry bodies. The man who spoke had the makings of an Aussie accent.

"Someone saved my friend yesterday like this," Lewis said, "so we were just paying it forward."

Elliot looked at him, said quietly, "I'm your friend now?"

"Shut up," Lewis said out the side of his mouth.

"Where are you heading?" the spokesman asked. One of the others climbed down and headed back toward the women and girls who had stopped to watch but ventured no nearer.

"The coast," Elliot said. "You?"

The man smiled experimentally. "Nowhere really. We've been here since the day before yesterday. Seemed like a good place to defend ourselves. We were totally wrong," he added. The smile turned wry. "Haven't seen that many zombies together for a few weeks. Maybe they came from one of the farms near here?"

Elliot glanced among the bodies. Four were children, dressed in shorts and expensive sneakers. Another had a big-name watch that would have cost him a mint if it was genuine. "More likely from the city."

"You see more on your way?"

Lewis and Elliot exchanged serious glances. "Not for a day or so," said Elliot.

Lewis added, "But there's plenty west of here. Thousands."

The cap-wearer's face fell.

"You hurt us?" asked the other man. He was older than his comrades, much older Elliot noted now he was closer, his consonants chopped short, his t-shirt yellow where the others wore black beneath their coats.

The cap-wearer backhanded his companion in the chest, exchanged words in their language and turned his smile on the newcomers again. "Sorry," he said. "Sorry."

Elliot shook his head. "Not gonna hurt you guys. Just spent a lot of bullets saving you." He indicated the bodies blocking the bridge. "But as we'd like to get through here, any help you can give us clearing the road would be much appreciated."

Lewis slapped the car's roof. "You can have one of our chickens."

"Lewis," Elliot growled.

"That leaves us two," Lewis said.

"Well, just don't give them away too. We might need some good will when we reach the island."

They kept the conversation quiet, smiling at the bridge defenders.

"We help you," said the older man. "You give us chicken. And some egg too."

Elliot opened his mouth but Lewis added, "Deal."

The two men smiled.

"Sonofabitch," Elliot murmured as he went around back to find some gloves among Jock's crap in the cargo space.

Elliot was three bodies into clearing a way through when he noticed Lewis wasn't helping. He heard his voice and then children's laughter. He and Heng—the taciturn wearer of the yellow tee—heaved a body onto the siding and Elliot climbed up onto the bridge stonework to see past the van.

Lewis had planted himself outside one of the tents with a notebook in his lap and pen in hand. The girls sat cross-legged in front of him, the women flanking him, squatting. They all leaned in, rapt with whatever he was producing on the page. He said something, tapped the book and the girls dissolved into giggles. The women exchanged glances, beaming. One of them picked up a white bowl from beside him, insisting he eat from it. He plucked something, popped it in his mouth and nodded thanks, returned to his drawing.

"The boy not helping," Heng complained, shaking his head. The lower half of his face was hidden behind the kind of face masks Elliot had seen people wearing in China against pollution. The other men had one also. They had given Elliot a strip of cloth to filter his breath.

"He's not a boy. But yeah, he's not helping. I'll kick his ass later." He got down carefully, glad when the tender ankle didn't give way under him. "Let's get the last few out of the way."

The younger men, Rit with the baseball cap and Kim without, lugged a body to dump on the pile, wiped their gloved hands on the grass siding where the slope plunged toward the river.

Kim indicated the gap they'd made in their barricade by moving the cement mixer. "It's not so bad. Three more, maybe, then you can squeeze the car through."

"You should move your barricade back along the bridge about thirty feet. Leave some room around this mess. Think about burning the bodies to deal with bacteria."

"Good idea," said Rit.

Kim pointed past the van. "It's a good thing Lewis is playing with the children. Good for all of them."

"Better things to do these days than play."

Kim shook his head. "It's even more important these days. I haven't seen my daughter laugh in a long time."

"Me too," agreed Rit.

"Boy should help," Heng insisted.

"Boy should be a boy," Rit said and punched Kim's shoulder cheerfully. The two returned to the spread of bodies to pick a new one. He glanced up at a fresh bank of grey clouds creeping their way. "If we're lighting them up, we should hurry. Might rain again soon."

"You and me, Mr Heng," said Elliot, trying not to limp as he slowly followed them. "I think we're the only ones here gonna agree on matters like this."

"Heng. Not Mister. Just Heng."

Elliot almost said *whatever* and only just caught himself. "But you need to treat the boy like a man," he said instead and bent to the next body.

"What are you eating?"

Lewis peered up at him, squinting because Elliot had chosen to come in at him from sunside, like a Battle of Britain Spitfire.

"Riceballs they call them." He waggled the bowl, put it back on the asphalt without offering any to Elliot. And Elliot didn't want any. The golfball sized clumps of rice were speckled with something that might have been vegetable matter or even insects. Or poison. The girls watched the exchange fascinated by Elliot rather than frightened. On seeing him approach, one of the women had hurried back to the van and now tried to press a similar bowl with six of the tidbits into Elliot's hands.

He shook his head and waved it away. "No. No thank you."

"You need to eat."

"I'm good. Not a fan of rice."

"Not a fan of manners," muttered Lewis, biting into one and returning to his sketch. Elliot could see now it was a pretty good image of a horse frolicking with a young girl. Both figures had big round eyes like those on Japanese cartoons. But the grass and the tree he'd sketched looked pretty lifelike.

The woman pushed the bowl at him and he stepped back out of reach.

"Talk to you for a sec."

Lewis sighed, handed the notebook to one of the girls. "Maybe you could get your crayons, and color this in?"

The girl squealed and dashed back to the van with the book clutched to her tummy while her friend or cousin or whatever chased her.

"What?" Lewis demanded. He hadn't moved.

Elliot asked the two ladies, and the men who'd now crowded closer, "You mind if we talk in private for a minute?"

"No, no, all good," said Rit and flicked his hands at the women, waving them away.

"He should eat," said the one with the bowl.

"Shhh, leave him alone."

Kim and Rit herded them back to the van, enduring a barrage of displeasure in their language while Heng pottered past, nodding in approval. "Kick boy's ass," he said.

When he was gone, Lewis said, "You're going to kick my arse?" He stuck the pen behind his ear and leaned back on his hands. The SIG lay four feet away. Elliot squatted and pointed to it, then the bowl.

"How do you know they don't want *that*? And aren't poisoning you with *this* to get it?"

"Seriously? Because they're not."

"Man, you have to stop trusting people. How do you know they're okay? If anyone knows the world is full of bad folk, it's you."

"My parents weren't bad."

"No, but they might have gotten desperate enough to turn that way. To protect you."

"Birdy wasn't bad. Jock wasn't bad."

Elliot swallowed. "And those women at the train looked like ordinary chicks—ordinary people like these folk—but they weren't. They were desperate. And desperation broke them bad."

"Maybe you're bad folk then."

"Sure I am, but I'm on your side. Maybe these folk are too, but what if they decide they want what we've got and hurt us for it. Like the railroad chicks."

"What do you care? You *want* to get rid of me. So now is your chance."

"You don't get off the hook so easy, pal."

"But you're taking me to some island. There'll be people there. Maybe they'll be bad."

"Sure. But we get to check them out carefully before we start trusting. Same as these folks. Someone gives you food, you have them eat it first or you watch them make it from starters."

They both looked up as the people started shouting. The girl without the horse picture was running back with a fresh notebook and some pencils in her hands. She ignored her guardians' protests. Rit waved apologetically. Lewis waved back and Elliot growled as the girl bobbed down by Lewis.

"Can you draw me a dog? I used to have a dog. A labrador."

Lewis made a face. "I'm good at beagles. Is a beagle okay?"

She shrugged. "Sure. Can I name it?"

"Whatever you want," he smiled, taking the pad. "As long as you look after it."

She giggled. "It's a picture, silly."

"No, it'll be a dog. Until you get a new dog, it'll be *your* dog. And you have to look after it. So you'll have to draw food on the page after I've finished, so he doesn't get hungry."

"I can't draw food. I can't draw anything."

"I'll teach you." He raised his eyebrows at Elliot. "Is there something else?"

Elliot put a hand to his stubble and rubbed at it, stood up. "Sure there is. But I'll wait until there's no kids around before I say it to you."

"Mr Grumpy Pants," Lewis told the girl and she laughed and gazed up at Elliot unabashed.

"Mr Grumpy Pants here wants to get to the coast," he said through gritted teeth. "He's so close to it, he can smell the surf."

"Then go, I'm not stopping you."

He opened his mouth to respond, but the little girl was prevented from hearing a bunch of foul language by the lady returning with the bowl.

"Please. You have lunch with us. You saved us."

Elliot turned his back and headed for where he'd parked the SUV. "I've got my own," he said over his shoulder. He knew it for an insult in any Asian culture, just as Lewis had sensed. But it was no more insulting than them mollycoddling Lewis, letting him be soft, encouraging him to draw goddam children's pictures.

He stomped past the SUV and climbed the barrier, M4 swinging at his shoulder. He watched the clouds covering what remained of the blue sky, erasing the light. He was almost as far from the western highlands as he could get and not be swimming. It was going to be one long journey back there, though the SUV would help.

He turned at the sound of more laughter. The little girl had the pad on her lap, pencils in her hand, pointing at something for her mother who knelt down and hugged her and nodded while Lewis gave her a thumbs-up for the piece of lettuce or the dogbone or whatever the hell she'd drawn with her crap-brown and piss-yellow crayons. Heng had come over too and he picked up the bowl meant for Elliot, wandered to the side of the bridge and started eating, watching the river below. The rest of them—he still didn't know what country the adults were originally from and didn't really care—had clustered by the side door of the far van, sharing a meal and discussing something while the second girl sat in the passenger seat coloring in. She called to the adults and they looked at the picture she was holding up and made cooing noises.

Elliot eased himself down the outside of the barrier and bent over one of the dead still lying there. The guy was in business shirt, a tie hanging skewiff and too tight around his neck. Definitely no farmer. He wore an expensive Citizen multifunction dive watch, silver and sapphire color scheme. It was still ticking.

The girls and Lewis shared another laugh, the girls' squeal of delight rising up and up like a violin played well. One of the men, said, "We have three artists here now!"

Elliot put one foot on the deader's forearm and grabbed its hand. He pulled hard, wrenching it off like a drumstick from a Christmas chicken. He slipped off the Citizen and turned it this way and that. "Nice watch," he said and headed for the river to clean it.

16

The SUV's cargo seat made a half-decent bed when the junk in the cargo area had been pushed to the side and the rear seatback pushed forward. He sat cross-legged in there while a light rain set in to depress the afternoon, cleaning his M4, eating spaghetti straight from the can and sipping bottled water. The Cambodians—he'd heard them explain as much to Lewis at one point—fussed over Lewis who had taken his pack into what appeared to be Heng's tent. As the gloom curdled into nightfall, the young man sat with the other men on camp chairs while they stirred a large wok over an open burner. The women had vanished into another tent with the girls. No one was watching the perimeter. No one but Elliot, who kept checking out each window, watching the road, the river banks, the far side closest the coast.

The families gathered around the cooking area and ate together, still chattering good-naturedly. When Lewis stood to clear dishes, Rit and his wife Chariya pressed him back to his seat and did it themselves. Heng wandered to the side of the bridge with his raincoat on, his hood up, spat over the edge and lit up a cigarette, stealing glances to the SUV. Maybe he wondered if Elliot was taking aim at him. Elliot didn't know. But he certainly respected the suspicion. Heng called something back to the tent annex and Rit acknowledged it, picking up a bowl and an umbrella and making a beeline for Elliot's SUV.

"Oh, fantastic. Visiting hours."

When Rit drew near, squinting like an idiot through the windows, Elliot called out, "Door's open!"

Rit dropped the umbrella, opened the front passenger door and climbed in. Whatever food he was carrying smelled great and Elliot's traitorous stomach gurgled at it.

Rit settled himself sideways, pulled the door shut behind him and offered the bowl through the gap. This time he took the bowl. A broth of thick vegetable chunks and pink meat steamed up at him, an agony of temptation.

"There's no rice," Rit smiled. "But Lewis says you like veggies."

"What's the meat?"

"Fish. Caught it in the river here."

"You ate this?"

"Sure. Very nice."

Elliot held the bowl back to him and angled it so the spoon swung Rit's way. "Taste it."

Rit started to laugh, then it caught in his throat. "You … you think we're poisoning you?! Why the bloody hell would we do that? You saved our lives today."

Elliot didn't move. "Humor me."

Rit blew out a breath, took the spoon, ate a chunk of fish and something that looked like cabbage, dropped it back in the bowl with a *plop*. "I better head back to the tent and get the antidote quick." This time he didn't smile.

"Wise ass." Elliot spooned some broth and a little fish into his mouth. Flavors exploded. He kept the pleasure from his face and ate a little more, then put the bowl aside. "I'll finish it later."

Rit shifted in the seat, faced front. "See them out there? That's my family. All of them."

"Except Lewis."

"He could be."

"Not for long if you're staying out here in the open. This bridge is as much a trap as a base."

"We should come with you to this island then. We don't have any maps. We've been making it up as we went along."

"In that case, he'll be all yours. Just one request. Stop babying him."

"Babying him! You mean feeding him?"

"I mean stopping him clearing up dishes. Letting him out of cleaning up corpses. Getting him to draw pictures with your kids and giggle like a child."

Rit turned back, eyes narrowing. "For your info, he's the first ray of light our kids have had since the shit went down. And you know what he was drawing just before we served dinner? He was drawing the Sydney Opera House. Two months and our girls have already forgotten what it looks like. Can you believe that? But he made it real to them, brought it back to life. He's a bloody good artist and without the freakin' internet, someone like him's important to keeping our history alive."

"History's for grade school and grade school belongs in civilization. This world smell like civilization to you?"

"It doesn't smell like the end of the human race. Not if we hang on."

"He'll hang on fine if you stop babying him. Let him be a man."

"Like you?"

"No, better than me. He's just getting a grip on it and you're undoing all that progress."

"What, by being kind to him? Do you know what he's been through in the past week?"

"Pretty sure I was there. Lemme check my blog."

"And you've kept him safe till now which is amazing. But he tells me you've been hard on him."

"I've been *real* on him. He's thinking better, acting safer, using a firearm properly, making hard decisions. Gimme another week and he might actually start catching and cutting up his own food instead of getting a bunch of mommies doing it for him."

Rit held his gaze for a moment, sniffed and faced front. They were quiet a while, then Rit said, "I get you."

"You *get* me?"

"Yeah. I get you. You play the tough guy, the angry guy. You keep everyone at a distance. You set low expectations for yourself so everyone else will too. Can't fail then, can you?"

Elliot put his hand to his cheek, rasped his stubble and said, "And I get you too. You're the guy who spends his life talking crap and getting smacked in the mouth. Why don't you put Heng in charge? At least the old coot's got some balls."

Rit scratched hard at something on his face. "Bring the bowl back in the morning." He got out, picked up his umbrella and stomped through puddles back to the tent.

A little over three hours later, when Elliot's glowing wristwatch told him it was exactly 11.30, and the lights had been out in the tents long enough for everyone to be asleep, Elliot got out and went to the barricade. The rain had stopped, the clouds had parted, the moon was three-quarter full and high in the sky. He could see well enough to muscle the cement mixer out of the way. The air was heavy with deader stench and he gladly returned to the car. After backing it out of camp, he got out and replaced the barricade securely.

He turned the car on the shoulder and headed west.

The headlights lit up debris like Mardis Gras aftermath—leaves and twigs and trash blown in from God knew where. He took it easy, although he knew the route from earlier that day. What he had in the back of the car would see him through a week without rationing. But if the hosts of undead refugees were still making their way from north to south—or worse spreading out—he was better to find somewhere to wait it out. Lie low for up to a month before finding a tourist information center or library like he'd planned.

Jock's house would make as good a place as any in the meantime, even with that unholy shit in the cellar.

The windows were barricaded. It was defensible and he could escape up into those hills if needed. Food was growing in the back yard.

MISSING! My boy. Adam. 8 years old. If you see him, return him.

"Wish I could, honey."

Please!!! All I have left. CAN'T live without him!

"Baby, you shoulda taken better care of him. You're all *he* had. All he had watching his back."

He yawned long and loud and pushed himself back into the chair, stretching his legs. What he wouldn't give for a piping hot espresso right now. He sipped water instead, screwed the cap on one-handed.

Would those Cambodians be good enough to watch Lewis's back? Would he be enough to watch theirs? Lewis was resourceful. He was smart and now he was emerging from his shock and from his childhood both, he was starting to put things together. He'd be okay. He was a good learner. Probably been an A-grade student.

Like Tommy Harrison.

Hell, his fringe looked like Tommy's and he was always swiping it aside like Tommy did instead of just getting it cut off. He even drew pictures all the time like Tommy had.

"Man, you could draw for like Marvel or DC or somewhere." He'd told Tommy that once. He winced now at the sound of it, like he was a fanboy or something. And my, hadn't Tommy glowed at that praise, though he'd preferred to draw animals and street scenes rather than the cooler more masculine comic book stuff. There was plenty about Tommy that made other guys suspicious and from time to time Elliot himself felt a little uncomfortable. Pinky swears especially had seemed girly to Elliot even when they were younger. But the pair shared a sense of humor, a love of *Land of the Lost* and *Ninja Turtles* well into their junior high years, and Tommy made really awesome brownies. And his Mom had made even better stir fry, the best meals of Elliot's youth.

Elliot's home was casual violence and child labor. Tommy's home was refuge.

He was also the only kid Elliot knew who owned a remote control plane, something Tommy wasn't interested in and was happy for Elliot to play with. Hell, he hadn't even cared when Elliot crashed it, though Elliot made sure he stole enough money for his friend to have it fixed. Tommy was the brother he'd never had, his mom a surrogate aunt or something, always nice, always fussing over them both.

"Shit, Tommy," he said in the dark, his mouth abruptly dry again. "Why'd you do it?"

The memories were fresh as morning dew. The words were clear and accurate like a cassette had been jammed into the back of his head to punish him.

"My Uncle John's away again, driving," he'd told Tommy. He was lounging across his buddy's bed wadding up notepad paper and flicking it at the ceiling fan. Tommy was at his neat and compact desk, sketching and coloring. He didn't even look up at Elliot's words, so Elliot upped the ante.

"And he left some new magazines. Wanna come over and check em out?" Wasn't often he'd invite anyone to his own home. Only when John was on a trip. He'd only ever brought a friend home once while John was there. Seven years old and forced to fight his friend while John watched and drank and laughed and berated him for losing, though the other boy was bigger.

Tommy wriggled in his chair, rummaging through a pencil box for a better color. "Not really. Not this time."

"Seriously good shit, man. Come on. I have money for soda too. Or beer. Like, ten sodas or two beers. We could toss a coin for which."

"Thanks, but I'm not really up for it."

"C'mon man. You have to *see* these magazines. Whoo, boy."

Something was wrong. He sensed it. It was like the moment was frozen, but it was really Tommy who'd frozen, his drawing hand halfway between the page and scratching his face with the pencil. "I think those guys at school are right," he said so softly Elliot had to get him to repeat it so he caught it.

"About what?"

"About me."

Elliot chucked the notepad, sat up. "What're you talking about?"

"I don't like those magazines."

Elliot snorted. "Sure you do." When there was no response, he ventured, "Well. We can still do those beers … "

"Elliot, I don't think I like girls."

The moment, the revelation, hung in the air like a fart on a bus. Eventually Elliot said, "Sure you do." But his heart wasn't in it.

Tommy half-turned on his chair and the only place Elliot had seen a face so forlorn was in his own mirror after a beating.

"I think … I don't know, Elliot, I'm so confused."

"You're not queer, Tommy. You're not."

"I might be."

"You're not a fag! It's just … It's all that *bullshit* those idiots keep on at you with. They're messing with your head. Don't listen to 'em. Look, some guys develop their interest in women a little later than others that's all." As if Elliot knew anything about adolescent development.

Tommy had turned back to his art pads and his pencils, working the colors like his life depended on it. Elliot sat on the edge of his bed suspended between two realities—the long warm summer of their friendship and an approaching winter of doubt and fear. What if Tommy saw them as more than friends, or brothers. What if …?

Elliot left the house so fast he didn't even say good bye to Tommy's mom. And two days later, Tommy Harrison had thrown himself in front of a goods train.

Elliot combed his fingers through his hair and squinted at the fallen tree in the headlights. He didn't remember arriving at it. He didn't remember stopping the car and shifting it into park.

The dashboard clock said 12:17. Another eight hours or so and Lewis's new family would break camp to head for the coast. There they'd find a boat and make for the island.

And who knew what awaited them there?

"Ah shit," he said.

Throwing the shifter into reverse and backing up onto the shoulder, he turned the car around and started back. Even an asshole could have a conscience.

V

Barnabas Island

17

There was little conversation between him and the others when they started stirring in the morning. Heng had been pacing the bridge when he'd returned, watching him park the car outside the barrier. Elliot had remained out there, taking some shuteye before dawn when the cacophony of birdlife made further sleep impossible. When the others started stirring, he got up, went down to the river with a towel, upstream from the bodies. He washed armpits, neck and face, dried, put the t-shirt and hoody back on, did some pushups, squats, burpies, some stretches. A baby carriage floated by in the river like Moses down the Nile, but there was no savior inside. By the time he trudged back up and around, the adults had gathered around their burner while Kim stirred a tall pot and Lewis pointed to the map he must have taken from the car.

They put it away when he wandered over, the men avoiding eye contact, the women smiling in their gracious way and pointing to an empty bowl. He nodded in answer of the unspoken question and peeked at the map. It had been folded so that the island and their vicinity sat dead centre.

The term *dead centre* put him in mind of Jock's lame jokes and he pushed that memory away as he had done with so many others over the years. "You all heading there?"

Heng—folded into a camp chair with his knees under his chin like a child—said, "Yes. Look like good place. Good idea."

Kim started ladling a thin porridge into bowls. Heng was served first, then Lewis, then Elliot. He lifted a spoonful, blew on it and ate. It was salty and nutritious and he dipped the spoon in for more.

"I'll get the girls," one of the ladies said but Rit waved her to a chair.

"Let them sleep, they can eat later."

"What time we leaving?" Elliot asked.

Kim regarded him hard-eyed. "We'll eat. We'll wash up. We'll leave." He gave his porridge a stir and then another. "You coming too?"

"I'll drive ahead of you. Check the marina out before you get there."

"Me too," said Heng.

"Just me," Elliot said.

Heng leaned forward. "Me. Too."

"Okay, okay. You too. But—" He tapped a spot on the map before the road curved to what might have been an open view of the ocean. "—the rest of you drive a few hundred meters behind us and stop at this point here. If we're not back in an hour, you turn around and find somewhere else."

"You think it's dangerous?" Rit asked.

"Everywhere's dangerous."

"Why would you do this for us?"

He glanced at Lewis, thought about what the Druids had done to him, thought about Jock and his trophy shelf. He thought about a mother waiting for someone to bring her little Adam home, thought about a mother in the Middle-East wailing at the child in her arms and wiping at dust and blood. He thought about the ideal of *leave no man behind*, about Tommy Harrison. Lewis blinked back, regarding him frankly, whatever anger he'd felt now forgotten.

"You have kids," he told Rit. "In my book, kids come first."

Heng said nothing for the first ten minutes though he kept turning in his seat to check on the vans following. The larger vehicles kept a respectful distance. Eventually, he settled and fingered his bloodstained cricket bat.

"Boy not bad," he said.

"Pardon me?"

"Boy not bad. Good brain. Good artist. You should let draw."

"Let draw? I've never stopped him."

"You shouldn't stop."

"I just said I don't. What's this—?"

"In my country, the Khmer Rouge kill all artist. They put me in prison for ninety day when I same age Lewis. One room. The soldier in black uniform, they come and wash us with hose one time every week. I lucky. They take me out to farm, not kill me or torture. About twenty people one room. Very bad. One man, my friend, he artist. They find out, they take him away. I scare, I think they kill him, but find out later they make him draw picture of Pol Pot. Many many picture.

After war, he paint picture of torture, of killing, of the room we all sleep in, of the black uniform, the boy soldier, the baby killing. We have what you call—history? He make history for us. Your boy same. He can make history for us."

"He's not my boy. He's not *a* boy."

"You want make boy soldier. Maybe good. I don't know. Maybe bad. I see boy soldier in my country. This boy should be artist, keep his mind strong, his heart strong."

Elliot thought long and hard about that while the miles crept past as he travelled slow, keeping it way under the speed limit for reaction time. He didn't owe Heng an explanation. He didn't owe anyone anything. Except maybe Tommy. So finally, for Tommy's sake, he said, "He's drawing for you. He's soldiering with me. We give him choices and chances. Choices and chances. Then Lewis will be in a position to make up his own mind about who he is and what he wants to do."

Heng grunted, checked the map on his lap and pointed to a black-and-yellow traffic sign a few hundred feet ahead. "Around that corner there."

Elliot double tapped his brakes, the signal. In his mirror the two vans slowed to a stop and dwindled. He took the curve slowly, crossed the coast highway with a quick glance each way and pressed on. Gradually the world changed from a land of grass and bushland. The narrow strip of road swept in graceful curves down and around gentle slopes toward a green-grey ocean frilled with wave crests. The highway was lined with high dry grasses, wattle, malaleuca and coastal pines. A thin strip of service buildings hugged the coast near a modest marina. The island they'd targeted was visible way out like a green-brown smudge.

Elliot started down the sloping road and pulled over into the gravel, leaned out the window with the field glasses. An asphalt parking lot with a jetty off one end of it and a boat ramp off the other. A large fishing-and-boating supplies store that had been open when the shit went down: overturned postcard racks, fishing tackle spread out through the doors, a half-dressed mannequin toppled against a window. A fast food van. Four vehicles, *five* if he counted the burnout car skeleton over by the pier. Trash and sand piled against the storefront. Weeds attested to the slow reclaiming of Earth by nature.

The only things moving were birds. Birds and a smoky smudge that might have been a cloud of flies. The thirty-odd human corpses around and on the jetty probably accounted for that, giving mute testimony to some past violence. Large pockmarks in the wood and the asphalt indicated one hell of a big gun used against them. A gun rather than a firearm, since only something mounted on a naval vessel or armoured vehicle boasted rounds that large. Sure enough, many of the bodies were chewed into small pieces—a smorgasbord for scavengers.

Nothing was moored to the pier. One car had a boat trailer hooked up, but the trailer was empty. Further down the beach to their right, a wrecked rowboat languished against some rocks. Past that, on a brief curve of sand-beach, a skiff had beached itself like a whale carcass with a motor hanging off the back like loose skin.

He passed the glasses to Heng.

"No one there," said Heng.

"Except scavengers and bacteria. You bring your face mask? Well never mind." Elliot nudged the car out onto the road again and let it roll down the hill without touching accelerator. "I've got towels in the back of the car. We'll cover our faces and inspect that skiff on the sand."

"Boat? Maybe doesn't work."

"It's not the end if it doesn't."

"You can swim across?" Heng laughed. Elliot didn't see the humor. "Maybe I sit on your back?"

"If it doesn't work, we check up and down the coast, wise ass. Find another way."

Heng nodded. "Not bad idea. Not bad. But maybe boat will be okay."

"Boat is shit," Heng told the others.

The women and Kim spoke in unison as if the line were well-rehearsed. "Swearing. The children."

"Children fine," Heng said, but he modified his comment to: "Boat doesn't work."

"Whichever way he states it, it's true," Elliot confirmed. "Good news is, the coast looks deserted. No pusbags. Bad news is, no way across to the island."

He and the Khmers spent the better part of a quarter hour arguing about which direction to go in: up the coast or down it, until Elliot lost patience with the way Lewis sat there shaking his head and wearing a bemused expression.

"What the hell is it?"

Lewis took a deep breath for a theatrical sigh, studying his nails. "Don't you people ever use your eyes?"

"What eye?" Heng snapped.

"Why would we only find boats along beaches?" Lewis pointed back over the hills. "We passed a property about three kays that way with a great big sign on the front gate that said *Hammond Bay Fishing Charters.*" He looked at each of them in turn with almost comical smugness. "You don't think maybe they have a boat or two? On trailers? In their sheds?"

There was a moment's perplexed silence, then the Cambodians broke up laughing.

"Lewis help us," Heng said, clapping his shoulder. He nodded at Elliot. "Lewis help like a man." He lifted the hand to wag an index finger in Lewis's face, smiling coyly. "So if you a man, next time we kill lot of zombie, you help clean up."

The others laughed again, Lewis joining in. Even Elliot had to smile.

18

The heavens favored the three of them with clear skies and little wind for their trip across the bay. The swell was low, the sun hot enough to burn unprotected skin. Lewis stood at a rail, sketching in one of the girls' notebooks. The chickens clucked and complained from their cage inside the wheelhouse. Heng stood behind the wheel, humming a happy tune. At least, it sounded happy to Elliot.

Leaning beside the young man, looking out across water, he said, "Progress. Finally. Been a helluva long trip but suddenly you're nearly there."

"Yeah, nearly at a place I don't want to go. You know I still want to go to Minchenbridge, right?"

"And in a year or two—when the dead, er, die off—you can."

Lewis wiped spray off his cheeks, blew on the notepad and dropped it to his side. "And where will you be then?"

"A long way from here, pal. I'll make sure you and these folks are okay, then I'll be on my way."

"You'll blow off a safe island with food and clean water?"

"Probably." His mind was once more on the wilds of the west. If it was anything like the woods of his boyhood, he'd do fine.

"You really don't like people, do you?"

Elliot turned his back on the wind. "Maybe people don't like me."

"Wonder why that is."

Elliot had never felt much like explaining himself. When under army disciplinary action, he would simply nod and accept whatever penalty was dealt him, deserved or otherwise. When Uncle John had dealt it out, he'd learned to take it without a sound. School teachers had never cared for excuses. And he never much liked blaming others for his own behavior. And yet, from time to time a comment like this would unsettle him, would remind him of origins, of events that set a person on a path they could never quite pull themselves back from.

"Not everyone gets the chance to start life on a good road."

"What do you mean?"

"I mean that we get dealt our roles in this life and we just play 'em out until the story's done."

Lewis was quiet a moment then he said, "Sometimes you talk a lot of crap, you know that?"

Elliot chuckled. "Proves my point, don't it?"

"You're saying I was destined to be nice and make friends and you weren't?"

"Well, not like that, but you have to admit, you started out with better chances than me. At least you had a good family. My Dad cut and ran when I was born. My Mom did the same when I was seven, left me with an asshat trucker named John."

"Oh. I didn't know that. I'm sorry. But … my parents were useless. They couldn't survive in this world."

Elliot frowned at him. It was the last thing he'd expect Lewis to say. "Survived longer than ninety-nine per cent of the world's population. They did their best, pal."

"And made sure I got left here without knowing what to do. If you weren't around …" He slapped the notepad against his left thigh. "Dad didn't teach me anything useful."

"He taught you to take responsibility. And your mom taught you first aid and some herbal medicine. That'll be damn useful from now on." Lewis didn't respond. "Your dad gave you an education. He paid for your school books so you could learn to read, so you could learn to keep on learning. He didn't take a belt to you whenever you looked at him wrong. He didn't call you names. I'd say you got a lot to be grateful for there. Honor the man's memory. Your mom too. They were good people. Smart people. I'd say they served you well."

There was silence, a silence revealing the voice of the planet itself: wind and water and the hopeful cry of gulls. A conversation millions of years in the making.

When Elliot looked down, the knuckles of Lewis' right hand were white on the handrail.

"What is it, pal?"

Lewis lifted the notebook, handed it to him. He'd drawn two people, adults judging by the clothes, seated on a couch, holding hands. There was a blank place where the heads should be.

"I can't remember what they look like. When I try to imagine them, I can ... picture their clothes, that's all. What's wrong with me?"

Elliot—who had a perfect recall for the size and shape of body parts he'd picked up from conflict zones and the wounds he'd treated, but had a similar block in remembering dead comrades' faces—said, "Nothing. Nothing at all."

"I can't even see Birdy's."

Me neither.

Elliot said, "You carry them in your heart. The mind's a screwed up thing. Plays tricks on you all the time. But your heart—your heart, Lewis—can carry a lot of people."

"My heart is a mess," he said softly.

"Your heart is a whole lot cleaner and clearer than most. Trust me. And no matter what anybody says, even me, you listen to your heart. You trust it. You follow it. If you can do that, your family lives on in you. And you'll do fine, whatever world we end up with here."

The island didn't rise much above sea level; the ground was low beyond the stone breakwaters on one side of the pier and shallow sand beach on the other. Two small recreational boats had been tied up on the beach side, mirrored on the breakwater side by a larger rigid-hulled inflatable boat, a Navy boarding vessel, twenty-five feet long. Stenciled on the gunwhal: *HMAS AUBURN.* The mother ship would no doubt be anchored on the far side of the island away from prying eyes, and its deckgun was no doubt what had chewed up the deaders back on the shore.

"Maybe someone official's here," Elliot told Heng. "And maybe that'll actually be good."

Beyond and around the dock, the commercial and parking area came into focus: a service kiosk, a boat ramp and some storage buildings surrounded by chainlink plus enough space for twenty cars to park. The boat juddered as Heng cut the engine. It coasted toward the inflatable boat, slowing. He'd timed it well and as it drew alongside the pier, it was a simple thing for Elliot to toss a rope over a cleat post and cinch it off quickly. The hull bumped against a pontoon, bounced away in slow motion, was pulled back there by the tautness of the line and the laws of physics.

On the island, a thin ribbon of aged asphalt led from the dock's small parking lot through the storage buildings, disappearing into waist-high scrub. No one greeted them. No one was anywhere to be seen. No corpses, moving or not. The island was two miles long he knew, so a small population could be anywhere. Or they might all be various shades of dead. Wind made banshee noises through the trees and the service kiosk eaves. Down in the water, a bottle clinked against a pier stanchion. Three seagulls hopped up the pier toward them, carping for a feed.

"Didn't get the email, fellas?" Elliot said. "Feast's on the other side of the bay."

The three men stood at the edge of the boat and exchanged nervous smiles.

"Who first?" Heng finally asked.

"That'll be me." Elliot got a foot on the bulwark, stuffed a tire iron he'd brought along through his belt, then stepped over. Lewis handed Heng Jock's rifle, then Heng handed over his cricket bat. Elliot helped Lewis across, the SIG waggling precariously in the back of the young man's waistband.

Shit, don't lose that on me.

As Elliot turned toward Heng, he heard the unmistakable sound of a car approaching at moderate speed. No, not *a* car; *several* cars. He motioned Heng back from the bulwark. "Maybe stay there a little longer, Mr Heng. And close to the wheel. Lewis, stay close enough to jump over if you need to." He picked up the cricket bat and took a step closer to the post where he'd tied off the boat.

A late-model white Mazda came into view around the bend through the trees, followed closely by an electric motor scooter ridden by a fat man, and then after a moment, a flat-bed ute-pickup with three figures—a dog sitting in the back and two people in the cab. The bike peeled off near the storage sheds and parked there, facing back the way it'd come. The other vehicles came to a stop at the top of the pier, disgorging passengers, all of whom swung around to the far side of the cars. The dog remained where it was, barking once to get its point across before planting its ass. The helmetless motorcyclist killed his engine and pulled a .22 from a makeshift holster on the motor housing. The passengers also sported non-automatic rifles. The male and the female drivers straightened their polo shirts over their jeans and stepped onto the very end of the pier. Both were tall. The woman raised an arm and beckoned him and Lewis forward.

None of the gun-toters pointed weapons at him. Not exactly. The bike rider had settled into a kneel behind the bike, elbows braced on the saddle and the barrel pointed out to sea to Elliot's right.

"Your call, Lewis. We go say hi. Or we wave goodbye and get back on the boat."

"If they're bad guys, we're screwed either way, eh? So let's say hi. Smiling all the way."

Elliot liked that and grunted a laugh. He leaned across the water, handed Heng back the cricket bat. "Can you get out of here if you need to?"

Heng nodded, face taut. He had a knife in his back pocket and could cut the mooring line in a pinch.

Elliot painted a smile on his face and started down the dock after Lewis, picked up his pace to catch up. As they approached, something in the lead couple's body language told Elliot the woman was in charge here. She was strong-featured, the well defined muscles of her arms showed beneath her sleeves. Her hair was growing out of a short, utilitarian cut—like Elliot's. When the red-haired man beside her flicked her a glance she didn't return, Elliot was sure she was the boss. She watched them approach with her hands clasped behind her butt. Definitely from the naval vessel and an officer; it was still there in her posture, the tilt of her head, the set of her eyes.

At thirty feet away, Elliot murmured, "She's in charge."

"Don't say anything derogatory," replied Lewis.

"My, how our vocabulary is coming along."

"You know what I mean. We don't need your rudeness toward women."

"I wasn't rude to Birdy."

"That's different."

"I'll behave, Pops. Promise."

"Get stuffed."

"Thought you learned to swear better."

"That's close enough," said the woman when ten pier boards lay between them.

Lewis jerked to a halt and Elliot came to rest beside him, mirroring the woman's stance.

"Hey there," Lewis said. "Permission to come aboard?"

Her mouth flicked up in a half smile, quickly gone. "Not just yet. Weapons on the deck."

Lewis pulled Kim's pocket knife from a hip pocket and dropped it, shrugged as if to say *Not much, I know.* Elliot hesitated then tossed the tire iron, wondering if he should've kept the SIG for himself. It still made a slight bulge beneath the back of Lewis's baggy tee—a risk, but so far it was unnoticed. He didn't mention the lock blade in his side pocket.

"Thank you," she said. "Hope your friend on the boat's smart enough to not point that rifle this way."

Names humanized people, as he knew. It hadn't quite worked with the trio at the train wreck but it was always worth a shot, so he offered, "His name's Heng. I'm Elliot and this is Lewis. You are?"

"Not important," she replied.

"Get rid of 'em, Meg," called an old man behind the car. She blinked once and slowly in obvious displeasure, but slow breathed it away.

Well, that's one name at least.

Elliot got a good look at the speaker when the old man came around the car. His skin was ruddied from years in the sun, wrinkled like crushed linen. He'd shaved his head to a shiny pate, but his long white beard rivaled Santa's. Or Ned Kelly.

She raised one hand to shut him up without turning. "Your business here?" she asked.

Elliot gave up the smile. "Hoping for sanctuary. Got a healthy young man here. I'm healthy too. Friend on the boat is a resourceful guy."

Santa-beard piped up: "We got enough resourceful people here."

Meg's mouth puckered in mild sympathy. "Afraid he's right."

The red-haired man shifted his weight from foot to foot beside her. Nervous. Maybe. Or guilty. He kept his gaze moving between Elliot's midriff and Heng on the boat, avoiding eye contact. Definitely feeling guilty.

Elliot scanned the small crowd a dozen people, all male but for Meg. Was she the island's only woman? Testing dynamics, he said, "We have more people a short way from here. Two women, two men, all young and fit. Plus two young girls. Children."

Not a flicker from the men at that. Not a sign of lust; that was good. But not a sign of compassion either; not so good. Except for Red Head: he dropped his gaze to the toes of his own sneakers.

Meg puckered her lips again and shrugged like *What's that to me?*

"We don't want any of them here," said Santa Claus Beard. "Not these people."

"I know, Bill, I know," she replied.

He went on, and she rolled her eyes, enduring it. "Look at 'em: a Yank, a towel-head and a gook back there. First the gooks came and took Australian jobs away from Australians. Then the Muslims did. No way they're gonna take Australian food away from Australian mouths here." A chorus of "Too right" and "Yeah, mate" from the crowd behind him.

"Keep a lid on it," said the woman. "Still thinking it through."

Bill sucked at his teeth in displeasure but obeyed her. What she had over them Elliot couldn't tell. Maybe just the ability to make good decisions in a crisis? And maybe Lewis was right about Elliot, that he was rude to women. What did it matter which chromosomes she'd received at conception? A leader was a leader.

He was doing pretty well, he felt, keeping his temper under control, forcing his patience while Meg's gaze kept tracking across the three of them. And then Bill put his fingers to his eyes and pulled them sideways in a Vaudeville caricature of Asians, playing for the crowd.

"Have some respect," Elliot said. "You've only been through one holocaust. This is Heng's second." Ignorant Bill blinked at him, not getting it, so Elliot tried a frontal assault. "This *gook's* more of a man than you'll ever be, Santa."

Bill puffed his chest out baboon-like, used little jabs to the air with his rifle to punctuate a sudden tirade. "You're just lucky Meg's a soft touch, or we'd have shot you three and been bloody well done with it. You stole that boat and all."

Someone behind him added, "That's Reg Davies' boat."

Meg ignored everything happening behind her, assessing Elliot with a cool eye. She said, "Here's my offer. You, we'll take. You look like you could do a hard day's work. You get a three month trial. The kid can get back on the boat and they can both piss off. We see them again, we shoot."

Elliot rubbed at his jaw stubble. "Let me get this straight. Meg. You want me to join a bunch of people who'd throw an old man and a teenager out on their asses?"

Red Head blushed but kept silent. His sneakers had become objects of fascination to him.

Meg's expression hardened a little, but she showed no similar embarrassment. "You're one of us, despite the accent. Americans have always been our allies. We can trust you. But we can't trust them."

"Bloody oath," said Bill, turning to face the crowd. "Bastards destroyed a beautiful country."

More murmurs of approval and support. This time he got lots of eye contact.

Lewis shifted, about to say something, but Elliot put a hand on his arm. Then he raised his voice and pitched it past Meg and her red-haired lapdog. "So it was *this guy* who unleashed an undead plague upon Australia. Geez, Lewis, that was more than a little thoughtless."

Lewis rewarded him with a smirk.

"Not what he means and you know it," Meg snapped, an eye on her restless disciples. She nodded at Lewis, but said to Elliot, "You're not the poor prick who had to stop the refugee boats and saw how messed up those people are."

No, but I saw how messed up the region they came from was. And how we did a lot of that messing up.

Lewis bristled. "My dad wasn't a boat person! He came here as a uni student, then got a job."

"An Australian job!" snarled Bill.

"Shut the kid up," called someone else.

Red Head looked at Lewis with more than a little pity and made a hand motion to keep quiet.

Meg told Elliot, "Time's up. Choose. With us or against us?"

And that's what it boils down to these days. At least life's simple.

"I guess it'll have to be *against*."

Meg looked over her shoulder. "Tony, you recognized that boat? Said they stole it?"

"Bloody oath. Reg Davies' boat."

"Then search it. You too," she added to the man beside her. He squirmed, discomfort growing. "You'll stand right there," she told Elliot and Lewis, "and your friend back there will give them room. They find anything indicating you harmed this Reg Davies person and our conversation will change tack dramatically."

19

They took the trip back in silence with the wind and the sun in their faces. The small marina was as they'd left it, the birds worrying at the carnage on the pier. Their SUV and trailer sat at the far end of the lot near the ramp; no one had been by to steal it. They pulled the boat up far along the dock to bypass as much of the human detritus as possible, moored, climbed up and tiptoed through the mess with birds flapping and complaining. In no mood to love animals, Elliot swung a fist at one that flapped too close, almost connected. If they hadn't been picking at the unholy undead, he'd have considered bagging a couple for dinner. He had to do something to take his mind off this. And luckily, Lewis had coolly evaded any discovery of the pistol in the waistband of his jeans. Lewis had the SIG out now, studying it like he couldn't believe he still had it. Elliot couldn't either. He was certain the red-haired guy had noticed, but he hadn't said anything. The .303 and the pocket knife they'd kept, but perhaps in the interest of good sportsmanship they'd handed back the bat and tire iron.

Assholes.

But really what had he expected?

Thought you'd find an impregnable island fortress where happy people would welcome Lewis with open arms and let you ride off into the sunset with a clear conscience.

Idiot.

Turning left, Elliot dragged his feet onto the asphalt lot with the others flanking him. Their misery was palpable, a cloud at his back. After unhooking the trailer, it would be a fifteen minute trip back to the boat-owner's house to break the bad news to the other Cambodians. Their best choice short term would be to fortify that place—or more painfully, consider returning to Jock's. Beyond that, Elliot needed a good night's sleep before plotting options.

They were halfway across the parking lot when a male voice called from the door of the tackle store.

"Stop there and I won't shoot you."

Instinct kicking in, Elliot dropped to the ground, putting one of the parked cars between him and the store. He craned his neck to see Lewis and Heng still upright, hands climbing toward the sky. Heng faced the store but Lewis was turned toward their right. Elliot looked that way and gave up hope. A second man had appeared from behind another car, double-barrel shotgun covering him. A goddam ambush. He got to his feet. The man at the store walked out into the sunlight, brandishing a bolt-action rifle. Elliot's chest itched where the barrel was pointed. Light glinted on the hill above where a third man also held a rifle on them. All three wore faded work pants and long sleeve cotton shirts, their grey hair stuffed under cloth sunhats. Two wore glasses. None of them a day under sixty.

"Boy's got a pistol," called the man with the shotgun. Elliot noticed a walkie-talkie on his belt. A guy on the island had been muttering into a similar handset; Elliot had thought him communicating with others on the island. Instead he'd been tipping these farmers off, his comrades searching the boat to stall for time.

But for what purpose?

The guy at the store told Lewis to put it on the ground and for all of them to drop whatever other weapons they had. Exchanging glances, Heng and Elliot tossed the tire iron and cricket bat.

"Keys to the car too."

Elliot said. "We walked here."

The man pointed in turn to the cars hooked to trailers. "One of them's yours. You drove the boat here with it. So. Keys. Now."

Elliot dug them out and tossed them on the cricket bat.

They were directed out into the open and ushered by the guy at the store up the road out of the parking lot, while the shotgun-bearer collected the 9-mil. The guy on the hill stayed there covering them until they'd passed then fell in beside his mate, while the guy with Elliot's SIG started up the SUV and followed them in first gear.

"You farmers?" Elliot asked. "We can help you. We're fit, healthy-"

"Shut it," one said. The radio crackled at his belt.

"Must be immigration service then," Elliot said, nodding at the walkie-talkie. He received no answer except a gesture with the shotgun to keep him moving.

One trio followed the other up the hill. The older men were steely-eyed and weather-worn, capillaries showing in their cheeks and joint pain in the way they walked, but they weren't stupid, keeping a reasonable distance and keeping their prisoners to the centre of the roadway.

Around the bend and over the crest, the top of a long truck showed, dull steel or aluminum panels with long gaps between them. A livestock transport. He smelled them, then heard them. Sheep. Ten or twenty maybe, about a quarter the potential load of that trailer.

"So you *are* farmers," Elliot said.

"I said shut up."

"You said shut *it*," Lewis said.

"Smart arse kid. Gonna get shot."

Lewis had the sense to leave it at that, but Elliot wondered—as the other two must have been—why they *weren't* shooting them, doing it here, getting it over with. The truck gave off an aura, as if there were worse things than a bullet in the head on a country road.

The only times in history that people were herded into livestock cars …

When they were a hundred feet away, they were ordered to stop. One of the farmers skirted them and opened the back gate. There were sheep in the topmost level. The middle two decks were empty. Someone moved in the gloom of the lowest deck, the trailer floor, and Elliot hoped to heaven there weren't deaders in there.

"Back, you," the man at the gate told whoever was in there and Elliot's blood pressure dropped to a slightly healthier level.

"In you go," said the other man.

"Figured you'd say that," said Elliot.

And with no option, he and the others complied.

A young couple, male and female, crouched in the middle of the forty-foot trailer, their heads ducked beneath the floor of the deck above.

A gridwork of steel bars had been laid across the trailer's floor, for no purpose Elliot could see unless it was to stop fallen animals from sliding around. The way he'd seen livestock crammed into similar trucks over the years, normally there wasn't any room for animals to slide, held in place by the press of bodies. A couple of planks the size of suburban fence palings lay against the right-hand wall of the trailer; a tuft of wool had snagged in one where the wood cracked like a hangnail. The welded framework had been there for years, judging by the chipped paint, dried feces and rust. Each bar was a little thicker than his fingers and each square was fifty by fifty inches. And the framework made it impossible to sweep out the trailer if the farmers had been so inclined. "This is useful," he murmured, inspected the detritus fallen inside it.

"This bullshit," Heng said, fists wrapped around the thick side panels and rattling them hard.

"Won't get out that way," said the young woman at the far end. "We tried."

"Not try everything," Heng said.

Elliot gathered three bolts the size of index fingers into a pile and added, "Damn straight."

Above them sheep shuffled, complained. It stank bad in here, the air so thick it was almost solid.

Lewis crawled closer to the young couple. "I'm Lewis. This is Heng and Elliot."

The young couple closed the gap and offered him their hands in turn. They were college age, the male with heavy beard and long hair tied in a man bun, the female with her hair clipped shorter than Elliot's and eyes the color of a clear sky. They were in good shape, not an ounce of fat on them but well fed and toned, dressed in shorts and tees with hoodies tied round their waists. Stress had hollowed out their cheeks, painted dark circles beneath their eyes, while the sun had tanned their skin the red-brown of clay.

Each sported a different ankle tattoo above their sockless sneakers.

"Angie," she said.

"Dylan," he said. "They got us on the road. Maybe half an hour's drive from here down the coast. Tricked us into coming closer." He shook his head in rue.

"Looked like safe people," Angie explained. "Old people. We're so stupid."

Lewis made a sympathetic face. "Not many safe people around anymore."

Elliot noticed then that Dylan's left hand was bandaged as tightly as his own ankle. "You bit?"

"What? No! Cut my palm on barbed wire."

Something warm and putrid gushed through the gaps between decks, spraying near the three young people who cursed and made space around it.

"Do you know where they're taking us?" Angie asked from the striped sunlight in back of trailer.

"Didn't stop to ask them," Elliot muttered. "Too busy being herded in here with the rest of you sheep."

She flinched, then squinted blue death at him. Not one to tolerate disrespect. That was good.

Heng shuffled around, squatting, one hand on the outer panels for balance. "Doesn't matter where take us. Matter what we do when we get there." He turned Elliot's way. "You got plan?"

Elliot started unlacing the boot from his injured foot. When he had it off, he tugged at the long woollen sock he had there damp with sweat. He shook it and slid the three bolts inside it down to the toe, tied a knot above them. He lay it beside him and got the lockblade from his cargo pocket the dumb farmers hadn't bothered searching.

"You ever fire a rifle?" he asked Heng.

"Yes. No problem."

Worrying the hangnail piece of wood on the plank with his blade, Elliot told him, "Then I got plan."

20

The truck slowed around a bend in the road, grinding back through the gears, air brakes firing. Elliot pressed his face to a gap in the right side of the trailer, saw a steep drop off to narrow beaches, rocks and ocean, a skinny automated lighthouse.

"This side," said Angie and Elliot scooted across to the left.

The truck slowed to a crawl as they came up on the fenced-off property. The side fence, running off at a right-angle to road, seemed to go back a half mile or so before vanishing over a rise. A farm came into view then, fortified, the ten-foot-high chain link topped with rows of barbed wire. Razor wire had been strung along and through the grass to prevent approach. A rustic sign near the gate read *The Downs*. A homestead took up the corner closest to the road with maybe seventy-five feet between it and the fence line.

"Is that a *double* fence?" she asked. She smelled like sheep piss.

"I can see why," Dylan groaned and pointed. "Check out the local exhibits."

As the truck made to turn through the gates, the fence did resolve as one set inside the other with a consistent fifteen foot gap between them. And in that gap, the undead loitered. Easily thirty of them, in various states of decomposition and undress, fingers through the fence, fascinated with the turning vehicle, this giant noisemaker.

In the deck above, the animals shifted, bleating in fear.

"They smell them," Heng said.

"So do I," Lewis added, t-shirt over his nose. "Imagine living with that near you."

"Nice extra layer of defense though," Elliot told him. He kept his fingers hooked through the gaps in the panels as inertia tried to throw him to the other side of the trailer. The toes of his sockless foot scraped against the leather seam inside his boot. His ankle was sore from the angles he'd been forcing it to maintain, but it was holding, the bandage a godsend as a brace.

The makeshift kosh now had six bolts in it, since Dylan had found him three more. Hot as it was in here, he thanked God he'd worn his hoody on the trip across the water; the sock-and-bolts were hidden inside his left sleeve. A wooden shiv he'd carved from the plank was down his left boot. Heng had another one in his back pocket and Angie had turned from the view, distracted as she tried wedging her wooden blade in the back of her shorts.

With Jock's SUV bringing up the rear and driven by the guy from the hill, the truck eased through the double set of gates in low gear. It entered a large compound, the entrance to the farm, a broad courtyard or turning circle for trucks surrounded by buildings and corrals for animals. The corrals were empty, but there were more sheep visible in the paddocks beyond. Cattle too. A locked garage sat beyond the homestead, large enough for four tractors. The homestead on their side of the truck was big enough for a large family, about the size of Jock's ground floor. Elliot moved to the other side as the truck pulled straight in to park side-on to the house. The SUV swung in between house and truck. On the right, across a hundred-and-fifty foot gap, an open barn, four cars parked nose in to a low wire fence between barn and an empty steel-fenced pen. One of the cars was a pickup with the business name GNM Fencing emblazoned along the side. Beside the pen, piles of fencing wire, chain link and barbed wire, metal stanchions, a couple of hay bales. At the far end of the compound, a long shed and several holding pens behind a maze-like sheep run where trucks presumably loaded-unloaded the animals. No trees or garden beds apart from those fringing the house. A tank of diesel fuel and an orange tractor sat in front of the barn and parked in front of them, a lowrider Harley and a black muscle-van. Two bikers in leather vests lounged against the van in full sunlight, chatting with another farmer-looking guy, early middle-age this time, five or six years older than Elliot. And the bikers …

His heart constricted, lurched. He'd seen both before. Riding out of the Oussefs' health retreat. And one of them again, in Harrietville. Even from here, the pandora bracelet was visible on his belt, catching the sunlight. And that van had carried away Lewis's sister.

Lewis gasped, "No." He lost his shit, trying to tear a panel from the side of the truck, screaming nonsense. Heads turned. The bikers laughed, eyebrows raised.

Elliot grabbed him, pulled him back, held him close like he had in the tower. "Control it. Control it,

Cochise. Channel it. We'll get him. Okay? We'll get them. But you have to control it. You have to bury it deep. You lose it now, and the bastards win." Lewis went limp, catching his breath, forcing it to slow. Elliot let him go. "We'll get em."

"What the hell is going on?" Dylan asked.

"Trade. That's what's going on. Human trafficking. The island has an agreement with these gumbies. 'You can have the people we don't want'. The gumbies have an agreement with the Death Druids: 'don't kill us and we'll find you slaves'."

"Holy shit."

"Question of my own," he wondered aloud; "how'd these maggots end up out here? Harrietville's a long way from here. How'd they know about Barnabas Island?"

"Not so hard to figure," Angie said. "We've seen a few of them around, travelling in packs. Pretty small island if you have vehicles. If you have the numbers, the guns and the sociopathy—if the deadheads have killed off a lot of society and if there's no cops—a place like this is ripe for picking."

"Jesus," he breathed. That made him wonder about the actual strength of the Druids. Had he seen all of them at the Oussefs' home? Or was that merely a raiding party? He let Lewis go, the teenager retreated into the gloom, face hard, hands twitching.

Heng wriggled a little more. "Lewis told me about those men. You killed their friends." After a moment, he asked, "How many their friends you killed?"

"Two. Two very bad men. Bad like Khmer Rouge."

"No one like Khmer Rouge."

"Lewis tell you they raped and murdered people? They beheaded people? And here they are looking for slaves."

After another pause, Heng said in a more subdued tone, "Okay, maybe like Khmer Rouge."

Elliot scooted from side to side, checked the terrain the best he could, started giving targets designations in his head. Farmers One and Two were climbing from the truck cab, One armed with a bolt-action .303 similar to Jock's and wandering toward the bikers, Two coming to the back of the truck, double-barrels resting against his left shoulder and with a lump under his shirt Elliot hoped was the SIG. The fools had not only missed the Shrade in his pocket, but also the spare mag. Farmer Three exited the SUV, holding a .22 with a 5-round mag. He too headed for the back of the trailer. A chubby woman in her forties finished securing the inner sliding gate, leaving the outer one wide open. She carried a sawn-off double-barrel plus a machete on her belt. The two bikers and Farmer Four—who was maybe the fencing contractor; Elliot adjusted his designation to Fencer—watched with interest but came no closer. Between them, they had Waxer's sidearm revolver, Fencer's sawn-off .22 and the other biker's pump-action shottie; the latter weapon leaned unattended against one van tire. One grey-haired pot-bellied woman stood on the porch, weaponless. There may have been more people in the house, the fields, the outbuildings. If these eight were all there was, Elliot's group stood a good chance. If not—well, what choice was there?

He touched the sock in his hoody sleeve and said, "Here's what we do. This is a rough outline only; you all need to follow it while it works, then improvise if you need to. Remember the main idea is to take the house if we can. It's a good place to keep them at bay while someone makes a hole through the fences behind it. At the very least, the house will have ammo and food.

"Heng is first man out the door. Angie second. Me third. Dylan and Lewis hang back as long as you can, don't come out till I call if you can help it. Heng, Angie and I get close enough to take out the nearest gumbies, get weapons. The compound is my responsibility and Heng's. Angie, the house is yours as soon as you have a weapon; make sure you clear it fast, but careful." She nodded, her limbs twitching with adrenaline. "The house is our fallback point. Dylan, you'll be with Lewis, keeping him alive."

Lewis bristled. "What?"

"Because you'll be busy," Elliot told him. "Remember the bolt-cutters in back of the SUV?"

"Yeah."

"When I call your name, you come out of here fast, get to the SUV, grab the cutters and sprint around the back of the house."

"Wait! You're not sending me away. I want to shoot those biker bastards—"

"Oh? You're a sharpshooter now? Or maybe you want to run across forty yards of open ground toward three men with guns." A pause while Lewis fumed. "You'll help with a distraction. I'll take care of those biker bastards." Images of headless corpses flashed through his head, a crow pecking at eyes. He ran his fingers across his head. "Be sure I will."

"Firearms," said Lewis.

"Pardon me?"

"You said guns. They're called firearms."

"Point taken. So, you'll have the boltcutters, right? Round back of the house, you find a sheltered bit of fence where it's hard for people to shoot at you, and you cut the inner fence. Dylan's your support."

Lewis nodded. "And we make some noise, right? Bring the zombies around to the gap?"

"Exactly."

"Fine."

Dylan's gaze whipped between them. "You're kidding me!"

"The enemy of my enemy et cetera," Elliot told him. "Good news is, Dylan, you'll be armed with whatever weapons you can find in that SUV. Just be smart. And you better have Lewis's back. Against the dead *and* the living." He eyed the guy till he swallowed and nodded.

"Not like you haven't killed anyone," Angie told him. Dylan blushed, dropped his gaze.

"Speaking of killing people," Elliot said, "I'll take the woman at the gate."

"Woman?" Heng asked, surprised.

"She's armed. She's complicit in this. I take her out."

"Or I will," Angie suggested, still messing with her shiv. She couldn't find a comfortable place for it. "Believe me, I don't mind."

Elliot beckoned her closer to the door. "How much do you want to live?"

She shuffled over, gave him that *you're-a-dead-man* stare again. "Seriously?"

"Then take your shirt off."

"What!" Dylan choked.

"Shut up," she told him. She slid her tee up and over. "I get it."

Heng chuckled at the sight of her tiger-print bra. "Stay away from angry tiger."

She glared at him, then decided the back of her bra strap was a good place for the shiv which was small enough to slip in there sideways.

"Keep the bra on if you want," Elliot told her. "Just make sure you have their attention."

"As if I wouldn't," she snorted.

Farmer Two was fiddling with the door latch now, while Three aimed his rifle at it. Elliot slipped sideways, to let Heng take his place closest the door, with the girl beside him. Her bare skin gleamed with sweat.

"Lewis," Elliot said with a grim smile and without needing to look back. "Eyes down."

The two farmers kept back from the door as it swung out. Without much breeze, there was no danger of it blowing shut again and neither of them bothered securing it against the truck's side. They kept in a tight cluster, rifles pointed at the soil between them and the people emerging.

As Angie and then Heng slipped out ahead of him, Elliot pulled his hood over his head, hoping to avoid Waxer's immediate notice.

"Hi, boys," Angie said and minced closer, her hands on her ribcage, chest thrust out. "Surely you don't want to give this away, do you?"

"Bloody hell, girl," the middle-aged woman grumbled and marched over to where the two farmers stood frozen with eyes popping, slipping off the workshirt she wore over a tanktop one sleeve at a time, juggling the shottie awkwardly. "What are you, a bloody stripper?"

Angie's gaze brushed Elliot's for the barest of seconds, telling him to wait. He slipped his fingers into his opposite sleeve, pretended to scratch, cinching the length of sock into his palm. Heng shuffled at Angie's heel, shoulders stooped in feigned defeat, hands on hips. Elliot mimicked the old man's posture, slumped over.

"Get this on, ya little slut," the woman said, holding out her shirt. The shotgun hung loose from her right hand but her trigger finger was still inside the guard.

"Or maybe I'll take this off, huh?" Angie said. She winked at the blushing men with one hand at her bra clasp, the other reaching for the shirt.

She lunged, snatched at the woman's wrist, pulled her close as the shiv came around. The wooden spike buried itself up and into the side of the woman's neck. Red squirted, eyes widened, mouth drooped. Angie swung her around with great grace, laced an arm over her shoulder, and grabbed her gun-hand from behind, slipped her own finger through the guard, brought it up.

Heng and Elliot started moving. In shock, neither Famer Two nor Farmer Three paid them heed. Three hadn't raised his .22; Two had his own double-barrel up, hesitating, not wanting to shoot the woman blocking Angie.

Angie shot him in the chest. He crumpled, falling on top of his weapon. Farmer Three finally thought of using his, but Heng was on him, shivving him twice in the stomach, then wresting his rifle free and swatting him to the ground with it. Spry as ever, the old Cambodian knelt, aimed at the four men across the compound who, stunned, were only now reaching for weapons. He squeezed off a round and they scattered for cover, the bikers heading around the van, the Fencer toward the pens at the back of the yard. Only Farmer One stood his ground, firing, working the bolt.

"Make your shots count," Elliot told him, then shouted "Lewis!" while he tossed his useless kosh and scrambled to get a grip on the squirming, keening Farmer Three. He got a handful of shirt and another of grey hair and pulled the injured man back toward the cover of the truck. Farmer One's second shot whizzed over his head, passing between him and Angie who was still fighting to hold the chubby woman up as a meat shield. "Drag her back here! Then check her pockets."

Lewis and Dylan slid from the trailer as Elliot got back behind it. They sprinted around the side toward the SUV and Elliot put them out of mind, slipping his own shiv from his boot. He rolled the farmer onto his stomach and plunged it into his brainstem, left it there while he started checking pockets.

"Got him!" Heng cried after his third shot and Elliot didn't care which one.

He yelled, "Under the truck, Heng!" and hit pay dirt: a full five-round mag, and eight spare rounds. Plus his SIG. As Angie continued struggling with her opponent, trying to put her down, Elliot met Heng by the back of the truck and lay the ammo down on the ground for him. "Behind the tire," he said.

Heng nodded and squirmed his way underneath, dragging the spare rounds with him.

Elliot cast a longing glance at Farmer Two's body. There was a shotgun there, maybe spare shells, but it was too risky. "Shit."

Angie and her opponent struggled on the ground now, Angie underneath with arm locked around the woman's heavily bleeding neck, squeezing. The woman clawed at her. The shiv was out though Elliot couldn't see it, leaving the blood to run free. A minute, maybe less and she'd die on her own. They didn't have that time. The woman saw him coming, her struggles increasing as he got the Shrade out and unfolded the blade.

"Hold her!"

She sobbed then, and Elliot saw her for who she was, not wanting to. Just a country girl, gotten older and lost her looks, finding herself in a bad place and a bad time, doing what the others told her in order to survive. And Elliot was just a soldier, performing another in a long line of shitty things this shitty life had made him do, and damned if he'd apologize for it. He got on top, grabbed her chin as Angie dropped her arm, stuck the blade's point into her throat and put his weight on it, felt it pop through, pulled it back, rolled off as her breath turned to choking. He went back for the SIG. Halfway to it, light flared around the edges of his vision. His chest constricted. And he was no longer there.

He was in an arid place, sandy soil and tiny rocks and a wide black crater with his team in pieces and—

Stop this.

He was in a dusty village hovel with a baby hugging the leg of its mother who lolled half-on-half-off a beanbag with blood streaming from a hole in her chest, diving back out into the street as a hand grenade rolled from her hand—

Stop this. Please.

He was in his classroom listening to the teacher explain that Tommy Harrison had met with an unfortunate accident at the train tracks and the room lost its air and it spun around him and all he could think was it was his fault his fault his fault—

STOP THIS!

He sucked in a breath, hands on knees and centered on the grey dirt of an Australian farm, the tire-print between his feet, a stick with black ants running along it. Blood thumped in his arteries. Tinnitus screamed in his ears. The vision was gone from his left eye. The world had lost its oxygen. It wasn't working. Not fast enough. People were counting on him. He was in danger. There was—

He felt the ghost of a slap across the head, Uncle John's punctuation to his favorite saying. *Too much thinkin', not enough doin'.*

He felt a light touch on his shoulder, Tommy's mom rubbing it, asking him if he was okay, if he needed to talk, if he'd like to join them for dinner. The hand moved to his hair, massaged his scalp.

"You're okay," Angie was saying. "You're okay."

He pushed himself upright, forcing oxygen into his lungs. "Yeah," he said. "I'm okay."

"She had it coming."

"She did," he said. He squeezed his eyes closed and opened them. The vision in the left one was back but stippled with white. "And she didn't."

Angie let go of his head, looked down, realized the same moment he did that one side of her bra had slipped up; under the circumstances, Elliot found he could care less. She pulled it into place, the fabric sliding easily on a lubricant of sweat and blood. She cracked the double-barrel open as Heng changed mags under the truck. She pulled out the spent shell, checked the other was good and replaced it.

Elliot pointed to the now dead woman. "Shells in her pockets. Get 'em and take that house."

The Shrade was still in his hand. He could see and hear well enough. And John—goddam him for all the wrong things he'd done and said in his life—had been right about this one thing. He wiped the blade on his sleeve, folded it, dropped in his pocket, found his SIG. His head pounded like a bitch, but he'd deal with that later. Vision clearing, he took a peek around the truck. Farmer One lay wounded on the ground, chest heaving.

The Fencer was visible between the rails of the sheep run. It had been maybe forty-five seconds since Angie had fired the shotgun. Lewis should be on his way to the fence by now. The Fencer had a sawn-off; though he'd briefly have an angle on Lewis from there, it was unlikely he'd hit him over that distance. Waxer was nowhere to be seen, but his friend popped out from behind the black van, fired his pump-action, ducked back.

Elliot squatted and reached in under the truck for the empty mag Heng had ejected, started loading spare bullets as he picked them from the dirt. "Don't shoot the van: may be people in there."

If the Druids were collecting human chattel, it was certainly possible. Shit, what if Lewis's sister was in there; what if they took her on long trips as entertainment? That was one lie he'd no doubt have to face up to one day. Well, if it meant surviving *this* day, he could live with that.

Heng grunted. "Then what I shoot?"

"Can you see the asshole in the sheep run, behind the steel fence over there?"

"Wait. Oh, yes." Heng squeezed off a shot. Elliot's ears rang with the crack of the .22.

"Get him?"

"Not yet."

"Wait. The fuel tank, the diesel tank. Put a round through it."

Heng twisted around to frown at him. He had black road dirt smeared on his cheek and shoulder off the tire. "Blow up?"

Elliot shook his head, got the fifth round into the mag and tossed it beside Heng. "Only in movies. But that idiot doesn't know that. Might panic. If he runs, then—pow!"

"Waste fuel," Heng said.

"We're not staying to use it."

Leaving Heng to it, Elliot got up and ran around the back of the truck, 9-mil ready. Another crack from the .22 and Elliot wondered if it would work. No sign of Lewis or Dylan, the pot-bellied woman on the porch, or even Angie who'd sure moved fast. The front door of the house was wide open as were the back doors of the SUV. He checked the inside—Dylan must have taken the tomahawk Elliot had taken from Jock's home.

A shotgun blast from inside the homestead. He ducked, waited, heard nothing else and left it to Angie, moving further up the side of the truck. Nearing the cab, he caught a flash of flannelette shirt along the holding pens, vanishing behind the garage. The Fencer. Working his way round. Heng could hold off the bikers; Elliot would have to—

The window in the cab shattered above Elliot's head. Then he heard the gunshot. He ducked, swung the SIG round in a two-handed grip, found the woman in the open door of the garage, working the rifle bolt. Elliot squeezed twice, watched her drop. He moved to the garage at a run, put shoulder to the door, checked the room and moved inside. He kicked the 30-06 away from the hostile's reach, realized she was dead already, trotted past a tractor to the rear door of the garage.

A shotgun boomed from the direction of the barn. A shot from Heng, then another.

He risked a look, leant out and swept the pens beyond for hostiles. Nothing. Nothing but a woman with grey hair lying dead behind him, a woman who'd lost her life at his hands.

Tinnitus. Nausea.

Later. Deal with it later.

The pens on this side ran into a long shed, maybe used for shearing, all aluminum sheeting, with a couple of dirty windows set five feet high on this end, perfect place for Fencer to pick him off if he broke cover. He pulled back, squatted by the woman's body and checked her for spare rounds, then the rifle itself. Nothing. No more rounds. She'd had one chance and blown it. And the weapon was useless to him.

He listened. There was nothing for a time, but the pop and crackle of temperature change in the tin garage, the hoof-clatter of frightened sheep in the truck. Heng and the Bikers had either reached an impasse or one side had killed the other. Nothing further from the house and there was no telling if that was good or bad. What if Angie was down? What if someone was slipping out their back door now, taking aim at Lewis by the fence, finger on the trigger …?

Lewis hollered at zombies as planned and Elliot flinched. The young man shouted again and hammered a metallic rhythm on chain link fence with bolt-cutters. Elliot let out his breath. Time to get into the house and let the undead clear the yard.

He stood one side of the open front door, Heng the other. Despite the rows of solar panels he'd glimpsed in the yard behind the garage, there were no lights on in the house. A single hallway split the dwelling down the centre, gloomy without skylights. A window in a room at the far end flared with light, making it hard to see down the corridor. But one body was visible face down at the end. He and Heng had left the bikers under cover on the far side of the compound and had to hope the zombies would take care of them while they took the house.

"Angie," he called softly.

A moment, then from one of the side rooms, "In here! House is safe."

"Go to the end and see if Lewis is coming," he told Heng and followed him down the hall.

A head appeared at a door halfway down on the garage side of the house. "Got two in here," Angie said.

He stood in the doorway and regarded the two old women with disgust. They sat pressed against each other on an aging couch in an aging living room complete with lace doilies, porcelain dolls and a china tea set in a glass cabinet. They wore murderous expressions. Angie's sawn-off was on a sideboard by the door and she held a long-barreled pump action on the women.

Angie handed him the sawn-off. She was buzzing with adrenaline, her breaths short, voice husky. "Loaded. I got the rest in here." She raised the pump-action.

He jerked his head at the female body painting the hall runner red. "Her?"

"Tried to shoot me. I got in first. Haven't seen any other weapons but there's no one in the house."

He put the SIG in his belt, got out his lock-blade. The two women whimpered. He pulled a lamp's plug from the wall socket, cut the cord at both end, tossed it to Angie. "Tie one of them up, hands behind her back, tight." From the same power board, he unplugged a DVD player and cut its cord too, covered Angie while she set about tying them.

Clamor at the end of the hall made him lean back, poke his head out. Lewis and Dylan came inside in a tangle, forcing Heng back from the door and slamming it, then dragging a chair over to jam beneath the lock.

Heng went back to the window and swore.

Dylan limped down the hall, breathing hard, tomahawk dragging along the wall. He muttered curses under his breath.

"Problem?" Elliot asked. He checked Angie had the women under control and came out into the hallway.

"Yeah. You could say that. Instead of going round to the compound, the damn eaters chased us to the back door, didn't they?"

Elliot kicked out in frustration, puncturing drywall. Now they had the bikers out front and the deaders out back. His brilliant plan had gotten them trapped. That was the problem with decisions made in haste. And now he'd have to make another.

Heng and Lewis watched him from the room at the end which seemed to be a kitchen. Thuds and scratching came from behind them as the undead reached the door there. Angie eyed him from behind the second woman as she trussed her up. Dylan just leaned against a wall, moaning in fear.

Elliot made his decision.

"Angie watch the front door, Heng watch the back. Lewis, come up here and take the sawn-off. I'm going back out there."

Dylan gasped, "What! Why?"

"With the undead beating down the back door, they're our problem not the assholes who brought us here. If I can get the deaders on *their* trail, we can cut our way out the back fence and the barbed wire and get away."

"Bloody hell, you're gonna pied piper the dead? What if they kill you?"

"I'm a lot more scared of thinking men firing bullets than brainless undead. It's the only way I can think of for us to get out of here."

Coming toward him, Lewis offered, "Maybe we should stay. Our SUV is here with our stuff in it. This is a good place."

"You're going to cut the throats of these old ladies in here? 'Cause if we kill those three hostiles out there, then that's what we gotta do to take this place."

Lewis swallowed. "No."

"Then we're not staying, are we? We can find our way back to the place we left the other Cambodians and hole up there. Might take a couple of days to get there, but we got through worse. Shit, we're getting through worse now."

Trouble was, along with the swarm of deaders, he had those three live hostiles out there—since Heng hadn't been able to pick off either biker, and Mr Fencer was somewhere on the sheep pen side of the property. As he'd indicated to Dylan, three living targets were far less predictable than thirty pusbags, especially since he'd lost track of their actual locations. And they might have radioed the island for reinforcements.

Time was short, but there was no way he was going out the front door again when anyone could have taken position at the waist-high hedge around the front garden of the house. He went back to the living room.

He said to Angie, "Open that window. I'm going out there."

21

Tomahawk in one hand, SIG in the other, he squatted beneath the window as they locked it tight behind him. The ankle twinged but held strong. To his left, movement: two zombies wandering away from the main pack along the fence line and toward the solar panels. Maybe they'd seen something. Maybe they were bored. Improvising, he trailed after them keeping low. Without knowing where Fencer was, the two deaders might make solid cover—so long as they didn't hear or smell him. The rest of the pack seemed content to pile against the back of the house in search of the prey they knew of. For the moment that was fine.

His breathing was shallow, about the only sign of nerves as he trailed two monsters toward an armed opponent. For Elliot, action had always cured anxiety. Until the action was over.

He maintained a fifteen foot gap between him and the pusbags as they weaved through the solar panels headed for the shearing shed. He shifted position, keeping the deaders between him and the shed windows. As he thought of the windows, one shattered, glass flying outward. A hand appeared. He caught a flash of revolver and slid on his belly beneath a row of solar panels. His shoulder cracked against one of them and he dropped the tomahawk. A shot. Another. A zombie fell at the end of the row, head streaming black ichor. He shuffled sideways, risked a glance at the window. The gunhand wasn't pointed his way. It fired again and the second zombie went down.

"Gotcha!" he heard as the hand withdrew and knew it for Waxer. The bastard had moved position.

"No, got *you*," he whispered and fired through the wall twice.

There came a yell. No return fire. He rolled out into the gap between two rows of panels, and crawled beneath another, edging closer, then hurrying the pace a little when the groan and scrape of zombies came along the rows behind him. He'd dropped the ax, he realized, and was doubly glad he'd reloaded the mag before going out to the island. Six rounds left and more than a dozen pairs of rotting legs stumbling past and around him. The shambling legs began to halt, the undead piling up in the spaces between panels, uncertain of where the noise had come from and where their prey could be. It reeked like a slaughterhouse. His hand roamed around, landed on a stone. He lobbed it against the aluminum shed. The pusbags turned that way, started forward. He threw a second to make sure. A side door flew open. Through the forest of undead legs, he saw a living pair sprint out and across the open ground toward the garage; they made it to cover before he could get aim with the SIG. He swore. And a second set came running out, not as fast. He fired twice, plugged a zombie knee with the first and the fugitive's leg with the second. A scream. Between the milling dead, he caught a glimpse of flanellete shirt, the Fencer getting up on one leg to limp away before zombie hands and faces blocked Elliot's view, the deaders as keen on the wounder as the wounded. Elliot shuffled around, crawled fast beneath the cover of the panels the way he'd come, dragged himself out the end.

The truck started up, lurched into gear and started moving. He ran to the front of the garage as Fencer came hopping out of it, headed for the truck, .22 clutched to his chest. Elliot brought him down with one shot. The sawn-off rifle went flying. The man writhed and groaned. Blocked by the turning truck, a bike started up. Elliot leaned against the end of the garage, aimed and squeezed off two more shots. Missed the cab completely as it turned, punched a hole in the passenger side window before it was too far around to have a prayer of hitting the driver. He turned as two zombies reached for him, uncomfortably close. He shot the first in the head and then the hammer came down on an empty chamber. Dropped out the empty mag and reached for a new one. Ran toward the turning truck.

The fresh mag slapped home as he reached the fallen Fencer. He safetied the 9-mil and shoved it in his pants, scooped up the .22.

"Please," Fencer wheezed.

The bastard had been ready to sell three young people to the Death Druids to save his own ass. Elliot kicked him in the face and turned his attention to the truck as it straightened out on the far side of the yard. It gathered speed, headed for the gate. On one knee, he fired at the cab. A flash of face glancing his way, of graying ponytail. Waxer. Elliot had missed.

He worked the bolt. The truck cleared the barn on the other side of the compound, revealing punctured diesel tank, black van and the other biker straightening the front wheel of his Harley. Shifting aim, Elliot fired at him, missed, cursed. The bike lurched forward, the rider getting his right foot on the footrest. Elliot worked the bolt then fired again before the Harley could shelter behind the truck. One of the rider's arms jerked high, the bike toppled and slid. Elliot worked the bolt, swung toward the truck cabin, squeezed. Nothing. Out of rounds. He drew the SIG as the vehicle hit the gate and knocked it flat. The truck shuddered and jounced. A tire blew. Elliot ran across the compound to make sure the injured rider stayed down. The truck made it on to the road, but Waxer turned too hard too fast, lost it. With shrieks of stressed metal and terrified animals, the rig vanished over the slope beyond the road toward the lighthouse and beach. Twenty yards from Elliot, the biker struggled to drag his leg from under his bike. Elliot put two in his ribs.

There was a scream behind him. He turned back. Fencer's arm rose above a scrum of zombies. A short blade slashed once. Another scream. The hand vanished.

And near them, Lewis burst from between the hedges in front of the house, sprinting for the gate. Elliot called his name, got no response. The teenager was giving it everything he had, the sawn-off shotgun slashing the air as his arms pumped. A latecomer zombie started in Lewis's direction, ignoring the feeding frenzy. Two more—unable to get at the free meal—caught sight of Elliot and staggered his way. Ignoring them and a spike of pain in his ankle, he jogged toward the gate.

"Lewis!"

But Lewis slipped over the hill and out of sight.

Elliot picked up the pace, putting down the zombie between him and the gate. Those other deaders might keep after him or they might turn their attention to the house. There might be more farmers hiding on this property. But he cared about none of it.

Elliot's only concern now was Lewis.

He was forced to take the slope toward the beach more carefully than Lewis had. His ankle throbbed.

The truck had jackknifed, rolling. With trailer still connected to cab, it lay on its side, belly facing up the hill toward the road, wheels spinning, metal ticking and tocking. It blocked a straight approach to the skinny lighthouse, resting thirty yards from the low chain link fence intended to protect the tall structure from nosey tourists and vandals. Sheep cried in pain and terror.

He called Lewis's name a third time, but the young man didn't acknowledge him. He had reached the truck by the time Elliot crested the hill, now moving in stealth along the base toward the cab, weapon ready.

Behind Elliot, shots boomed and cracked from The Downs: Angie, Heng and Dylan taking care of the deaders now the farmers were gone. He hoped. He navigated the slope with a balance of care and speed, SIG trained on the cab.

Lewis peeped around the nose of the truck through the windshield, shoulders relaxing. Evidently, Waxer wasn't there. He vanished around the side.

"Lewis, wait!"

Elliot's good foot came down hard in a divot, almost upending him. Twice in a week—but he made it to the truck unscathed. The screams and bleats from the sheep were so loud he couldn't hear the crash of waves on the shore a hundred yards further down. He followed Lewis's route. The gate was wide open along with the lighthouse door. No sign of Lewis or Waxer.

Without the need for manned lighthouses for many decades, this one had been designed slim, twenty feet across at the base and tall, a minimal helix of narrow skylights set into the walls to provide light for repairmen climbing the interior. Despite the fence, a vandal had tagged the wall beside the access door, a red motif he couldn't decipher, if it was a word at all.

He reached the gate, ears straining over the sounds of surf and sheep, thought he caught Lewis's voice from within and bounded to the steel access door. Lewis was a step inside, shotgun braced at his shoulder. His breath steamed in and out like he was heading toward hyperventilation.

The lighthouse interior stank of stale habitation, the floor littered with proof of past camping. A sleeping bag, air mattress, a pile of towels for a pillow, two duffel bags, empty food cans—pasta, soup, cat food, a beer bottle. A gang of roaches competed with a swarm of ants for the scraps. Why someone had sheltered here so close to The Downs was impossible to know. As was their whereabouts; maybe they'd joined the farmers; maybe they'd been caught and sacrificed to the Druids. There was also blood and the blood was Waxer's. The biker had crawled through the detritus, squashing an abandoned duffel bag against the ladder up the far wall.

There he half-lay, half-leaned. His long hair and beard were slick from a running head wound, and his right leg was twisted at a painful angle. He gripped the knee with one hand while the other hand warded off Lewis in a *stop* gesture.

"You!" Waxer said, catching sight of Elliot. He tried to get up on his good leg, gasped and collapsed, out cold.

"Concussion," Elliot told Lewis, coming round the side, but the teenager wasn't listening. His breath remained heavy, face red, pupils dilated. His finger tightened slightly on the trigger.

Doubt struck Elliot like a fist. Elliot had been raised by a cruel man and while he'd never considered *himself* cruel, he was certainly broken. This world needed *hard*, this world need *brave*,but this world already had enough *broken*.

He made to put a hand on the shotgun, to push it down. Lewis pulled aside, stepped away.

"Let me, Cochise."

"He killed them."

Spittle flew from his mouth, but his eyes were dry. There was no sob this time. No catch of breath. Lewis seemed clear, determined, focused, channelling his pain, ready to kill—all the things Elliot had wanted for him.

And it saddened Elliot to see it.

"Probably his friends, not him."

"I saw him! I saw him out the side of the car when they took me. I saw him at my home. He dragged Alyssa away. She was screaming. He was laughing."

"Cochise. Remember how your dad said brain-power is better than firepower?"

"*You* said follow my heart."

"Who the hell am I to dispense advice?" He'd been leading him—this man-child—in the wrong direction if the result was to erase all of Lewis's sensitivity, his mercy, his grace with one act of revenge. John had tried to make Elliot hard-shelled, brutal, a fighter. And Elliot had been trying to do the same to Lewis.

This wasn't mentoring. This was a form of abuse.

Elliot had a lightning-bolt-clear flash of insight: *I'm the guy who does the dirty work.*

And he did it for people who needed it done. Two medics puking in the dust outside Al Kasrah needed Elliot to pick up the body parts belonging to his former comrades. The "free" world had needed him to go fight terrorism and oppression, so they wouldn't have to. John had certainly relied on him but it was because he needed the help, being a drug-and-alcohol affected asshole; Elliot had helped him keep the show on the road, keep his shit together. Nobody else had befriended Tommy Harrison, so Elliot had taken it on—until the day he didn't.

And Lewis? Lewis needed him now, not to help him be a man, but to stop him killing one.

Elliot had been twenty years old when he'd first taken a life. Lewis was thirteen. Elliot could be brutal so Lewis didn't need to be.

"Listen. You want to do this *now*, but … "

He saw them again, still images whipping across his own mind's eye—people he'd killed and injured—some of them with names, most without. A woman—a farmer's wife—held to the ground by a college-age girl while he jabbed a blade in her throat …

"You do this and it'll chase you all your life. It'll hound your dreams, it'll flashback when you're making dinner, making love. You don't want to live with this, trust me, Cochise."

"Stop calling me that. My name's Lewis."

"Okay, Lewis. Okay." He edged closer, hand out. Waxer remained out cold. Elliot couldn't see his chest moving. Perhaps he was gone already. He couldn't take the chance. "Give me the weapon." Lewis tightened his grip, hands shaking. "Shooting a man in cold blood? You're better than this."

Lewis hesitated. "He killed my family," he whispered. "He *hurt* my family."

Christ, what if Waxer woke, told Lewis the truth, that his sister had survived, was stuck in some living hell servicing the rest of Waxer's buddies? It would break what was left of the trust between them. It would be too much for Lewis to bear.

"He did, Lewis, he did." He got the flat of his palm on the barrel, exerted a gentle pressure downwards. The barrel didn't move, Lewis resisting. "I believe in an eye for an eye. I do. But Heng out there, Kim, Rit, their wives, their girls. They're your family now. And they need you in your right mind."

The barrel dipped then Lewis let him push it all the way down to point at the air mattress. "I don't want to let them down," he whispered. It was so soft, it took Elliot a moment to piece the sounds together into a meaningful sentence, and that he meant his parents and sister, not the Cambodians.

What should he say? What would Lewis's dad have said? He had no idea. He couldn't know. He'd never

301

had a parent or role model like that. And goddam it, it was Hollywood had conditioned the world to believe there was always the perfect thing to say, the thing that someone like Lewis needed to hear, that would heal his wound and change his life.

Elliot did the only thing he knew to do and gently pushed Lewis toward the door. "Watch the hill in case any deaders followed us down here. I got this."

Lewis went, shoulders slumped, shotgun hanging from his right hand. Elliot waited till the door clicked and fired the SIG.

Outside Lewis squatted, picking blades of grass, jaw working. Up the hill near the road, Heng peered down with exhausted eyes. Haunted eyes. The battle for The Downs must have been over. Having him there was like a sign, if Elliot believed in such things: his plan had worked. And he'd done the right thing for Lewis.

"It's done," he said.

"Why were you in there so long?" Lewis's voice was soft.

"Patting him down. Checking him for useful gear. Checking the bags in there." Elliot showed a cigarette lighter he'd found, then handed over the pandora bracelet. "And getting this."

Lewis turned it over in his hand and stood, pushed it into his pocket. "What about them?" He indicated the sheep truck.

Elliot sighed in relief: Lewis was still Lewis. "We'll check the compound, make sure everything's okay.

Then come back and let out the ones who can walk and euthanize the others."

Lewis grunted, cast one long look at the lighthouse door and set off up the hill toward Heng, with Elliot struggling to keep up. At the top, Lewis told Heng what had happened.

Heng accepted this without a reaction then said, "You not believe this."

"Believe what?" Elliot asked.

Heng led them back through the gates, pointed. Bodies littered the compound, including those of the zombies who'd once protected The Downs. He felt a pang of something, maybe sadness, at the woman's body—the one he and Angie had killed—homely clothing, cheap and utilitarian, no style, her greying hair mussed in death.

You picked the wrong side.

Past the carnage, the Druid's black van door was open. Two young women in jogger gear—strangers—sat on the running board, Angie squatting before them, talking while they rubbed at their eyes and nodded. Elliot froze for a moment thinking one of them with black hair was Lewis's sister. She wasn't. Ten years too old. He wondered if Lewis had the same reaction; nothing showed on his face.

"Goddam," he said, thinking of stray bullets. "Lucky them."

"God on their side," said Heng.

Elliot frowned at him, unsure if it was a joke.

They weaved through the mess of bodies, gathering Dylan in their wake. He looked lost, exhausted. The women fell silent at their approach, the newcomers' eyes kept diverting to Elliot's handgun. He was opening his mouth to suggest heading back to the boat-owner's house when Angie spoke first.

"Better get the gate fixed again."

He squinted one eye at her and then Heng. "You want to stay."

"Good place," Heng said.

Elliot chewed his cheek, thinking it over. "Then we've got work to do," he said.

"Work?" Dylan said. He sounded like he wanted to lie down and nap.

Elliot pointed the SIG at the other biker's body where it slumped near his side-lying Harley. "You want to stay? Then this place needs organizing. These animals will be back sometime. Question is when and in what strength. Last I saw them in Harrietville, a couple were complaining about running short of ammunition. That might mean their whole gang, or it might've meant those two individuals. We have to base our plans on the latter."

"What the hell are you talking about?" said Dylan. "You had us ready to run out that hole in the fence twenty minutes ago. I don't know what's wrong with you," he aimed at Angie. "I'm definitely happy to get the hell out of here. I'm not staying here." One of the girls was nodding agreement. Lewis looked unsure.

Elliot took a moment to think and realized the safety was off on the SIG. He castigated himself for the lapse, made a show of safing it and slipping it in a cargo pocket where it clacked against his lockblade. "You all have a choice now," he told them. "You could scatter like cockroaches, find new rocks to hide under. Or you can band together, fortify this place, learn to defend it. You stay here, the first thing needs doing is fixing those gates. Heng here, he knows what he's doing. Lewis too. And Angie. I'd be making their opinion on these matters high priority."

"What about you?" Lewis asked, stepping in front of him. "You're not leaving?"

"Not short term, Cochise. Tonight and tomorrow, I'll do whatever you folk decides needs doing."

"You wrong," said Heng.

Elliot eyed him hard. "How's that?"

"First thing we do is get my family."

VI

Choices and Chances

22

The dawn smeared the east with grey and orange and pink. Birds rioted along the orchard behind the barn and The Downs' makeshift parking lot, greeting the coming day. The washed out color of the farm environs emerged from the gloom in stages. Sipping black instant coffee the taste and consistency of battery acid, Elliot watched The Downs' new occupants emerge from a shaky night's rest to continue the work of the previous afternoon and evening. The gates were back up after a lot of whining from Dylan about his injured hand and after Heng had safely brought in his family. The various dead bodies no doubt still smoldered in the pyre they'd lit in one of the back paddocks; Elliot didn't think he'd ever clean that particular smell out of his nostrils as long as he lived. Angie and one of the van girls had kept busy walking the fenceline looking for weaknesses, and creating an inventory of the stores, while the third girl who looked like Lewis's sister had helped the men pick up bodies.

Elliot had seen a shitload of communities in his years, in all shapes and sizes and variations of economic wellness. This one was going to be a first. Two office workers, two college students, seven Cambodians, and one thirteen year old Syrian-Australian. Not much to hold off a concerted assault from outlaw bikers. But with the fences and with their weapons, it was a start.

Angie emerged from the house with shotgun gripped in one hand and coffee mug in the other, veered off toward the sheds to start whatever work she had in mind for the day. She was a concern. She reminded him of himself: she'd do what it took in the moment and worry about the guilt later. Or maybe she'd feel zero guilt; she didn't seem at all fazed by what she'd done. That could bode well for the new community or it could turn out to be very bad. She was either exactly what they needed or she was a loose cannon. He'd ask Heng to keep an eye on her.

The remaining woman farmers had been locked in the black van for the night. Elliot was going to let someone else decide what to do with them. He knew what he'd do, but it wasn't up to him. Probably the others would drive them a fair distance and let them loose to fend for themselves. He shrugged as he thought of it, but the idea still niggled at him.

He was regarding the spindly windmill that climbed above the garage and solar panels when Lewis came out, sipping a coffee of his own. Following Elliot's gaze, Lewis asked, "Sniper nest?"

Elliot nodded in approval. "A lookout at least."

They sipped their lousy coffee shoulder-to-shoulder and let the dawn come. Silence stretched between them. Lewis had his sister's bracelet in his other hand, fingers tracing the various charms. He'd added a new one, a bird he must have made from fencing wire.

This boy should be artist, Heng had said.

And Elliot had replied, *We give him choices and chances. Then Lewis will be in a position to make up his own mind about who he is and what he wants to do.*

Elliot might have a lot of regrets from the life he'd led, but preventing Lewis from blowing Waxer's head off would never be one of them.

Lewis heaved a heavy breath, slipped the bracelet in a pocket and said simply, "I want my family back."

Elliot—who would have given anything to get Tommy Harrison back, and even assholes like Radler and Eames—reached up and squeezed the teenager's shoulder, then dropped his hand to his side. What the hell was there to say about it?

He sipped coffee and heaved a breath of his own. "Need more people here."

"To defend it?"

"And farm it."

"How about Jock? And the people he went out visiting?"

Elliot's gut tightened. It wasn't time yet. But he'd have to tell him before he left. If he didn't, then any day now Lewis would grab a vehicle and find his way back there. He'd walk into the pedo's study and find a body. He might even investigate the cellar. Elliot shook his head to clear it of the images. He didn't want those stuck in Lewis's head. He'd have to tell him. Tomorrow.

"Give it a day, Lewis," he said. "Get settled first, then we'll think about who else. But, you know, those idiots on the island had one thing right: you have to be careful who you include, who you invite in. It might be as simple as if anyone's gut says no, you all say no."

"You keep saying 'you'. You're staying. Aren't you? You don't really want to go all the way out west and live in the bush on your own."

He'd walked out on Tommy for all the wrong reasons, for an ignorant kid's reasons. He had different reasons for walking out on Lewis—he didn't get along with people, he was a serial asshole—and *maybe* that made those reasons better.

"Gimme a couple of days to decide on that, Lewis," he hedged.

"Just tell me now."

"Impatient little bastard, ain't ya?"

"Yep."

"Ask me again tomorrow." He sipped and grimaced. "Anyway, I have a couple more ideas about defense. One is we use the radios here to contact the island."

"Seriously? The people who sold us out!"

"That red-haired guy didn't seem too happy with Meg and Bill doing that to us. Maybe there's others who feel the same. And I'd think Meg still has some conscience in there somewhere. She might have enough to consider a new deal."

"What deal?"

"Instead of allying *with* the Death Druids, they ally with us against them. Druids will be here some time when their boys don't return. Probably in force. There's at least ten of them. We can ask to borrow the red-haired guy and a few more to help us defend the place for … pick a timeframe. Maybe a month."

"They won't do it."

"We pay them in sheep."

"They won't do it."

"They might. It's worth asking. But. We need to make sure we don't use too many of them so that they outnumber us. Four maybe. And I get to look Red Head in the eye when he arrives and make sure he's on the level."

"You're always thinking, aren't you?"

"That's the nicest thing you ever said to me, Cochise."

"Didn't say you were thinking smart things."

"You're a helluva wiseass, know that?"

"Takes one."

"Guess so."

They returned to silence until both their mugs were empty. Elliot handed his over.

"Take this back to the kitchen for me?"

"Where are you off to?"

"One more body to take care of." He indicated the top of the lighthouse visible above the road.

"Want help?" Lewis asked but his heart wasn't in it.

"You need to get your people together and plan your day. I'll take care of that prick."

"Be careful, eh?"

"Sure will, Pops."

Lewis rolled his eyes and moved away. He stopped, turned to speak, seemed surprised Elliot was just standing there watching him, froze up.

"What's up, pal?"

"I, uh, I guess I wanted to thank you."

Shee-it. There's a first.

"No need."

"Yes need. You …" He stared a while into an empty cup. "I could be dead by now, but I'm not. So, you know, thanks."

"So pay it forward, Cochise."

"I will. Believe me."

Elliot cleared his throat. "You know, I should thank you too."

"Huh? What for?"

"For teaching me that a man should keep an open mind."

And there it is, folks. Another first.

A wan smile emerged through the dirt on Lewis's face. "Wish my family could have met you. Dad, Mum, Alyssa. They'd like you."

He winced at the sister's name, covered it by running a hand over his stubble. "I doubt that, Lewis."

Lewis' smile grew cheeky. "Yeah, I doubt it too. Seemed like a nice thing to tell you, though."

Elliot chuckled. "Asshole."

"Ass*hat.*"

"Wash my cup."

Lewis straightened, snapped off a salute and strode away. The young man's shoulders seemed broader than even yesterday, his stride longer and more sure. He waved at Angie in the shed and she gave him a thumbs up.

For some reason that escaped him, Elliot felt proud.

23

Fresh off the ocean, the sea breeze hit him in the face like aftershave as he navigated his way down the hill to the Lighthouse. Against all reason, he felt good, real good, as if by breathing that breeze he was imbibing optimism. An albatross hovered just off shore. Silver gulls pulled at the remains of sheep, but even that felt natural; far better than deaders doing it.

His next task was clear to him, but unlike the gulls and despite what he'd told Elliot, it wasn't getting rid of a body. Not yet.

He cracked open the lighthouse door, SIG ready. No danger. He relaxed a little.

Waxer struggled to sit upright, shimmied his shoulders up the whitewashed bricks, *mmm*-ing against his gag, eyes wide beneath the bloody brow. The bonds Elliot had cut from the pile of towels still held. Waxer croaked something that was probably "Water".

Elliot shoved the door closed, stuck the SIG in his left hand cargo pocket and reached into the right one. He took out the lockblade. Waxer's eyes: a brief widening in fear before a narrowing of hateful resignation. Elliot nodded to confirm it. He crouched in front of the biker, right by the trussed-up man's feet. Waxer wouldn't lash out, not with that messed up knee.

Elliot clicked open the blade, tapped it on Waxer's boot. He said, "And now you're gonna tell me *exactly* where to find his sister."

Acknowledgements
&
Notes

I used to read novels and wonder why authors thanked so many people at the end. Surely they wrote it alone, I thought. I pictured them as tough lone wolves (like Elliot), working in their own strength, relying on no one, gettin' it done.

Now I know better.

You can't write anything half-decent without the generous support and advice of others. And I was blessed with the help of incredible advisors and professionals as I wrote and polished Doomsday's Child.

I offer heartfelt thanks to…

Janine: for supporting me through author-tantrums, for your awesome fact-checking and proofreading, for the colour scheme in my writing office, and for your love and optimism and partnership. *We* did this.

Author JR Jackson: for advice on things military and nautical. Elliot was a mere character sketch until you stepped in, JR. Other authors, seek out JR online at The Ward Room.

Author and editor, Jason Nahrung: for his kind and thoughtful mentoring through the Australian Horror Writer's Association … and for continuing to guide and sharpen *me the writer* once the mentoring program was over.

Joy Killar: for helping me further Americanise (excuse me, Americani*z*e) my American protagonist. Apparently he came across as British in the first draft. Which might have been interesting too.

In order of last name, authors Peter Cooper, D Robert Digman, Kevin Ikenberry, EJ McLaughlin, Ian Welke: good friends, writing buddies, gifted authors in their own genres. These magic five read (and sometimes reread) my late drafts, and hammered me hard on making improvements.

Andrew Spong and Tamra Crow: for proofreading, especially for picking up the various ways I'd misspelled *Elliot*.

The 20 people who voted on the title: sorry if you didn't get your number 1, but your voting certainly crystalised both the name and the theme of the story for me.

Author Keith C. Blackmore: for kind advice and giving me courage to do the indie thing, but do it well. And for introducing me to Captain Morgan.

Some errors and untruths in this novel represent an author taking liberties, bending Truth to serve Story. Others, I'm sure, are simply errors.

Read on for an excerpt from Pete Aldin's supernatural thriller…

Black Marks

Jake darted into a vacant lot as the roar of the car came up behind him. The vehicle missed him by inches. The wind of its passage nearly buffeted him from his feet. He careened off a corrugated iron fence, regained his balance and pelted across debris and gravel toward the rear fence. Pain lanced through his bare feet. Gaps in the fence were large enough that he didn't break stride to leap through into the high grass of someone's backyard. He knew the area - had checked it out the first day he'd come to Angelo's. Across the next street was a patch of wasteland and beyond that a disused railway track: lots of scrub there, ditches, culverts, places to hide. The sedan - it hadn't been Eddie's van as he'd expected - was growing fainter but that didn't mean he was safe. They'd be circling the block, and they would be in the street within seconds.

Three teenage boys lounged on the back porch, passing a joint. "Hey!" one yelled at him as he passed. He hurdled the low brick fence onto the sidewalk. The motor noise leveled out then grew louder as he crossed the street. The Chevy appeared at the crossroads to his left, slewing around to face him with another screech of tires on asphalt. He plunged into the wasteland and tried to dodge bricks and other detritus hidden like landmines beneath the sedge grass and thistles. Up ahead the silvery line of the railway's chain-link fence announced refuge. Thirty yards.

The Chevy growled in protest as the driver mounted yet another curb. Gears crunched. Jake glanced over his shoulder. The car bounced and drifted, struggling to find traction on the fallow ground. Who the hell were they? More of Zee's crew?

And what had happened to Eddie? That was definitely his van back there.

His foot turned on a piece of wood and he stumbled. Almost fell. Numbness spread around his ankle, but there was no pain. Not yet. The Animal complained within him, surging. On four legs, a wolf could cover this ground twice as fast and more sure-footed.

He tucked the bundle of clothes under one arm like a wide receiver and pushed on as hard as he could. Soil and stone crunched as the car slid to a halt twenty or thirty yards back. They couldn't crash through a fence, not if they had any brains; they weren't going to catch him.

He leapt and landed high enough up the fence to avoid using his toes, grabbed the top and swung a leg over. The cold metal bar at the top of the fence pressed painfully against his inner thigh and he narrowly avoided tearing his scrotum on a wire-end. Something pinged off the bar below his gut. The next moment he was on his back, flattening a patch of thistle, with what felt like a heavy weight on his hip. He touched it; his fingers came away bloody.

They hit me!

He had to get up. Now, while the car's transmission complained as someone hurriedly put it in gear. Now, while their aim was off.

Get up.

Pain pinned him to the ground, a white-hot wire above his right hip.

Get up*!*

He turned over. Somehow. Got on hands and knees before the pain in his gut sucked him back onto the earth. So bad, so bad he sobbed.

The car crawled closer and someone fired. He heard the shot this time. The bullet whined past to his left. Down amongst the weeds like this, they maybe couldn't see him. He pressed his right hand over the bullet wound, hot blood slicking it like treacle, while he looked for his clothes. He scrabbled towards his bundle.

A squeal of brakes and a car door groaned open. Another shot and someone snarled, "Don't waste them!" A voice he didn't know. Not a pusher. Not a gangbanger.

Hunters. Had to be.

He felt it then, just as his hand closed on the parcel of clothing. A creeping, prickling malignancy, spreading deep inside from the epicenter of the bullet wound, bubble wrap inside him inflating and popping, sending poison through his system.

Silver.

They'd hit him with a silver bullet.

Black Marks — *available now in eBook and paperback from all good online bookstores.*

About The Author

PETE ALDIN is an Australian-based writer and a member of the Australian Horror Writers Association.

His professional life has involved empowering people with disabilities, helping professionals shape their career and work-life balance, working with migrants and with youth, as well as designing courses and courseware for training companies.

He follows Chelsea FC in the English Premier League. He is obsessed with Breaking Bad, plays FIFA games on xBox, and reads way too much when he should be writing. He owns a sonic screwdriver, a Dalek and a TARDIS.

His short fiction has found a home in publications including *Andromeda Spaceways Inflight Magazine*, Orson Scott Card's *Intergalactic Medicine Show*, *Niteblade* and Poise & Pen's *ABC Anthologies*. He has written for several parenting magazines including Kindred and Natural Parenting.

Connect with Pete at www.facebook.com/PeteAldinAuthor and www.petealdin.com. On his Facebook page, you'll find a link to music Pete listens to while he's writing in the About section.

One Last Thing…

If you enjoyed this book, please post a short review on Goodreads and your favourite online retailer.

Your word-of-mouth support makes a difference (it *really* does) and your feedback helps make the next book even better.

Thanks again for your support!

…By the way, keep your eyes open for Elliot's return in the novel: *Came Monsters* and in the Kindle short story *Rescue Mission*.